Praise for
SOCORRO

"Leman's story of separation and hardship details the isolation, lone-
liness, and courage of those who are invisible, underserved, and then
turned into convenient political scapegoats. This is a tale that brings
light to these crimes and offers empathy and humanity to the victims."

—Daniel Ruiz
author of *Coconut Versus* and *The Life of Jian Ciervo*

"Sara A. Leman's novel explores concepts of familial relationships,
identity, and sense of place while implicitly asking the reader, 'What
secrets are okay to keep from those we love? Are we protecting them
or ourselves?' This novel will keep readers guessing until the end and
leave them wondering about their own family's mysteries."

—Anne Marie Wells
author of *Survived By*

"Sara A. Leman's novel *Socorro* bristles with tension as it explores the
steadfast love and determination of a family snared by hostile immigration politics. After her mother is picked up by Immigration police, the
novel's central character, Silvia, a college student, faces the challenges
sustaining her family, maintaining a protective facade of normalcy,
and raising her younger sister and brother. Though her mother had
carefully prepared her for this possibility, the import and burden of
her responsibilities is deeply moving. Silvia's journey is neither entirely
uplifting nor depressing—it is real. It resolves and unravels right to the
novel's conclusion. Leman's characters bring to life what most people
only know as dry news reports and political battles. She shows how

current immigration policies trap families, shred aspirations for safety and opportunity, and deny American society generations of talent, energy, and beauty."

—Susan Suntree
author of *Sacred Sites: The Secret History of Southern California*
and *Dear Traveler*

"Sara A. Leman is empathetic and sensitive to the issues of Mexican immigrants. Founded by immigrants, this is after all, the United States of America and "justice for all." She cleverly sets the stage in the city of Socorro, immediately alerting the reader of a potential hazard. Leman parallels the lives of different generations. Is there any ambiguity to the American Dream? Is there justice and fairness for all? This novel forces you to evaluate facts and prejudices."

—Elda Mejia
Mexican immigrant with dual citizenship

"*Socorro* is a most remarkable novel from the headlines, where borders have become battlements and the uprooted must find home in strange and often uncaring lands. Read *Socorro* to understand the great global story of migrants and refugees in a world imprisoned by the nation state."

—Luis J. Rodriguez
author of *Always Running, La Vida Loca, Gang Days in L.A.*
and *From Our Land to Our Land: Essays, Journeys & Imaginings from a Native Xicanx Writer*

"*Socorro*, by Sara A. Leman, cleverly mingles the story of a modern-day teenager caring for her younger sister and brother when their mother is deported, with the story of their great, great-grandmother's life in small town, Depression-era Mexico. Skillfully blending historical details, (especially those about migration and repatriation), fine descriptions, and the tropes of adolescent behavior, Leman weaves a dismaying indictment of ICE and other programs that have been used in the United States, for years, to discriminate against people of Mexican descent.

Among the historically interesting anecdotes and descriptions are those of a region in west Texas, between Texas and Mexico, whose ownership was disputed until the 1960's; several portrayals of times the Rio Grande flooded; and the depiction of the plight of many women left to fend for themselves and their children when their menfolk went north for work.

Leman is particularly good on the day-to-day feelings and struggles of adolescence. The novel has some faults of a first book: certain incidents are repetitive; the weight given to a few of the descriptions might be excessive. But this is minor in light of the moving, present-day story of Silvia and her siblings, set against the traumatic events recounted in the old diary that she finds."

—Joan Goldsmith Gurfield
award-winning author, English professor

"*Socorro* is a beautiful glimpse into life on the margins and offers an authentic-feeling view into a world not often shown. This staggering narrative of struggle and hope is timely now more than ever ... It offers an authentic-feeling view into a world not often shown."

—Debra Moore-Muñoz
Co-executive producer and writer, FX's *Mayans M.C.*

SOCORRO

SOCORRO

a novel

SARA A LEMAN

 Nervousghostpress.org

SOCORRO

PROLOGUE

At 10:45 in the morning they came to get her. She had already messaged MigraWatch when the two white vans pulled into the parking spot outside the brown single-story apartment building in San Marcos, Texas. She stood in the center of the living room, suitcase in hand, as they strode up the walk. She calmly answered when they knocked.

"Coming!"

Mechanically, she opened the door and checked the officers' badges as she had been trained to do, then asked to see their warrant. Heart pounding, she followed the "do not speak, do not sign anything" admonition from her MigraWatch training and simply locked the door and followed the men down the walk. She absolutely would not give them the satisfaction of seeing her break down or even tremble. She climbed into a van. The departure that she had so long dreaded was over.

Rosa had known that this day was coming, as, one by one, her acquaintances at work and church had been arrested. That was why Rosa always kept a safe wall of distance around herself and her family, just as her parents had done as undocumented migrants decades before. *Keep a low profile*, her papá would say every morning as he left the house. Rosa interpreted that to mean that she should never stand out in any way: Neither a terrible nor a great student. Neither a mean girl nor a best friend. Not an athlete. Not a musician. Always walk away quietly; never run. And now, never act jumpy, even when the Border Patrol agents come around to arrest people.

Not arrest—"detain," the agents always said, trying to make it sound temporary and innocuous. Indeed, Rosa herself had allowed Silvia to believe their separation would be temporary while she was preparing her eldest to take care of the younger siblings "just in case." During one of their last planning talks, Rosa had said, "Silvi, I know you don't like discussing this, but it's all just in case I'm ever detained. It would probably be only for a short time, so I'm trusting you not to worry your brother and sister about this. They don't have to know anything until it happens."

"You mean unless it happens," Silvia said.

"Right," said Rosa. "But just for me, let's go over the plan one more time."

Silvia sighed and brushed back her unruly chestnut hair. "Okay, one last time. If you were away, I'd have to pay the bills."

"On time."

"Yes, on time so we wouldn't get any calls or visits." Silvia busied her hands straightening up a toppled stack of papers on the kitchen table. "Second, I'd clean the house. Third, I'd cook the foods that Lucy and Seba like best. Mami, I know all this. We'd be fine for a few days."

"Querida, it would be more than a few days. They'd have to release me to Mexico and then I'd need time to file documents to come back legally." Rosa glanced at Silvia's face, then quickly added, "But the application can be done quickly if I pay an extra fee. Anyway, it would probably be weeks, not days."

Silvia hesitated, her hand on the pile of papers. "Okay, weeks, then."

Just then the doorbell rang. Rosa heard Sebastián's bedroom door slam shut as it always did when someone came to the door unexpectedly. She knew her youngest child was now crawling under his bed. She turned her eyes up to the ceiling in a silent prayer and walked to the door.

A minute later she returned to Silvia in the kitchen. "Just a boy selling candy. Now. What's fourth in our plan?"

Silvia grabbed a paper towel and began wiping the gold-flecked Formica tabletop, stained here and there with brown coffee rings. She sighed. "Fourth. Shop for food."

"Fifth."

"Go to meetings at the kids' schools," said Silvia.

"Because …"

Silvia recited, "Because you're at work and I'm going to be eighteen, so the school can talk to me, too."

"Así es, muchacha. Phone calls are always best, but if you have to go in to meetings, go."

"I know, Mami. But anyway, it's almost summer, so they'll be out soon. No more meetings until fall." Silvia turned her left hand up in the "no problem" gesture, then began wiping faster circles with her other hand.

"Right." Rosa blinked. "So that's all five steps. Run through them every day, and you'll always have everything in order."

"Great. Can we change the subject please?"

"Not quite yet. I have to give you two updates. First, I went to the bank today and paid the rent for the rest of the year using the money I've saved working at the deli and cleaning."

"The whole year?" Silvia left the paper towel on the table and straightened up, holding on to the back of a kitchen chair.

Rosa tried to put her hand on Silvia's shoulder, but she stepped to the side, staring back with eyebrows raised. Rosa let her hand drop and reached into her pocket. She took out a Visa card with an orange sunset on the front and held it out toward Silvia. "And I opened a credit card in your name and mine so you can use it for grocery shopping if the cash runs low."

Silvia swallowed, grimacing at the card as if it were a cockroach in her mother's palm. Then she looked up and tried a smile. "But you'd be back in plenty of time. We have plenty of cash."

Rosa swallowed her guilt about having to train her daughter like this, about not being able to shield her from the pain that was coming. She pushed the credit card toward Silvia. "Sure we do, mija. This is all just in case."

Silvia took the card between her thumb and index finger and set it on the damp table.

"Most of all, Silvi—"

"—keep a low profile," they said together. And then they laughed to break the tension, Rosa brushing the back of her hand across her eyes. It was just too impossible to tell her daughter that their separation could be anything but temporary.

That was days ago. This morning, the day that Immigration and Customs Enforcement came, Rosa had awoken calm. She had been lucky up to this point. She knew from her neighbors that the officers' visits had become more frequent while she was out during the day. Like her acquaintances, she also knew that she would have no choice but to go when they came for her. Today, she was going to be prepared and not caught by surprise, just like her father had taught her when they first crossed the Rio Grande under cover of darkness and started their new life.

She kissed the kids and sent them off to school calmly and without tears. "Sebastián, be a good boy today. Listen to your teachers. Don't forget to drink your whole bottle of water."

Sebastián pressed his cheek against hers, his long lashes brushing her face. "I will, Mami. Te quiero."

"Lucy, come here." Rosa looked her in the eye and smoothed her daughter's shoulder-length dark hair. "You are my sweet girl. Remember to be good to all your friends today. No arguing, okay? Don't be an enemy to anyone."

"Okay, Mami. It's just that some girls—"

"No excuses, Lucy. Don't make waves."

"Sí, Mamá."

"And Silvia ..." Here, her voice almost broke. She was afraid that her oldest, her salutatorian, her big girl, would see through her tranquil demeanor and would know that today was likely to be the day. "Silvi, I love you so much and I'm so proud of you."

Silvia glanced toward the door and then back at her mother. "I know, Mami."

"Take care of your brother and sister. You know we talked about that."

"Of course. You remind me every day."

"And all of you—"

"Keep a low profile," they said in unison.

"We know, Mami," said Silvia. "We've got to go or we'll miss the bus."

"Okay, corazón. Just one more besito." She kissed Silvia on the forehead.

And then they were gone. Her babies, her heart walking outside her body, soon to be separated from her by a border, a river, a wall. Only then did she cry.

01

"Hurry up, you two, or you're going to be late. Again!"

"I'm not ready!" called Sebastián from down the hall.

"Just grab your shoes from yesterday and get out here!" yelled Silvia, trying not to let the stress of the morning routine make her voice shrill.

"God, Silvi, you sound just like Mami," complained Lucy.

At Lucy's comment, Sebastián's thundering footsteps suddenly ceased. From where she stood holding the front door open, Silvia saw his face fall.

"Come here, Seba. She didn't mean it. We all miss Mami." Moving to hug her brother, Silvia glared over his slumped shoulder at Lucy.

"Yeah, Sebastián, sorry. I wasn't thinking." Lucy rumpled his hair. "Come on. Let's go."

Sebastián unwrapped his arms from his oldest sister and wiped his eyes.

As Silvia straightened up, she saw her sister's eyes go to her chest. Quickly, she pulled her flannel shirt around her body, but it was too late.

"What are you wearing?" Lucy demanded.

Sebastián stood looking from one sister to the other.

"Nothing," said Silvia. "Just my pajamas."

Lucy took three steps and pulled open the lapel of Silvia's plaid shirt to reveal a navy-blue T-shirt with silver lettering on the front. "That's Mami's. We agreed we wouldn't touch her stuff!"

"It's been over four months, Luce. It's none of your business what I wear when I'm home studying. You don't know what it's like taking care of you two all the time!" Silvia felt her face grow hot. She swallowed and glanced at Sebastián's face. "Sorry, Seba."

Sebastián gave her another hug. "Can I wear Mami's things, too?"

"No!" yelled Lucy. "Nobody's touching her stuff."

Silvia glared at Lucy, then bent down to her brother's eye level. "We'll talk about it later. Now you've got to get going." She kissed him on the temple and turned him toward the door.

Straightening, Silvia handed Sebastián his brown bag from the table by the door. Lucy snatched hers up before Silvia could touch it and slammed out the screen door.

Silvia closed the steel door and doubled over, pressing her hands against her face and growling out her frustration into her palms. The fighting was getting to be too much and too constant. This wasn't supposed to be her life. They weren't supposed to be her responsibility. Not for this long.

While she was crouched over, the memory of the day Mami was taken returned to Silvia in a flash. She had arrived on the bus from high school, always the first in the family to get home. Like every other day, she'd planned to do her homework and start dinner with her normal self-discipline, but also with her customary nagging sense of dread. *What if today was the day?*

As usual, she had dropped her backpack on the recliner on her way in and headed to the kitchen to see if there were any special instructions from her mother. Checking the kitchen table, she saw an envelope instead of the usual Post-it note. Instantly she lost her breath. Her stomach seized as she grabbed the envelope. Holding back tears of panic and grief, she ran down the hall to her bed, clutching the envelope to her chest. She coiled defensively into a ball like a worm unearthed onto scorching-hot pavement.

As she opened the envelope, three pictures slid out. Each was of Mami with one of her babies. Silvia pressed the picture of herself to her lips, frantically blinking her tears away, and read the letter with her name on it. By the time she finished and crawled out from under the quilt, her jaw was set in determination just like her mother's so often was. She knew from Mami's words that she had to somehow gather

her strength and prepare to be in charge for a little while. Her mother had done her best to steel her for this day, and Silvia was absolutely determined to live up to her expectations. No, she would exceed them, like the overachiever she was. And surely Mami would straighten this out and apply to come back across the border legally to be with her children as soon as she could. Silvia figured she had to hold it together for five or six weeks, tops.

Silvia straightened up and, with a twinge of guilt, opened the front door again, craning to see her brother and sister as they waited by the main road. They were basically good kids. It was not their fault that seventeen weeks had passed and she was losing it.

She saw Lucy, a middle schooler, dressed in skinny black jeans and a black hoodie, her stuffed backpack slumping down well below her waist. With her dyed-black bangs peeking out from her hood, she looked the part that she was trying to play, the rebellious teenager. But Silvia knew better. Lucy had always been a good girl who knew that certain things, such as homework and housework, were nonnegotiable.

Still, this fall Silvia had noticed some concerning changes in Lucy's behavior. She did her homework quickly, but often left sections sloppy or incomplete. Lucy complained more than ever about having to help out around the house. And about once a week, as soon as she was done with her work, she would run out of the house and not return until nearly bedtime, avoiding eye contact and with her backpack bulging. She refused to tell where she went or with whom, instead shouting, "You're my sister, not my mother!" or "Get off my back!"

Pressing her lips together, Silvia moved her gaze to Sebastián, in his favorite green windbreaker, holding his reluctant sister's hand at the bus stop. At six years old, he was a sweet boy to be around. A blonde in a family of brunettes, Sebastián attracted compliments from young moms and whispered adoration from bigger girls. He loved rocks, maps, anything involving trucks, and he was learning to ride a bike. But last week Silvia had gotten her first call from school about him:

"Mrs. Castillo?"

"No, I'm sorry. She's not available right now. May I help you?" Her heart was pounding.

"Yes, please tell her that the school called about Sebastián."

Silvia stifled the panic she felt rising in her chest. "Yes, I'm Sebastián's big sister and my mother has left me in charge while she's out. I can talk with you about Sebastián."

"Oh, is this Lucy? This is Ms. Adams, Sebastián's teacher."

"Hi, Ms. Adams. This is Silvia. I'm sure you don't remember me; I'm in college now," she said.

"Silvia Castillo. I remember your name, for sure."

"Yeah, it was a long time ago. Could you tell me about Seba, please?" Silvia asked. Then added, "So I can tell my mother?"

The teacher hesitated. "All right. He hit a girl in class today."

Silvia's mouth fell open. "He did? What happened?"

"She asked him to play, and he didn't want to, so he hit her on the arm and pushed her."

"Oh my gosh, I'm so sorry. I'll talk to him about it as soon as he gets home. And I'll tell my mother."

"There's no need for any punishment or anything, Silvia. We already settled it at school. He apologized and she's fine. But your mother might want to talk to him about treating others like he'd want to be treated."

"Of course. I will. I mean, she will."

When they had hung up, Silvia's face was burning, and cold sweat dripped down her sides from the strain of the lie she was living. And her sweet brother had developed a temper. *Understandable*, Silvia had thought. *Just like me, he's starting to realize that Mami is not coming back any time soon. She hasn't even called.*

Silvia watched the kids until her view was obscured by the school bus. She checked that the bus stop was empty after the vehicle pulled away, carrying Sebastián to Travis Elementary and Lucy to Goodnight Middle. It was fortunate that they rode the same bus so that they could look out for each other.

Squaring her shoulders to get her emotions back on track, Silvia closed the door and walked across the living room to her computer desk. If there was one word that defined her, at least until recently, it was *disciplined*. Her self-discipline had gotten her through high school nearly at the top of her class, and had been getting her through life without her mother for the last four months. If she kept working hard, she wouldn't have time to think, to worry, to miss. If she kept getting up each morning and facing her siblings' needs and conflicts, if she kept powering through her own fear and resentment, just maybe she could stick to Mami's survival plan a little longer.

02

Silvia opened her laptop and pulled up her coursework for the day. She was an "Online Freshman" at Penn State, not a title she'd ever imagined for herself. No, she had dreamt of attending a school in the Northeast, where she would see American history firsthand and explore the original heart of the country, far from the border. She imagined weekly escapes into Boston, DC, or Manhattan after completing her assignments. She anticipated the thrill of independence, the joy of inhabiting the American stories she'd always read about in school, the America of George and Martha Washington, Clara Barton, Benjamin Franklin. The *real* America. Furthermore, she wanted a big university; she had been in little San Marcos her whole life and was ready to learn how to be a small fish in a much bigger pond.

The acceptances had rolled in: Boston University, University of Maryland, even New York University. The scholarships followed. Mami celebrated each one as if it were a birthday, cooking special beef stew one night, pozole another. She loved how her mother was always able to make even a dinner at home feel like a party.

"Mami! Another cake?"

"Sí, mi amor! I'm so proud of you. We all are!"

Sebastián had held out a construction-paper card he'd made for Silvia, in maroon and gold for Boston College, that day's acceptance. Silvia grinned as she took it, giving him a hug. "Thanks, hermanito," she said, ruffling his hair.

"So is this the one?" Lucy asked. "Or do we have to keep throwing you parties?"

Silvia ignored her sister's comment and paused, drawing out the suspense. At last, she opened her arms wide, announcing "This is the one! I'm gonna be an Eagle!"

"Clearly not a bald eagle," Lucy said, looking pointedly at Silvia's unruly dark waves.

"Actually," said Sebastián, "the name *bald eagle* comes from the English word *piebald*, meaning 'white.' They are named for their white heads and faces."

"Clearly not that, either," muttered Lucy, walking away.

Mami opened her arms, flapping her hands to gesture Silvia close. "Ay, un águila. Qué linda mi aguilita. We're all so proud of you."

Eventually even Lucy had offered her congratulations, and they had all sat down to dessert. Late that night, Silvia sat with Mami and they made the deposit to secure her spot at Boston College, her first choice.

Silvia shook off the bittersweet memory. When Immigration and Customs Enforcement took Mami, they took Silvia's dreams, too. Seventeen at the time, she had tearfully let go of her green campus in Boston, her meals in a long dining hall beside real friends from New Jersey and Connecticut, her afternoons studying Poe and Wharton in the grass under abstract sculptures. Those were probably romanticized notions, anyway, fictions themselves, those glossy brochures. All that mattered now was getting Mami back.

In the end, Silvia sent a remorse-filled email deferring her enrollment to Boston College for a year. Mami would be back long before then, and anyway, she could get some of her core requirements done in the meantime. She accepted the scholarship from Penn State, because it was the only one of her schools with an online degree program that she could begin from home. She would simply transfer for her sophomore year. It wouldn't be that bad.

In the meantime, she was studying history, English, and botany as an Online Freshman while her siblings were at school and while learning how to run a household. She believed in taking one course for fun (botany—she'd always had a passion for flowers) along with the hard classes, so that she would have a reward after she got her most difficult assignments out of the way. That approach had worked for her in high school when, alongside AP Spanish and Calculus, she had taken a seminar on the Thirteen Colonies that she hoped to see one day.

"Okay, we'll start with English." Silvia often talked herself through the details of her class work. It helped her focus and made it feel more like there were other students working alongside her. Online learning had its challenges, the greatest being isolation.

"Week three of Memoirs. Next week we write our own journal entries, to see what the process feels like … What could I possibly have to write about, the laundry? The credit card bill I can't pay? Lucy's attitude?" She laughed bitterly. "All right, we'll start with today's video lecture, and then the reading."

Silvia spent the next hour and twenty minutes listening to Professor Simon talk about the various styles and structures of some of the most famous published diaries: bravery and desperation from Captain Scott, innocence and voice from Anne Frank, intimacy and honesty from Nelson Mandela. Silvia began to think about chronology, detail, description, and dialogue. She opened *The Diaries of Nella Last* to begin the week's reading.

And then the dryer buzzed. Silvia put down her book and stood. Passing through the kitchen on the way to the laundry, she turned on water to boil for macaroni and cheese. She entered the back hall, pulled out the laundry, and sorted it. She walked through the kitchen again and turned right down the hallway to the bedrooms. She dropped the clothes on each kid's bed in turn, then noticed the messy bathroom. Toilet seat up, mascara smeared in the sink, towels needing to be washed. Shaking her head, she went back to the laundry room, stirring the pasta on the way, put the detergent in the washer, closed the lid, put the cover on the mac and cheese, and collapsed with her book at last on the recliner by the front door. Almost immediately the stove started hissing as the water boiled over. Sighing, she thought: *I guess the biggest challenge of online learning is distraction.*

Silvia planned to spend the afternoon on History of US Borders, a course that mainly dealt with territorial conflicts between the United States and Spain and then with independent Mexico. In an earlier unit, she had read about Spanish explorations in North America, including sixteenth-century forays by men whose names she remembered from fifth-grade social studies: De Soto and Ponce de León into the southern peninsula of Florida, Rodríguez Cabrillo in California, and Cabeza de Vaca in the Southwest.

The latter's was a voyage of adventure that Silvia loved to imagine. It started with two hundred fifty men exploring Florida and ended with four lone survivors walking from Texas to Mexico City during the course of seven years and 2,400 miles. Silvia was impressed by the survivors' determination but moreover, Cabeza de Vaca's various modes of survival—he was in turns a forced laborer, a hunter-gatherer, a merchant, a healer, and even a surgeon—reminded her of her father, who had been gone since before Sebastián was born.

Silvia realized with a pang that she hadn't thought about him since her graduation day back in May, when, against all logic, she had allowed her eyes to rove over the rows of proud parents, dozing grandparents, bored little sisters and brothers, scanning for her mother. Her stomach had dropped when she suddenly thought, *She's not here, but what if* he *is*? She began to run her eyes methodically up and down the rows of chairs on the college quad where the event was being held, left to right, front to back, looking for the leather fedora he always used to wear, like the Mexican Indiana Jones. Without it, would she even recognize him? Sure, he had her eyes, and Sebastián's crinkly smile, but how could she see details that small in a sea of faces on the Texas State quad?

That's how she always remembered him, wearing that hat and ready for an adventure. One early spring Saturday after lunch, he had put on his hat and taken her fishing along the muddy bank of Purgatory Creek.

"Okay, amor. Here's how you bait the hook." Her father pinched a wriggling brown worm between his thumb and first finger, then expertly skewered it onto the barb. It ceased its movements right away, as if shocked at the violation.

"Ay, ¡no! Papi, you're hurting it!" Silvia cried.

"Nonsense, mi hija," said Papi, lowering the worm toward the weedy edge of the water.

"Don't!" Silvia cried.

"You're big enough now to go fishing with me, and you know how your Mami loves trout."

She plopped her chubby seat down on the riverbank and crossed her arms. "Never. I'm never going to go fishing and I'm never going to do that to a worm. They clean our soil for us. You told me so!"

Papi's forehead creased as he glanced at Silvia. "He will be a nice meal for a fish. You'll see." He plunged the worm underwater.

Silvia burst into tears. "But you're taking him away from his family!" she wailed. "His family needs him!"

Her father's shoulders slumped and he balanced his fishing pole on a rock, leaving the line dangling into the river. "Okay, mi hija. As you wish." He sat down and pulled her onto his lap.

Silvia leaned against him for a few minutes, feeling his warmth. Then, turning to see his disappointed face, she brightened. "I know! I'll just fish without bait! That way if the fish wants to be dinner, he can come along with us." She jumped up and grabbed her little pole. Checking that the hook was firmly attached, she lowered it into the flowing water alongside her father's.

Silvia smiled a little at the memory, still holding her unopened Borders textbook. Then her smile faded as she remembered the whispered late-summer conversations that she'd hear coming from down the hall as a child.

"Do you really have to go back already?"

"They say it's just for four months this time, to work the vineyards. It'll go quickly, querida."

"But Silvia. She's too little to understand why you're gone, and it gets harder each week for her to remember the good times. All she asks is 'When is Papi coming home?'"

"Well, mi amor, we really don't have any choice. I can't make enough here working odd jobs or day laboring. We need the money to support our growing family." Here their voices would get softer, and Silvia could hear her mother giggle a little.

She remembered coming down the hall to leave for school and there he was, standing in the kitchen (not sitting with his café con leche like he should have been), and she noticed that his duffle bag and his fedora were in the corner. (Not on his head. No adventure today.) Still, he walked her to the door like the other mornings and kissed her on the top of her head.

"Be a good girl and take care of Mami."

"But I'll see you after school, right, Papi?"

Her father had just smiled down at her, but this time his eyes did not crinkle at the corners. Silvia had tried not to cling to him, had held back her tears. She knew he would be gone again when she got home.

It was the same every year. Papi was home all the time when Silvia was really young, but gradually he had to look for work farther and farther away. At first he was gone for only four months at a time, harvesting lettuce and berries in California. He'd come back for the cool weather, and during those months he'd try to do as much as he could with Silvia, and then with Lucy once she came along.

After a few years, the absences became longer. Silvia learned to feel complete on her own with Mami, Lucy, and, after the last visit, Sebastián; they didn't need anyone else.

Silvia blinked and looked down blankly at her textbook, as if unsure why it was dangling from her hand. She still hadn't opened it. *That was when Mami started showing me how to do everything around the house. At the time I felt grown up and needed.* She slammed her US Borders book down on the desk and palmed it away, no longer allowing her fingers to touch the cover.

03

Silvia was surprised to discover tears in her eyes when she finished writing her first entry about her family the next week. Professor Simon was right: journaling certainly was "an effective way to process emotions and reinterpret the past." She needed to clear her head.

Okay, time for lunch, but then I'm doing botany. I deserve a reward.

Silvia got up from the computer, stretched, and dried her eyes on her T-shirt. She walked into the kitchen, scooped some rice and beans into a bowl, and took note of the dirty dishes in the sink. She stopped in the hall, put some towels in the dryer, walked back through the kitchen and down the hall to her room. Grabbing her botany textbook and syllabus, she returned to the living room and stretched out on the floor on her stomach with her bowl at her elbow.

She glanced at the date and found her botany assignment for the day. "Page fifty-two, chapter seven, desert plants of the American Southwest. Now, this is going to be fun!" Then she thought, *I'm a total nerd.*

Silvia opened her book to begin reading about desert succulents, shrubs, and wildflowers, working to memorize each with its range and morphology. At first glance, she recognized some from hikes with her father when she was younger: agave, Texas sage, prickly pear. Others were new to her. As she flipped through the pages, she turned a few of the plant names around on her tongue: the cane-like *ocotillo* with its graceful arms tipped with vermillion flowers, the shrubby ground-cover *damianita* with its golden mane, the silvery *ceniza* with its purple blooms. The Southwest seemed to be absolutely tied to its Mexican roots both morphologically and figuratively, yet today's Mexican Americans had to hide theirs.

Silvia sat up cross-legged and instinctively retwisted her unruly dark waves into a tight bun. She had just pulled her book onto her lap to continue studying when her phone rang.

"Hello?"

"Querida?"

"Mami!" Silvia choked out, overcome with relief at finally hearing her mother's voice after all these months.

"I'm fine, bebé I'm fine. Don't cry."

"It's been so long." Silvia shook with tears.

"I know, amor. They didn't let me call until now. They've just let me go. I wanted to talk to you right away."

"They just let you out? Where are you?"

"In Piedras Negras, just across the border."

Silvia couldn't answer. Somehow she had convinced herself that her mother would not be sent to Mexico. She stood and walked over to the curio cabinet that hung on one wall of their living room, next to the couch. Her mother had always kept little Mexican pottery and wooden figurines there. When she was younger, Silvia used to love to dust them, taking each one down and gently polishing it with a cloth before setting it back in its spot. Now she picked up the tiny wooden box with a blooming pink rose painted on its lid. Silently, she stroked its shiny petals with her thumb.

"It's okay, mija. I'm okay, and nothing bad happened to me at Pearsall. That's the processing center for deportations."

"Oh my God, Mami, you were in detention all this time?"

Right after their mother was taken by Immigration, Silvia had read as much as she could about the processing centers that the federal government maintained along the border. Essentially, they were jails, and the crime (charged and punished, but rarely tried in courts) was illegal entry. ICE held detainees in these facilities for anywhere from a few days to several months, and then officers escorted nearly all of them on foot to the US-Mexico line and released them either into police custody or freely into Mexico. The freed ones found themselves walking into the harsh desert of a country they might not have seen since they were babies—if ever—with only the money and possessions they had with them at the time of detention.

"Yeah. I guess I was sort of lucky. Some people have to wait even longer."

"I don't feel very lucky."

"I know. But we have our plan and we're going to get through this."

Silvia was crying again. She set the rose box back in its spot, the only clean rectangle in a shelf thick with dust.

"Listen, Silvia. I know you're upset, but I need you to talk to me. I need to know how my babies are. I've been worried sick about you all."

"Oh, Mami," Silvia sniffed. "They're due home at three-fifteen, but they're not here yet, so …"

"Okay, but you're my baby, too. I have six minutes on this phone card," said Rosa, "so tell me how you are. And then I'll call again and talk to everyone when I can."

"Basically we're fine. I mean, we're okay."

As quickly as she could, Silvia filled her mother in on the big events that had happened that summer: high school graduation, choosing online college. She wanted to tell her about Lucy's attitude and mysterious outings, and to ask her what to do about the credit card bill and the shrinking stash of money, but there was no time. Plus, she'd probably burst into tears once she started sharing her fears and frustrations. No, she'd rather spare her mother the worry. It's not like she could do anything to help. "Like I said, things are fine, just weird. It's just weird without you." Silvia's eyes filled again.

"I know, bebé, I know." Rosa's voice was thick. Then brighter, "How are your classes?"

"Oh my gosh, I love them! At least, I love them when I have time to finish my assignments." Silvia glanced at the open botany textbook on the floor.

"What are you taking?"

"Botany, history, and English."

"English? Is it literature? You've always loved reading."

"It is. Well, it is and it isn't. It's Memoirs. We have to write our own, online, like a blog. And we've read some amazing examples of really good ones in class. Anne Frank and—"

"Amor, did you just hear that beep? One minute left on my card."

"Oh, Mami, there's so much to say! Sebastián's growing so fast and Lucy—" Silvia broke down into sobs.

"I know, Silvi. I'm so proud of you all. And I miss you so badly."

"We miss you, too," Silvia managed to say.

"But mira, before I get cut off. Write this down: I'm headed to San Francisco de Conchos to stay with family. When I get there, I'll call you right away, okay? Should be tomorrow, if I can get a bus."

Silvia was crying, into her sleeve rather than into the phone. She knelt by her school books, fumbling for paper and a pen.

Rosa continued, "Give my babies big hugs and muchos besos. Be strong and keep—"

And then she was gone again, cruelly cut off before even another beep or a goodbye.

"A low profile," said Silvia, crumpling over the kitchen table.

04

I thought the relief would last longer. The relief of finally hearing from him after he's been gone for so long. Instead, all I've had is nausea and nervousness. Perhaps even panic. The first time it happened, my mouth went dry and I couldn't swallow. I felt my heart racing and heard a terrible rushing sound in my ears. But I was able to talk myself out of it, to tell myself that I was not dying or in danger, that I was all right. Virgen María, protect me. Protect us.

Margarita stood from her chair and climbed the stairs to the attic to check the seedlings sprouting under the south-facing window that Jorge had cut in their slanted roof last year. Seeing the baby plants always made her breathe a little easier. The wispy first fronds of carrot rose toward the growing light from the skylight, reaching up and then diverging in opposite directions like a beautiful conundrum. The sturdier bean shoots, white, reached out of the soil and bowed in thanks to the earth that nourished them, gathering the strength and resolve to stand up straight. The slenderest chives anyone ever saw formed a silky lawn in their silver tray. Baby tomatoes were still indistinguishable from their nightshade siblings, the baby eggplants, peppers, and tomatillos. The miniature farm had once again begun to take shape in the rafters of the house. Looking down at it, Margarita thought that maybe somehow everything would be all right for their little family.

Her heart pounded and she closed her eyes against the memory of the second incident of panic, just a week after the first. Violeta had just left the house to do her outdoor chores. As Margarita had watched her cross the field, growing smaller in the distance, she broke out in a sweat. Her dress was instantly soaked under the arms and beads of water stood out on her forehead. At the same time, she began to shiver uncontrollably.

The closest chair was Jorge's. As she lowered herself onto its cushion, she had felt the nausea and accelerating heartbeat that she had experienced last time. "Oh no," she said. "Oh no, oh no." She tried to lower her head between her knees against the dizziness, but before she could, her thoughts started racing in time with her heartbeat. *There's going to be another flood. There's going to be a flood and Violeta is out there alone. I can't believe I sent her out there alone. She's only a girl and there's going to be another flood. We're only seventy-five steps from the rise above the river. I'll never get to her in time before the water comes rushing over. What if the snow in the mountains has melted early and is rushing downstream at us right now? That's what the newspaper said is going to happen. Spring is coming early and the river will run over Violeta before I can even get to her.*

The words had been accompanied by familiar images: brown frothy water carrying sticks, boards from the chicken coop, Violeta's mittens, then a little girl facedown in the murky rush. It was all absolutely real to her, completely logical, desperately inevitable.

Margarita's heart pounded in her ears. Tears ran down her cheeks while she tried to pray louder than the insistent words in her head, expelling them by force of volume: "God, please help us. Please save Violeta. Please save us. Socórranos."

Focusing on the words of her prayer seemed to help. Margarita opened her eyes but kept praying. "Please save us. Please save us." She forced herself to slow down the sentences, and felt her heartbeat relent slightly with them. Then she made herself take a breath between each repetition. Her heart calmed a little more. By the time Violeta burst back in the door, Margarita had tilted her head onto the chair's headrest and was breathing deeply, one hand on her chest and one on her head.

Her eyes had flown open. Seeing that Violeta was not wet, not hurt, she closed them again.

"What are you doing, Mami?" asked the little girl, unaccustomed to seeing her mother not in motion.

Margarita slid her eyes open. "Just taking a rest. I'm fine."

* * *

Blinking in the attic light, Margarita fought the fear that was rising in her throat with the memory of the panic attack. She forced herself to look to the far corner of the attic, where she nurtured a root of *Rosa floribunda*. When it had arrived in the mail the day before, Margarita had carefully unpacked it from the shipping crate and trimmed it according to the instructions. She had set it to soak overnight and was now ready to plant it, where it could warm up gradually with the surrounding soil. If all went well, she hoped that the rosebush would protect the secret that could safeguard her land and her family in the event that things got worse and they had to leave.

Margarita stepped carefully among the trays of seedlings until she arrived in the corner. She bent under the sloped roof and carefully removed the rose from the tin pail where it had been soaking. Picking up the towel that lay beside the pail on the floor, she gently wrapped the root and cradled it like a newborn in her arms.

Unable to hold the railing, she backed carefully down the steep steps from the attic and reached for her shawl near the door. Outside, she counted the seventy-five steps to the top of the rise, the highest point of her ancestral land. At the top, she looked down and nodded at the river, blue and cold and far below her. She breathed deeply, noticing the buds on the mesquite tree, the spiky yucca below it already greening up, the willows along the river acquiring their early yellowish cast.

She nodded, then turned her back to the river and set the rose atop its designated spot. Then she returned to the house and took a sheaf of papers out of her file. She folded them once, twice, then rolled them up. Stepping to the pantry, she removed the last of the crackers from a Uneeda Biscuit tin, tucking them into their waxed-paper blanket and setting them back on the shelf. She slid the roll of papers into the canister and replaced the lid.

Her pulse beating in her ears, Margarita walked to the kitchen counter, where she had a candle burning. She lifted the candle and dripped its red wax onto a sheet of tinfoil until she had a warm, soft lump. Then she flattened the wax into a round just slightly bigger than the biscuit tin opening, pressed it into place to form a seal, and put on the lid. Returning outside, she picked up the heavy iron shovel she had leaned against the house in preparation for the day's project and walked unbalanced, with the heavy tool in her right hand and the light tin in her left, back to the rise.

She checked the count again. Seventy-five steps. There, Margarita dug a hole twice as big as she needed. She dropped in the can and picked up the rose root. As she bent over to lower it into its spot in the earth, a pain stabbed through her belly. She froze, praying it would pass without incident. When she was sure, she gently set the root ball in place. Straightening up, she more cautiously filled the hole and packed the soil lightly with the back of the shovel. Finally, she whispered a blessing for the health of the rose, the protection of her family, and the safety and longevity of the documents hiding in the tin. "God bless this escritura," she breathed. "May these papers preserve the Rosas daughters forever."

05

The big assignment for Memoirs class was to choose a journal to read all semester and analyze, eventually turning the notes into a well-developed final paper. Silvia had already missed the deadline for submitting her proposal and was determined to do it today. She opened her laptop and started searching for famous diaries not included in the course syllabus. If she could find one housed at the Texas State library, maybe Melinda could take it out for her and she'd catch up on her work.

She pursed her lips at the thought of asking her high school best friend for any favors. In school, they always used to eat lunch together and see each other between classes and on the weekends. And even as recently as summer, Melinda had been Silvia's best support, helping her with the grocery shopping and talking through her feelings about her mother's deportation. She reassured Silvia that the separation would be temporary and that her responsibilities as caregiver to her siblings would be short-lived.

Yet as the weeks of her mother's absence passed, Silvia noticed that Melinda became increasingly distant. It was understandable, since, as a student at Texas State right in San Marcos, she had probably gotten involved in the academic and social aspects of campus life in ways that Silvia could not. But Melinda also seemed to have run out of patience for hearing Silvia's "parenting" woes. Or maybe she had just run out of advice, as a member of a family who would never really understand what Silvia was dealing with. Their frequent phone conversations had been replaced by less-frequent text messages, although they would still occasionally get together to go for walks or ice cream at Rhea's, despite the new unease between them.

"We'll cross that bridge when we come to it," decided Silvia as she typed in her first keyword search for diaries.

The house phone rang and she jumped. She closed her laptop and ran to the kitchen. Maybe it was her mother. She had only called once since arriving to stay in Conchos at Silvia's aunt's house. But in that first conversation, Mami had laid out a plan for the family's communication. She always had a plan. Although she had no cell connectivity in the house where she was staying, she would get to an area with service and call every Wednesday after the kids got home from school. There were no extracurricular activities that day, and the kids promised to be home. Today was Wednesday, but Silvia thought it odd that her mother would call so early, before Lucy and Sebastián arrived from school.

"Hello?"

"Hello ... Mrs. Castillo?"

Silvia's heart pounded, as it always did when someone asked for her mother. As a rule, the siblings were forbidden from telling anyone other than their closest family friends and Silvia's academic advisor at Penn State that Mami had been deported.

"Um, she's not available right now."

"Oh, Silvia? Is that you? You sound so grown up. It's Mrs. Black from Lucy's school. Your mom's not home?"

Silvia swallowed hard, trying to keep her voice from shaking. "No, she's not. She's actually out of town, but I can talk to you. Is everything all right with Lucy?"

"Well, not exactly. But I can just call your mom later."

"No, now that I've graduated, my mother has me taking over some of the care of my brother and sister." Silvia was trembling but said with conviction, "You may talk with me."

"Okay, I suppose. Well, Lucy has been having an ongoing conflict with her science teacher, Mr. McCloskey."

"Oh, I'm sorry to hear that. She hasn't told me about it."

Silvia walked toward the kitchen and grabbed a dish towel. She started wiping the counter in a circular pattern as she listened, biting her lip.

Mrs. Black continued, "He's been having to physically chase her down to get her to hand in her homework and labs, and I think he reached the end of his patience today."

"Oh. Yeah, that doesn't really work well on Lucy."

"Mr. McCloskey told me that she shouted 'Leave me alone!' and 'Get off my case!' at him."

"Oh, I'm so sorry." She wiped in faster circles now. "That's totally inappropriate. I'll talk to her as soon as she gets home."

"You know, you were always such a stellar student. I think we've been … surprised by Lucy."

Silvia swallowed, thinking of the unfinished journal entry and late assignments for US Borders sitting on her desk. She walked by her Borders text dozens of times a day, even sat in front of it to do other work at her desk. Yet for some reason she hadn't been able to open it in weeks. "Everybody's different, I guess," she said.

Mrs. Black went on as if she hadn't heard. "You know, if I didn't know Lucy better, it would make me wonder if she was trying to hide something."

"What do you mean, *hide*?" Silvia stopped wiping the counter, clutching the phone to her ear with both hands and feeling her face burn.

"Well, like hide drug or alcohol use. 'Leave me alone' can sometimes mean 'Let me do whatever I want, even if it's drugs.'"

"Oh, I'm sure that Lucy isn't doing that." Silvia smoothed her hair back with her left hand. "She's here with me every day after school. I check her homework myself, and I put her on the bus in the morning. She wouldn't really have time for … for that."

"Does she spend time with friends?"

Silvia thought of Lucy's evenings out and her bulging backpack. "Um, yes, a little, but she's always home by nine and she never goes out until her homework is done."

"Well, that's good. But she's got to address her science work."

"I'll speak with her. I promise. Thank you so much for the call." Silvia stiffly moved to hang up.

"Wait. There's something else," said Mrs. Black.

"Okay. What is it?"

"Lucy also pushed a girl on the playground today. Lucy claims the girl was bullying her and calling her names. She pushed her and the girl fell down."

"Oh, geez. I'm so sorry. Did the girl get hurt?" Silvia tucked a stray wave behind her ear with trembling fingers.

"A scrape on the knee. But between that incident and falling behind in science, this behavior is raising a lot of red flags. Can I ask you something?"

"Sure," said Silvia, with dread. This was the opposite of how their mother had taught them to live: above suspicion and making no waves. Since the election, even Mexican American kids born in the US were fearful of deportation, so they were all learning to be invisible. It simply meant doing well in school, not talking to the police or other officials, and never getting into trouble. Lucy was failing at least two of those tasks right now.

Mrs. Black went on. "Is everything all right at home?"

"Of course!" Silvia said a little too loudly, walking out of the kitchen and into the living room. "Why?"

"There was an agent here the other day asking about Lucy, asking for her attendance records, things like that."

"What?" Silvia froze.

"That's what I thought. You don't know anything about it. We didn't give the agent any information. He was very polite in asking for school records and made it clear that he didn't have a warrant. We just wanted to check with your mom, or I guess you, before sharing anything."

Silvia tightened her jaw. She could only imagine one agency that could possibly be checking on her family. "I appreciate that, Mrs. Black."

"Sure. Like I said, we weren't sure if you knew anything about it, so we gave him no access to her records."

"Thank you so much. Would you please let me know if he returns?"

"Certainly." Mrs. Black took an audible breath and cleared her throat. "In the meantime, if anything comes up that you or Lucy—or your mom—would like to talk about, you know we're here."

Silvia felt her face flush again. "Thanks. I'll tell my mother. I'll discuss the science class with Lucy when she gets home, but if you don't mind, I'm not going to tell her about the agent."

"That's up to you. And don't forget to remind Lucy to keep her hands to herself."

"I won't. Thank you for calling." Silvia clicked the button to disconnect the call and slumped into the waiting recliner.

So Lucy was possibly under investigation for her citizenship status? Was it because Mami had entered illegally as a child or just because they had a Mexican last name? And that meant the whole family was probably being investigated. All three kids were born here and Mami had placed their birth certificates in a safe-deposit box in the bank, but Silvia wasn't entirely sure that would be enough anymore since they were closely associated with an undocumented person.

She thought of the article that she had just read on a growing movement to eliminate birthright citizenship, the policy that all babies born in the US are automatically American citizens. If that happened, US-born children of undocumented immigrants would have their citizenship revoked and could be deported to a country in which they had never lived, and which likely didn't consider them citizens, either. Lots of Mexican American children didn't even speak Spanish and certainly didn't have a home in Mexico. Silvia could hardly think of anything scarier for a family — even if they had relatives they'd never met in Mexico like she did — and she had absolutely no idea how to deal with it.

06

Silvia wasn't sure how long she'd been sitting in the recliner thinking about the danger that Lucy and perhaps the whole family were in. Her laptop sat on the desk across the room, snapped shut like an unyielding oyster. Beside it, her stack of books and notebooks stared back at her, but she made no move toward productivity. On the other corner of the desk were two envelopes from the electric company and an unopened one from the water board. From where she sat slumped in the chair, the bills and laptop were at eye level and the books towered above. Both blurred before her eyes and she blinked away tears.

"Mami, what am I supposed to do?" she groaned, covering her eyes with the heels of her hands. She wished she had been able to talk to Mami in private, to ask her for advice and not feel so alone. She peered beneath them at her pajama bottoms and yellow ribbed tank. Irritated with its cheery color, she pulled her flannel shirt closer across her body. She hadn't worn any of her mother's clothes since Lucy's outburst before school a few weeks before, but right now she felt the need to access her, to somehow channel her mother's ability to deal with disaster through planning.

She stood from the chair and walked slowly down the hallway to the bedrooms, unsure what to do next. Her siblings would be back from school any minute and she didn't want more conflict with Lucy, nor to have to tell Sebastián no again.

She pushed open the door on the right, hearing the bottom of the hollow wood swish across the tips of the dingy beige carpet fibers. Silvia rarely went into her mother's room these days, except to get something like tweezers for one of Sebastián's splinters or a shoebox for organizing her note cards for class. The curtains were pulled, shutting out any intrusion by the Texas sun through the south-facing glass. The air was stiflingly still but the silence somehow made Silvia feel her mother's presence.

She opened a drawer of her mother's low dresser, then closed it again. She lifted the lid of the oak jewelry box, then gently lowered it. She lifted it again and took out the shallow tray to see if there was, by chance, any money stashed underneath. Nothing. Sighing, she sank down on the floor and stretched her legs out in front of her, her back leaning against the hard steel of the bed frame.

She remembered the stack of bills on the desk. To stretch the family's money until Mami came back, she had resorted to paying the electricity and gas bills every other month, figuring that as long as the power company was getting some money, they wouldn't shut off service. At this point, she had a small stack of blue envelopes sitting next to the computer, the ones that the company sent to mark late payments. She had put the phone bills on the credit card, and was also using the card to buy their food now, conserving their cash for emergencies. Maybe she could put the gas and electric bills on the credit card as well. If only she could find something here to tide them over.

The cold metal bedframe on her back made Silvia remember another place to check, and she swiveled onto her knees. She reached under the bed and felt around. Just then, she heard keys in the lock down the hall. Not sure whether she felt guilty about looking for money or just for being in her mother's room, she grabbed the flat plastic box that her fingers bumped and hurried to stash it in her room next door before the kids came in.

Her heart was still pounding when she walked as nonchalantly as she could down the hallway. "Hi, you two. It's Wednesday! I'll get the laptop. Sebastián, run to the bathroom."

"Okay, hermanota!" Sebastián grinned, then ran down the hall.

"What are you up to?" Lucy asked, eyeing Silvia.

"Not much. I'm going to put on some soup and bread for dinner. Could you log us in, please?"

Lucy sighed exaggeratedly but did what she was asked. By the time

Silvia had opened a family-sized can of chicken noodle soup and started preheating the oven, she could already hear the kids chatting with their mother. Silvia smiled, glad that they had figured out a way of chatting online with Mami once a week.

When they were finished, they called Silvia to the living room for her own conversation. As she took her place in front of the screen, she was shocked to see how thin her mother had grown, even in the last week. Her eyes, normally dark and shiny, looked somehow dull above uncharacteristically yellow circles.

She plugged her headphones into the computer to hear her mother more clearly.

"Silvi, we've barely talked since I got out. I want to hear all about your classes."

Silvia hesitated, wondering whether to comment on her mother's appearance. Instead, she scanned the whitewashed wall in the background, adorned with a brightly painted cross with a calla lily in the center. "Yeah, but Mami, I just miss you so much." Her eyes welled with tears.

"I know, querida, lo sé. I miss you all so much, too."

"It's just so hard without you. Your plan—" Silvia broke off.

"It's longer than we wanted, right, mi hija?"

Silvia nodded, unable to speak.

Her mother rubbed her forehead. "I'm so sorry, Silvi. I'm afraid this is how life is right now. We have to be where we are. At least until I can get my papers filed." Mami smiled sadly at the camera.

Silvia swallowed hard. "You're right. That's what I'm trying to do, to be where I am and be patient. For the kids. For all of us. It's just—"

"I know. So just try to tell me about your classes."

Silvia recognized that her mother always felt more emotion than she showed. She had been raised in a family of women who powered through the hard times so that the good parts of life could follow. Silvia tried to emulate her mother, but after five months it was getting hard.

"Well, I did a little for my Borders class last week. I'm trying to catch up, but …"

Her mother sat up straight in her wooden ladder-back chair. "Catch up from what? You've always been an excellent student." She furrowed her brow.

Silvia began wiping tears as they flowed from her eyes. "I know. I just don't think I can do it anymore." She began to cry quietly.

Mami leaned toward the camera. "Escúchame, hija. This is your job. You, and Lucy, and Sebastián are students. Your education is very important."

"But I'm worried about money. I'm buying the cheapest food, mac and cheese and canned soup, but the money's not lasting. Your plan's just not—"

"No, I wanna take it out!"

Silvia heard a bang and a slam from the kitchen.

Then Lucy yelling, "No, stupid! You're just gonna get burned and I don't feel like a trip to the emergency room!"

Silvia pulled out one earphone and looked over her shoulder into the kitchen. She saw her brother and sister pulling on either end of an oven mitt, dangerously close to the open oven door.

She jumped up and pulled out the other earphone, already screaming. "Hermanos! Stop it. Can't you just work it out for once? Lucy, take the bread out of the oven! Seba, set the table! And let me finish talking to Mami!"

She turned back to the computer, pressing her hands to her cheeks and gritting her teeth. Her mother was looking at her silently. Silvia's cheeks burned red and she was near tears. She put in her earphones again. "I don't know what to do anymore. Lucy can't get along with anyone!" Silvia glanced over her shoulder then wiped her eyes on the sleeve of her flannel. Leaning toward the computer screen, she whispered around the lump in her throat, "I need to talk to you about that."

"Of course. But take a big breath first, Silvi. I've never seen you yell like that."

Silvia looked down and exhaled in a growl. "I know. That's what I'm trying to tell you. I don't think I can do this anymore. I just want to get out of here."

Her mother tightened her mouth, making her cheeks look even more sunken. "One thing at a time. What did you need to talk to me about?"

Silvia told her mother in a whisper about the call from Lucy's school earlier in the day. "So I'm not sure what to do about the teacher. He just needs to just let her be and she'll get it done."

"Sí, mija! She's always been like that. Remember the time she left her room a pigsty just because I kept pestering her to clean it? It was weeks! But once I decided to pretend it didn't matter to me and stopped mentioning it, it was spotless within two days! That's just how she is." She laughed.

"Right. That's what I thought. And I told Mrs. Black the same thing, that pestering Lucy just doesn't work." Silvia raised her eyebrows and glanced toward the kitchen doorway. Lowering her voice, she returned to the computer screen. "But there's another thing."

She told her mother about Lucy's playground fight. As she was finishing, she glanced again at the kitchen doorway and saw her sister there, just outside the range of the webcam, eyes narrowed in anger. Lucy turned and stormed down the hallway to her room.

"Lucy, wait!" Silvia spun back to the computer, growling in frustration. "Mami, I have to go."

"Talk to her, Silvi. She's a good girl. Or let me talk to her about it!"

"No, Mami, I have to handle this myself. I'm the one who's here, so … I'm sorry, I really have to go. Te quiero." Silvia didn't wait for her mother's response before clicking the button to end the call. She whipped out her earphones and got up to head down the hall after Lucy.

Glancing into the kitchen as she passed it, she called, "I'll be right back, Seba." She caught sight of the little boy standing in the kitchen with a soup ladle in one hand and an oven mitt in the other. Silvia's heart pricked, seeing him looking so small and alone, but she had to take care of Lucy first this time.

She knocked at her door. "Lucy."

No answer.

"Luce, I'm sorry."

After a beat, Lucy flung the door open. "Who told you?" she demanded.

"The school. Mrs. Black. She called today."

"So you just tell Mami? You don't even know my side of the story!"

"I know enough. You're talking back to Mr. McCloskey, not turning in your work, and you got in a fight!"

"Yeah, after she called me names!"

"Who did?"

"Libby Harding. She's in my class. She's never been nice to me." Lucy was still yelling.

"So what did she call you?"

Lucy's eyes flashed. "Just about every Mexican insult you can think of. And some Middle Eastern ones, too. Because, well, she's stupid."

Silvia almost smiled despite herself. "Still, you can't push her, or anyone. You can't even touch her. You can't let people like that win by making yourself lose."

"Fine, whatever. So I'm a loser. But now I'm a loser to Mami, too." Lucy bit her trembling lower lip while continuing to stare her sister in the eye.

"I didn't call you a loser! I said you lose, we all lose, when we let bigoted people win. They say we're violent, dangerous criminals. We can't afford to prove them right, even if we feel like we're just defending ourselves."

Lucy rolled her eyes, stalked across the room, and threw herself on her bed.

"Especially now, Luce, without Mami." Silvia continued in a gentler tone. She looked around the disordered bedroom. "There's no one here to take care of us. We have to protect ourselves."

"That's what I was doing!"

"No, you were retaliating. There's a difference. We have to protect ourselves from standing out. We can't make waves. Keep our heads down, keep a low profile, like Mami always said. For Seba, if not for yourself." Silvia jumped. "Oh my gosh, Seba! He's cooking all alone!"

She rushed back down the hall to find the little boy seated at the kitchen table with his napkin on his lap, three steaming bowls of soup, three plates of bread and butter, and three glasses of water laid out and ready on the table. "Wow, Seba!" she cried.

Lucy walked into the kitchen and stood staring at Sebastián as well.

"What?" the little boy asked. "And what happened to you two?"

Sebastián looked back and forth from one sister to the other.

Lucy took her seat. "Nothing, Seb." She glanced at Silvia, at last without evident hostility. "We're fine now. We just had something to take care of."

07

They say the miners are coming back to town tomorrow. All day, I've been cleaning and tending to Jorge's seedlings in the attic under the skylight. He thinks we'll be able to plant early this year, says he can already smell the spring in the air at the mine. I'm not sure I can smell it here, but I've been trying. Nevertheless, I've knitted him a new cap and scarf to welcome him home. I'm sure we'll still have some brisk days.

Planting will be heaven. Once the corn, barley, alfalfa, and cotton crops for selling are in, and the seedlings are sown in our own garden, I'll finally have leisure to plant my flowers! The order of flower seeds came in last week, on the train from Sacramento, so I'm ready. I've even been making window boxes to dress up our house. Our little house, full of so many hopes. And my biggest is that maybe Jorge won't have to return to the mines next year.

Margarita set her pen down on the rough-hewn dining table that Jorge had made of ponderosa pine for her wedding gift. It occupied one corner of their house, in the cozy spot between the iron stove and the central fireplace. She stood and walked over to stir the pot of beans that would be their dinner, and to put another log on the fire beneath it to keep the heat high.

Stretching, she pressed her fists on the small of her back and arched toward the ceiling. She saw that Jorge's repairs were holding nicely; not even the melting snow could drip through the thick tar he had spread on the angled roof of their little house before leaving in September. She smiled to herself. He had been so proud of the repair, the last little job he had time to do before he left for the mine.

"¿Ves, mi amor? It's so tight now that not a sliver of light shines through," he had said after coming down from the roof and pulling the curtains closed against the late summer evening's light.

They stood together staring up at the ceiling, which had dripped rain into a tin bucket on the floor during the sudden downpour the week before. Now it was dry and sealed.

"Gracias, Jorge," she had said, leaning back against his shoulder.

He slipped his arms around her small waist. "You'll be safe and dry all winter," he said, kissing the top of her head.

Margarita closed her eyes and tried to cling to the ghost of that embrace. She couldn't believe that it was nearly seven months ago.

Her eyes flew open as a cold breeze hit her from across the room. Violeta ran in, leaving the door open behind her. She held a basket of eggs in one hand and was blowing on the other to warm up her bare fingers.

Margarita opened her eyes. "Why didn't you wear your mittens?"

"I didn't finish them yet! Remember, I outgrew my old ones?"

Margarita looked at her daughter. Violeta was indeed growing. She was small for her eight years, but nevertheless was a great help around their house and little farm. Like other girls in town, she attended Mt. Carmel School at the mission during the day, and did a range of chores after school. In this town without men and boys half the year, girls had no choice but to pitch in.

Margarita took the eggs from her daughter. "Ooh! Your hands are freezing!" she said, squeezing Violeta's fingers. She glanced through the open doorway and saw the pile of firewood and kindling that Violeta had stacked on the top step before gathering the eggs. She stepped past Violeta and closed the door. "Well, you'd better warm them up quickly. You'll need them for your homework and your piano today."

"I know." Violeta took off her coat and boots and hopped toward the iron stove to warm herself. "But do I have to do my homework right away?"

"Say," said Margarita, "how about I help you finish knitting your left mitten right now before dinner, and you can just finish the right? Your homework can wait until after."

"Thanks, Mami!" Violeta skipped over and the two sat down at the long table.

They each picked up a set of knitting needles with a half-finished mitten attached, the light blue yarn leading from the wooden bowl across the gnarly wood like parallel rivers on a topographic map.

"I read today that they're going to designate more state forest land," Margarita said. She tried to continue her husband's current events lessons while he was away. It was something he'd always shared with Violeta. She remembered listening to them while father and daughter turned soil side by side in the field:

"They say that there's a terrible drought in the Midwest," Jorge had said.

"Where's that?"

"North and east of here. A long way off."

"Too bad that it's so far," Violeta said.

Jorge creased his brow and looked at her from under the brim of his hat. "What do you mean?"

"Well, if it were closer, we could take them some water. We have plenty right here in the Rio."

Jorge had straightened his back and laughed, throwing his head back. "That's what I love about you, Frijolita, my little bean. You have such a generous heart, even when it makes no sense."

Violeta scowled. "It does make sense. It always makes sense to be generous." She turned her back to him.

"There, now, I'm sorry," Jorge said, stepping toward the little girl and ruffling her hair. Then his eyes twinkled and he nudged her gently with the smooth wooden handle of his shovel. "It's why I tell you the news, you know."

Violeta squinted up at him. "Why?"

"Because you help me remember that there are people in the stories. Not just facts and numbers."

That was why Margarita wanted to continue sharing the news with her, too, while Jorge was away. She believed it was important for her daughter to know what was going on in the world, but also it helped Margarita to see Violeta's humanistic perspective on the stories.

"That's good, right, Mami? More forests?"

"In a way it could be good. I think the government is hoping that more parks will draw more tourists, and that will help our state's economy."

"So how could it be bad?" asked Violeta.

"Well," said Margarita, reaching for the long steel scissors, "some of the land belongs to private owners right now. Some of it is community property. So when it's protected forest land, rural families will have less access to firewood. Then they'll have to pay money to heat their homes instead of using the resources directly from nature."

"Hmm." Violeta scowled. "It probably won't cost a lot of money to buy wood, though."

"Hopefully not. But any price is a lot of money for many families. Most papis are away working now, and many mamis don't have a way to earn money." As she spoke, Margarita's knitting needle slipped out of its loops and fell clattering to the floor.

"Mami! Usually I'm the one that drops my knitting!" Violeta laughed.

Margarita frowned as she bent sideways to retrieve her needle. She was thinking of the many times in the past year that she had accompanied her friends to see their husbands off on the train to California to harvest berries, or to Colorado to work on the huge cattle ranches. Crying children clung to their mothers' skirts at the station, wiping their noses on their hands and waving bravely to their papás. Attendance in church on Sundays made Socorro look like a town of women. Only wives and children filled the wooden pews, with the exception of a few señores and those who owned businesses in town.

She slowly worked to untangle her yarn, still scowling. Their own family had been lucky. Jorge had gotten work six years straight at the mines, helping extract lead, silver, and zinc. This year, he had even been asked to work on bookkeeping instead of in the shafts, once the foreman had recognized his talent for computation. Although she knew office work was less dirty and dangerous, Margarita still grew increasingly nervous as the months wore on that Jorge was away. Perhaps if the crop sales went well this year, he wouldn't have to go back at all.

"Yes, I know. I guess I'm a little distracted today." Margarita laid down the knitting and moved to look out the small kitchen window over the sink. She craned her neck to peer toward the road.

"But people can just get a loan from the bank, right? If they need money?" Violeta continued.

Margarita sighed. "Yes, that sometimes helps. Some families borrow against their home's value to sustain them until the pay comes in." She thought of the wives she knew who had not yet received money in the mail from their laboring husbands. Many of the men might not even be paid for their work until the end of the season. She didn't tell her daughter that securing loans was becoming harder and harder to do. In the seven years since the crash of 1929, land values had plummeted, and with so many mines closing and families moving away, few savings and loan companies would risk lending money.

"So then the mamis can either get loans or figure out how to earn their own money! Like you!" Violeta grinned.

Margarita shifted her weight from one leg to the other, peering farther down the road. "It's true. We've been working hard, haven't we?" She turned around and smiled at her daughter, thinking of the money she'd earned selling the soaps she made from the willows on her property. "And lots of mamis do that. Some sell crops from their gardens, or eggs, or meat. Lots of women even go to town as vendors in the markets."

"Like Señora Blanco!" Violeta said.

"Exactly."

Violeta tossed down her knitting and jumped to her feet, running over to Margarita. "I'm big enough to do that now! I could go to town and sell our eggs and our vegetables in the spring! I could make enough money that Papi can stay home!"

Margarita put a hand on her arm and guided her back to her chair. "No, sweet girl, your job is to be in school. You're going to school, then you're going to college. You can't be at home making soap or in town selling eggs if you want to be ..." She turned her head to look questioningly at her daughter.

"A miner like Papi!"

"Well, no, that's very physical work. But girls study to be writers, nurses, scientists, teachers, even politicians! A woman could be president, you know!"

"No, thank you. I wouldn't want to be president. Too much time indoors. I need to be free!" Violeta ran in a circle around the room. Then she stopped and gazed at the ceiling as if it were the sky. "But being a scientist would be good."

"Then you may be a scientist. Now go do your homework, doctora Violeta. I'll finish up the mittens. Remember, Papi might come home tomorrow."

The black-haired girl whooped and ran off to grab her stack of books and a pencil from her canvas school bag. Returning to the table, she settled down to work.

Margarita tied and trimmed the last of the yarn on the mittens. Then she went to the stove and added the end of a ham to the bean pot. She stirred it, staring into the soupy depths, wondering what the future indeed held for her little daughter. She tried to picture her in a lab wearing a white coat and holding a steaming glass flask. A Mexican scientist. A Mexican woman scientist. She tightened her lips as the image dissolved into the brown murk of the pot.

She had read in the newspapers about the increasing anti-Mexican sentiment not just in New Mexico, but throughout the Southwest. There were protests in the cities and fights over jobs. The U.S. Immigration Service Border Patrol, formed only twelve years earlier in response to increased immigration from Mexico, had come through Socorro several times in recent months. Margarita knew a few families that suddenly left, and the gossip in town was that they had been "repatriated."

During the long winter months, she had begun to try to find out how she might protect her family and land, especially with Jorge away so much of the year. What she learned was that it all came down to documents. Once, Mexican seasonal and contract laborers could come into the United States to work on the railroads, in the mines, on farms, and in factories without a problem. But when the president created the Border Patrol and it started demanding documentation, suddenly there was a new category of Mexican in the US: the illegal migrant.

People who had seasonally traversed the border with no need for documentation were surprised to find themselves viewed as criminals and subjected to forced and immediate deportation. Margarita read that in 1930 alone, the government captured and returned eighteen thousand of these migrants.

Yet even legal residents and their US-born children were not immune from repatriation, once the president announced that they were not "real Americans." The government had already expelled 458,000 documented residents—many of them citizens!—since the crash. Traumatized by the financial hard times, it seemed that most Americans were blindly following the president's idea that Mexicans were "expendable" workers at best. While Margarita sympathized with Americans who had lost their jobs due to the financial hard times, she also recognized right from wrong. She was amazed at how the cruel words of one man could set the tone for the entire nation.

Her own family history in the United States was as long and continuous as the Rio Grande. Her ancestors received their land in Socorro in 1816 as part of a grant from Spain to Mexico just before its independence. When that land eventually became part of the United States of America, her family acquired instant citizenship. *I shouldn't have anything to worry about,* she thought.

"Done!" announced Violeta, pushing back suddenly from her homework at the table and banging her chair down in the process.

"Díos mío!" Margarita yelled, whipping around from the stove to face her daughter. Immediately her eyes filled with scared and angry tears.

Violeta righted her chair silently. "Lo siento, mamá." Then she closed her books and tiptoed toward her room, leaving Margarita looking down the hall after her, chest heaving.

08

Silvia stood up, stretched, and headed to the kitchen for a late lunch before her siblings got home. She grabbed a package of sliced turkey from the fridge and walked the two steps to the Formica kitchen table.

She had left her phone at the charging station, and now saw that she had a text from Dr. Cisneros, her academic advisor.

ICE raids in multiple locations in Austin. Over 50 detained. FYI.

Silvia sank down in a kitchen chair, forgetting her lunch. She knew that both of her siblings had become understandably fearful of immigration officers. And now the raids were coming closer to home. Austin was a mere thirty miles away. And an ICE officer was watching Lucy.

Thanks, she texted back.

You okay?

Yeah, just a little worried. Thx for telling me.

Silvia did a quick search on her phone about the raids and learned that some immigrants were detained on their way to work, some at fast-food restaurants, and others outside their apartments in several neighborhoods of the state's capital city. It appeared that most of the people detained had no past record of crime, despite the fact that ICE insisted that they were targeting "criminal aliens." Silvia shuddered at the term. She knew that once people were labeled as inferior, called *alien* or *illegal,* violation of human rights was easy. Too easy.

The screen door creaked open, then banged shut. Lucy burst into the living room, dropping her backpack with a thump on the floor, then ran down the hall to her room and slammed the door. A moment later, Sebastián came through the door, his face wet with tears.

Alarmed, Silvia met him in the living room. "Seba, what happened?" she asked, kneeling down to hug him.

"I caught Lucy hiding something in her bag and I told her I had to tell you and she hit me and now I can't tell you and she won't talk to me anymore." Sebastián sobbed on her shoulder.

"Okay, okay, hermano. Let me get you some chocolate milk and a Kleenex and we'll sit down, okay?" Silvia disentangled herself from her little brother's arms and went to the kitchen. She poured the milk into his favorite cup, the one with a cow stamped into the glass. She squeezed in the chocolate, grabbed a spoon and a Kleenex, and headed back to the living room. She plopped down on the couch next to her brother, wiped his face, and passed him the glass.

Sebastián stirred his drink pensively, watching the sweet syrup begin to turn the milk pale brown while his sister rubbed his back in slow circles.

"It's her phone, Silvi. She never puts it down. And she hides it or pushes me when I try to see what she's doing. I just wanted to play a game on it. But this time ..." Sebastián's face crumpled.

"Okay, Seba, it's okay. I'm sure she didn't mean it."

"I feel like she doesn't love me anymore. I used to be her baby brother and now—"

"Lo sé, Sebastián, lo sé," breathed Silvia into her brother's sandy hair, just like their mother would have done. "But you know she still loves you. Lucy's just going through a hard time, is all. Like all of us."

"And then I tried to see what was in the box."

"What box?"

"That little black case she keeps in her backpack." Sebastián indicated a rectangle of about six inches by three inches. "Not the one with the makeup. That's boring! The little black one with the tiny baggies inside."

Silvia's stomach dropped. First the behavior changes and the sneaking. Then hiding her phone from everyone's view. Now little bags hidden inside a case? Was it just as Mrs. Black had suggested? Silvia was going to have to confront her sister as soon as she was sure that Sebastián was okay. "Oh, that case." Silvia tried to sound casual.

"Yeah, but she doesn't have to hit me!"

"Wait, she hit you?"

"Yeah, she punched me and told me to mind my own business and stop being so nosy. It really hurt my feelings." Sebastián sniffled into his Kleenex. "And my arm!"

"I get it, Seba. I'll work on her. But you've got to give her some space, too."

Sebastián nodded reluctantly. "Okay, I'll try." He managed a half-hearted smile and she squeezed him around the shoulders before heading down the hall to talk to Lucy. She pushed open the door and stopped when she found that her sister had pulled the curtains to darken her space just like their mom's room: not to be disturbed. When Silvia's eyes adjusted, she saw that Lucy was in bed with the covers pulled over her head, seemingly hiding from the world. The covers rose and fell a little with her breath.

Silvia approached the bed. "Lucy," she whispered.

Nothing.

Then, "Luce." Silvia heard a gentle breathing coming from the pillow, in time with the rise and fall of the blankets.

"Geez, teenagers," muttered Silvia, then half smiled to herself because she was a teenager, too. Though she felt more like a mother and more than half relieved that she didn't have to have another difficult conversation with Lucy right then.

By dinnertime, Lucy still hadn't come out of her room. Despite her stress and frustration, Silvia decided to make a special evening with Sebastián to make up for his rough day and her short temper of late. They ate hamburgers and watched television, and Silvia served vanilla ice cream for his bedtime snack.

"Here you go, hermanito."

"Gracias, hermanota." Sebastián slid closer to her on the couch.

They sat together until his bedtime. Then Silvia took his empty bowl. "Come on, let's get you to bed."

Sebastián shuffled down the hall and dutifully changed into his outer-space pajamas. Silvia watched as he brushed his teeth with his favorite strawberry toothpaste. As was her custom since their mother had been taken away, Silvia read to him and stayed until he fell asleep. Then she tiptoed out, feeling like she had at least done one thing right that day.

09

It wasn't until the next afternoon that Silvia finally found the time and the privacy to return to the plastic storage box that she'd taken from under her mother's bed the week before. She had briefly checked inside the night she found it and, finding no money, had stashed it in her closet. But sitting in front of the computer once again trying to find a memoir to study for her research project, she recalled that, under some old letters and pictures in that flat box had been a book labeled *Diario*. Maybe she could get away with not doing any research after all. Since her proposal was already almost two weeks late, her grade was going to get docked anyway. What did the quality or fame of the memoir she chose matter at this point? At least it would save her from having to ask Melinda for any help.

She retrieved the box from her closet. Setting it on the bed, she rifled beneath the rough-edged black-and-white photos and the envelopes adorned with rose stamps until she found the little leather book. She brought it back to the living room and settled in the armchair to decide if it was worthwhile.

Turning it over in her hands, Silvia noticed that the book's worn brown cover felt warm and soft under her touch. The leather's finish was crumbling a bit near the binding, but apart from that, the volume was in beautiful condition. The binding itself was hand sewn with white cotton thread, and the pages, though yellowed, were thick and richly textured. Silvia stroked them with the reverence of the serious student that she once was, before she was saddled with the life of an adult. Then she began to flip through the pages, starting at the back.

The first thing she noticed was the drawings, done in pencil and shaded in what must have been charcoal, although it was hardly smudged at all. She paused at a map drawn from an aerial perspective, showing land lying along a river, which was labeled *Rio Grande*. She flipped to the next drawing, a view of a street lined on both sides with low buildings. Some had signs indicating that they were stores or restaurants. Next she turned to a drawing of a small adobe church in the middle of a flat field, its bell tower reaching up into the sky. It was labeled *La misión*.

"Wow," Silvia commented as she continued turning pages. She came to a sketch of a wooden cottage with a stone foundation, standing partway up a hill. She smiled at the tidy house surrounded by flowers, shed roof sloping at a perfect forty-five-degree angle. The next page showed what must have been a close-up of the garden, and then of several of its plants. Each was labeled in Latin. Silvia strained to see if she could identify the plants using her newly honed botanical skills. One was clearly a rose. Another was some sort of frondy, riparian plant, like a willow or a rush. Silvia felt a tingle of discovery as she used knowledge from her three courses. *Whoever drew this knew Spanish* and *Latin*, she thought. *Amazing*.

She flipped to the front of the book, and then back again, scanning through the dates. "April 1936," she read. "Right in the middle of the Great Depression."

Silvia's mind raced as she tried to figure out who the book might have belonged to—perhaps someone in her family?

She remembered asking her mother last Christmas about her grandparents' new life after their illegal entry into the United States. "Were they happy here, Mami? Were they glad they came?"

"Mostly. Your abuelo had to do more farm work in the US than he wanted, but he also did get into those air-conditioned offices that he'd dreamt about, even if it was only on the weekends for cleaning jobs."

"What about abuelita?" Silvia had stirred the beans and rice on the stove while they talked. She barely remembered her grandparents, since they had returned to Mexico when she was four.

"Well, once she had me registered in school, she found work as a part-time receptionist at a busy medical office that served mostly Spanish speakers. Her schedule allowed her to be home every day when I got home from school." Silvia's mother looked off into the distance as she talked. "I grew up with a house—rented, not owned—and a yard with a peach tree. No real friends, though, because abuelito always told me to keep to myself. But it was a good childhood."

"What about your brother and sisters?" asked Silvia, even though she already knew the story. She loved hearing about her family in Mexico.

Her mother smiled. "They were much older, so they stayed and lived their lives. My parents were never able to bring them, nor the grandchildren, across the border. They just didn't have the money and didn't want to take the risk." She paused. "Plus they also couldn't go back to visit since they had entered illegally. So they kept their relationships with your tíos alive through phone calls and postcards. I feel like I know my siblings, even though I haven't seen them since I was tiny."

Well, now you have, Mami. At least something good had come of her mother's deportation. Silvia returned her thoughts to the diario.

If her grandparents had come to the US when her mother was little, in the late 1970s, the diary couldn't belong to one of them. She had been hoping that maybe it was her abuelita's and she could get to know her through her writing, even though she had passed away years ago. But it could still be useful for her research project. It was already yielding potential questions about bilingualism in Texas, education, and the Great Depression. She began to feel more excited about her project.

Feeling for a moment like the student that she used to be, Silvia crossed the room to her desk and penned a preliminary to-do list. But she wanted to follow one lead now. Her curiosity was piqued by a word that had jumped out at her while she was turning the pages of the diary: *Socorro*. She knew it was a woman's name, and also a noun meaning "aid" or "help." But was it also something else?

On her hunch, she keyed in *Socorro*. The results included a map of Texas, which showed the blue dot for the town of Socorro, consistent with the diary's sketches, on the bank of the Rio Grande. She zoomed out and saw that the town was located at the very point of far west Texas, at the border the state shared with New Mexico and Mexico. Socorro was now all but gobbled up by the cities of El Paso, Texas, and Ciudad Juárez on the other side of the border.

She clicked over to see images of the town. Up popped photos of flat dirt roads, dusty pastures, and a single street that resembled the one in the diario. Below that, multiplied throughout the search engine's window like an Andy Warhol painting, was a single adobe church that matched the one she had seen in the book.

She clicked to zoom in for a closer look. It had a perfectly symmetrical facade with a central wooden door. Above that was a metal bell, and at the low peak of the structure, a simple cross. Silvia had participated in a few class trips to the historic sites of San Antonio, and thus recognized the church as an example of Spanish mission style. She clicked to read more and learned that the church had been built in 1840. *Interesting*, she thought. *Right at the very beginning of Texas's statehood.*

Silvia was surprised to find that it was after three o'clock, marked not by a clock chiming, but by the door swinging open and her siblings entering. Sebastián ran over for a hug and started chattering about his naturalists' club, which had held its inaugural meeting that afternoon.

"And look at this rock," he grinned. "It's pyrite, but I think it's also got some real gold!"

Silvia held the sparkly stone up to the light from the picture window while Sebastián opened the lid of a sturdy cardboard box with compartments for eight more minerals.

"We're going to get a new one each week!" Sebastián said. "At the end, all"—he counted the spaces with his finger—"nine of these holes will be filled!"

"That's fantastic, kiddo!" Silvia glanced down the hall in the direction that Lucy had gone without a word while Sebastián was talking.

When Sebastián paused for breath, Silvia held up a finger to him to wait, and turned to follow Lucy. "Be right back, kiddo." It had been a relatively smooth arrival from school, and she figured this was as good a time as any to have that serious conversation. Setting her jaw in imitation of her mother's characteristic determination, Silvia walked down the hallway toward conflict.

"Hey, Luce," she said, at once knocking and entering her sister's darkened room.

"Hey."

"Everything okay?"

"I'm fine!"

"Well, you don't sound like it." Silvia tried to disguise her annoyance.

"Just leave me alone! I'm fine," Lucy said between clenched teeth.

"I'm glad you're fine. But we have to talk about what happened yesterday."

Lucy sighed and swung her feet onto the floor, letting them thump heavily on the carpet. "It's over. Why can't you ever let anything go?"

Silvia took a deep breath, willing herself to stay calm. "Sebastián told me that you have a little black box in your backpack. Can I see it?"

"Help yourself," Lucy said, tossing her open backpack across the bed in Silvia's direction.

Silvia sat down, then reached into the pack and pulled out a black rectangular case that matched her brother's description. Hands trembling slightly, she opened it and a tampon spilled out.

"Happy?" Lucy said defiantly. "I don't know why everyone has to mess with my things. Tampons and makeup. That's all I have."

Silvia persisted, "Sebastián said that you had little baggies in here."

"You mean these?" Lucy roughly grabbed the case back from her sister, emptying out small plastic containers of blush and eyeliner until she pulled out a Ziploc baggie of Q-tips. "Oooh, scary. Big sister, may I please have your permission to clean my ears?" She pulled out one more bag, this one with the crumbs of a broken blue eye shadow. "And to color my eyelids? Do I have to check everything with you?" As Lucy tossed the baggies down onto her bed, the one with eye shadow in it came open, sprinkling dark powder on the cream-colored pants Silvia was wearing.

"You have got to learn to control yourself, Lucy. You're ruining everything!" Silvia shouted, scratching frantically at the blue-gray stain on her pant leg.

Lucy leaned toward her. "Oh my God. Are you wearing Mami's pants? What is wrong with you? You do think you're Mami." Lucy looked disgusted.

Silvia got to her feet, pulling herself up to her full five feet, five inches and leaning over Lucy, seated on the bed. She lowered her voice to a near growl. "I may not be Mami, but I am in charge here. Of who wears what. Of who has what in their bags. Of what we eat and what we do and when we eat it and do it. And I am in charge of both of you, whether you like it or not."

Lucy glared at Silvia, unblinking.

"If I can't trust you to be honest, do your work, not fight with people at school, and"—Silvia's voice almost broke, but she controlled it—"keep a low profile, you're out of here."

Silvia turned and walked out of the room more confidently than she felt, and bumped right into Sebastián, who was stationed outside Lucy's door, holding more rocks and ready to go on with his story. "Sorry, Seba, I just need some quiet for a minute," she said. She brushed past him, turned down the hall to her room, and slammed the door.

10

Last night I had another of my dreams. I dreamt of Socorro. I saw it first from the sky, like a map spread below me: the dark green trees atop red dusty land, the glittery brown Rio Grande. As I watched, the map briefly displayed our own lush green farm crisscrossed by irrigation ditches from the river. Then it was as if I was flying, soaring slowly above the neat grid of our town.

As Socorro grew larger in my view, I saw the wooden roofs and adobe walls arranged on both sides of the streets. The open-air market. Carlton's store. The bank. Then my sights rested on the dual steeples of the orange mission. For a moment I felt happy, joyous even.

Margarita stared absently across the open living room, remembering her dream. When she had seen the church, she had suddenly plummeted out of the sky, stopping just before hitting the street. But unlike with some of her other dreams, she did not awaken from the fright. Instead, her eyes remained riveted to the mission and she walked, almost against her will, down El Camino Real Street as the mission slowly grew larger in her view. Townspeople—her friends—started to emerge from the buildings to stare at her, as if they somehow knew why she was being drawn to the church. In her peripheral vision she saw skirts, dresses, parasols against the burning sun. Something felt wrong.

Mustering her strength, Margarita wrenched her vision from the mission to inspect the people she passed. Mrs. Carlton, but no Mr. Carlton of the general store. Willy's wife, but no Willy. She scanned the sidewalk. Little girls walked toward the mission school holding tiny versions of themselves by the hand, who in turn dangled rag-doll imitations of themselves from their fingers. A truck rumbled by, piloted by a girl in overalls who waved as she passed and smiled a macabre toothless grin. Margarita's eyes widened in panic as she searched the streets, seeing nothing but women.

Then Margarita saw the mailman come into view. He was limping down the street, his pace a slow-motion counterpoint to the pace of the girls and the pull of Margarita toward the church. He was lugging his heavy bag, bulging with newspapers and letters. Relieved, Margarita smiled and tried to call out to him. He turned to look her way, revealing a grotesquely lipsticked mouth and heavy pearl-drop earrings. She gasped and he looked away, laughing.

Her inexorable draw toward the mission continued, and now tears streamed down her cheeks. She tried not to see the carriages with only pink blankets inside, the produce wagons with red-painted fingernails on the handles, the bicycles with high-heeled feet on the pedals. She looked straight ahead at the wooden door to the mission, her haven. She must be going there to escape from this Town of Women.

At the end of the street she could see the church door swing open, Fr. Rodríguez's reassuring form filling the doorway, silhouetted by the candles blazing in the sanctuary behind him. Why were they lit on a Friday morning? Was it a funeral? A wedding?

When she was fifty feet away, the zoom accelerated and Margarita rushed as if jerked by a rope around her middle toward the open door. At thirty feet, Fr. Rodríguez turned to make space for her to pass into the church. At twenty feet, she saw, black against the golden candlelight within, his abdomen bulging with child. Screaming, she threw her hands and feet out front in a vain effort to cease the forward motion, then crashed into the priest's voluptuous form, and they both landed on the hard red-tiled floor, her legs astride his belly heaving with child.

11

The next morning, Silvia was back to work, hoping to catch up with her late assignments. She'd start small: a discussion board post for her botany class. But she didn't anticipate how distracted she'd be by the conflicts of the last week. Still facing a snow-white screen after more than twenty minutes, she realized it was time to ask for help.

She tapped over to Dr. Cisneros's faculty member page, where she confirmed that her advisor was holding online office hours. It wasn't the same as being able to appear in person in a beautiful redbrick college hall, but it would have to do. She opened a chat box and took a deep breath.

Hi, Silvia. What's up?

Hi, Professor. I wonder if you could help me.

Sure. What do you need?

At this point, Silvia's hands started to shake. Where could she possibly begin? With their inability to pay their bills? With the federal agent inquiring about Lucy? With her own temper that she couldn't seem to keep under control?

Hello? Still there? appeared on her screen.

She decided to keep it academic. *I'm having some trouble in my classes.*

What's going on?

I've fallen behind in Borders. My project proposal is late for Memoirs. Only botany is kind of going okay.

Kind of?

I have a B.

Is that what you were aiming for?

Well no, but … Silvia hesitated. *Dr. C., could we talk on the phone?*

Sure. Give me five minutes and call my office number.

Okay.

Silvia stood up from the computer and paced a path from the desk to the kitchen. Finally, she decided to just go make a cup of tea. By then it would be time to call.

She let seven minutes pass before ringing her professor, out of equal parts consideration and nerves. They spent the first minutes of their call strategizing for Silvia's classes and making a plan for her to get back on track.

"Good. I love plans," Silvia said. "My mom always solved problems by making plans with us. It worked really well. Usually," she concluded, thinking about the five steps her mother had coached her on before her deportation, and how that plan was never supposed to have lasted more than a few weeks.

"Usually?"

"Well, yes. I mean, until lately, when it turns out that some plans don't work the way they were supposed to."

"Are you talking about the deportation?"

"About that, about my sister and brother, about everything." Silvia's voice was thick as she told her professor about the conflicts at home, the unpaid bills, and her concerns about Lucy's behavior. "Then I find out that federal agents are visiting her school!"

"What kind of federal agents?"

"Immigration, I assume. I just don't know what to do with all of this." Silvia sank into the armchair, cradling her head against the phone.

There was a pause. Then Dr. Cisneros said, "Did I ever tell you how I got into teaching?"

"No, I don't think so."

"I was working as a lawyer in southern California after I got my law degree from UCLA. Like every lawyer in San Diego, I eventually started getting cases that involved immigrants, some legal, some un-documented."

"Sure."

"Even though my job was to represent laborers in workers' compensation cases, more and more of my caseloads began to include sticky situations involving the rights of illegal immigrants. I saw how I could be of more service to workers and families if I took on more immigration cases, and my work suddenly felt more meaningful."

"That's great." Silvia smiled at her professor's kindness. She got up from the chair and began to walk around the house, pausing at the family photos that lined the walls of the hallway to the bedrooms. She and Mami. Little Lucy and Sebastián posing in a tree. Her eyes filled with tears as she listened to her professor speak.

"Yes, it was. I had some pretty big successes, big to the families that they affected, anyway. I eventually worked in Tucson, and then in Laredo. My Spanish got better and better, and I felt like my work was important and true to my Mexican heritage."

Silvia stopped at a picture of herself with Mami and Lucy in front of a church. "Oh, I didn't realize you were Mexican, Professor."

"Yes, my grandfather on my mother's side was from Puebla, and my father was born in Oaxaca. So anyway, everything was going well, until one day I lost a case." She paused.

"Oh, sorry." Silvia looked down the hall at the line of family portraits that led to her mother's room.

"It wasn't my first loss, by any means, but it was my worst. The father was a legal resident who had let his visa expire and I was representing him in a suit for wrongful termination over an unrelated issue. The judge not only ruled against us, but ordered his immediate deportation."

"Oh no!"

"His wife, who had come from Mexico illegally, was deported as well, right from the courtroom, even though she was not involved in the case at hand. Their children, seven and four, were born in the US and were also present."

Silvia's eyes filled with tears, and she reached out her hand to touch Sebastián's face in the tree picture with Lucy. He must have been younger than that when the photo was taken.

Dr. Cisneros sighed and continued. "Being citizens, they were not allowed to be deported with their parents. Instead, they were placed directly into foster care. I'll never forget that mother's screams when they took her out of the courtroom through one door and her kids out another with CPS."

Silvia took her hand away from the photo and pressed it to her mouth. "That's awful," she managed to say.

"It's unconscionable," said Dr. Cisneros. "I quit my job that day. I knew I could never again see a family ripped apart over a border, feeling like I could have done something to stop it, if only."

Silvia turned her back on the hall of pictures and faced the living room, her mouth open.

The professor continued. "I'm Mexican, and I couldn't help Mexicans. I wanted to get as far from that border—and from those problems—as possible."

Those problems. Silvia walked to the living room and laid her hand on the leather diary sitting on her desk. She clenched her jaw. "So you just left?"

"I had to. I passed my other cases to my colleagues, handed in my resignation, and moved to the Northeast, as far from the border as I could get. Eventually I landed an adjunct position teaching social work while I got my PhD. I already had the experience I needed to apply for faculty positions; I just needed the degree."

"Yeah, wow," said Silvia, tightening her lips.

"All I'm saying is that, to the extent possible, I understand what you're going through."

Well, sort of, thought Silvia. *But then you quit.* Then she blinked and answered quickly, "I guess right now I just need to get back on track and try to keep our life together. Thank you for sharing your story with me, even though …"

"Even though I left, right?" Professor Cisneros asked. "Look, I'm not proud of it. Sometimes I hear that mother's screams in my dreams at night. Or see those children's faces in my memory. But I've come to realize that there are other ways I can help."

Silvia nodded. "Yeah, I guess. We haven't been able to talk about this to anybody."

"And you have to keep it that way, Silvia, especially if you think you're under scrutiny. Just try to keep a low profile for now."

Silvia blinked, surprised to hear echoes of her mother's admonition in her professor's voice. "Thank you. I'll try."

12

Silvia spent the rest of the day working on her courses with vigor fueled by anger and fear, after talking to her advisor. When the kids got home from school, Sebastián was brimming with excitement.

"Look, hermanota! I got another rock!"

Silvia blinked at the sudden change of roles that she had to make. She got up from the computer to try to be encouraging to her brother. "Wow, Seba, what is it?"

"It's quartz! A real mineral!"

"What does that mean?" she asked, watching out of the corner of her eye as Lucy passed through to the kitchen, not saying a word.

"Well, all rocks are all made up of minerals, but some rocks are just the pure mineral, without any sand or anything mixed in. Like this one. I think it looks like a diamond!"

Silvia held the double-pointed crystal up to the window. The light shone right through it, giving it a glassy appearance.

"That's really cool, Seba. How many rocks do you have in your box now?"

Sebastián knelt down on the floor and opened his collection. He place the quartz crystal in its compartment. "Three. Pyrite the first week, gypsum last week, and now quartz."

"That's great," said Silvia, ruffling his hair. "I'm glad you love your club."

"It's the best!" said Sebastián, gathering up his rock box with his school backpack and skipping down the hall to his room. A moment later he poked his head back into the living room. "Hey, Silvi? Can I watch a show on your computer?"

"Sure," she said, unplugging her laptop and handing it to her brother. "Careful, two hands."

Sebastián headed down the hall, this time at a more cautious pace.

Silvia entered the kitchen, where she found Lucy getting a snack. "What about your day?" she asked.

"It was okay," said Lucy, grabbing a small brown paper bag of sunflower seeds from an upper cabinet.

Silvia reached over Lucy's head and pulled down a package of crackers. Hoping that the mood was right, she decided to check in on her sister's behavior. "So, is Libby leaving you alone?"

"You mean am I leaving her alone, right?" Lucy snapped.

"Um, no … I really meant the question I asked," Silvia responded.

"Yeah, we're staying away from each other."

Silvia let a beat pass while she got a juice box from the refrigerator and calmed down. "And how's science?"

"Better, now that he's leaving me alone."

"I'm glad. I know you hate to have someone on your case."

Lucy turned to face her. "You mean like you are right now?"

"I'm just checking on how things are going. It's kind of my job now, as you already know." Silvia clenched her teeth.

"Well, 'things' are fine. I just can't wait until everyone can just leave me alone and let me do my own thing." Lucy sat down hard on a kitchen chair, sweeping a pile of mail to the side with one forearm. The letters cascaded to the floor.

"You know what, Lucy?" Silvia's eyes flashed. "Me neither. I can't wait until you're eighteen and I don't have to be your mother anymore. But right now I am. So pick up those papers." She planted her feet and pointed at the pile as if commanding a dog to obey.

"No," said Lucy coolly. She took a handful of sunflower seeds and began eating them one by one.

"Do it. Now."

"Nope."

Without thinking, Silvia punched her sister on the shoulder, hard enough that her knuckles hurt as she contacted the seam of Lucy's black denim jacket.

Stunned, Lucy clutched her shoulder with her opposite hand. Then she seemed to regain her composure. She stood up from the table, eye to eye with Silvia. "So you're going to start abusing us now? Is that what's next? Because I could tell Mrs. Black about this. About all of it."

Silvia was silent, eyes boring into her sister's.

"I will. I'll tell her about the crappy food you're buying us, the unpaid bills, and now the abuse."

"You can't!" Silvia raised her chin confidently. "You can't, because then you'd have to tell her about Mami."

"What does it matter?" Lucy yelled. "She's not coming back! Do you think I care where I live? I'll go to Mexico right now! It would be better than here!"

Silvia shouted without thinking, "Maybe Mrs. Black will help you with that, too! She can just ask the immigration agent to take you to the border! He's been watching you, anyway!"

Instantly, she knew she had gone too far. Lucy's face registered shock, betrayal, and worst of all, fear. Then she began to sob, loud, horrible convulsions wracking her body.

"Shhh, Lucy, shhhh. I'm sorry." Silvia put her arm around her sister, glancing toward the open doorway. She was glad that Sebastián was using his headphones in his room.

Lucy continued to cry, leaning over the narrow counter.

"Shhh. Please stop crying. I love you."

Lucy fell silent and stood up, turning to face Silvia. She spoke with control. "You don't. You don't even care about me."

13

Jorge came home last week. In some ways, it was just as I hoped. We ate the cornbread I baked for him, we talked about how well the new roof he installed has been holding up. We laughed about Violeta, how big she's gotten, and how she wants to be a scientist when she grows up. Jorge brought her a puppy and she was so thrilled! He even remembered to bring me a can of Uneeda Biscuits just like my father always did when he returned from travels.

All of that was good, but still, Jorge seems changed. He didn't react when I sliced the cornbread with the rosewood knife he made for me for our first anniversary. He doesn't return my affections. He seems preoccupied about the state of the economy and the recent mine closures. At least, I hope that's all it is. Maybe as he settles back in he'll be able to tell me more about it.

Margarita finished writing and closed her leather-bound diary. She closed her eyes and thought about her husband and how different he seemed. Sure, he had made the effort to change out of his work overalls into his black pants and shirtwaist. And his mustache was neatly trimmed. But his attentions seemed to end there. When Margarita had asked him if he needed to talk to her, his answer was curt.

"Nope," said Jorge in a grouchy voice. "Only that prices for lead are down and many of the veins have already run out. You must have read that several mines in New Mexico have closed already."

"Hopefully you won't be returning, anyway, like we planned."

Jorge looked at her. "No," he said slowly, as if talking to a very young child. "The plan is to see how this year's crops go, and then after next year's work I'll come home to stay. Maybe."

Margarita looked down for a moment, then moved to the table and began straightening the cheese and butter, busying her hands lining them up just so. "I just can't bear the thought of you living in that squalor, eating who knows what, away from your family …"

Jorge laughed, a single bark. "It's not all bad. Not at all."

Now what does he mean by that? Margarita thought. She felt her face grow warm.

Jorge continued. "I don't mind life in the boarding house. The men are good company." He sat down at the table and grabbed a chunk of cheese. "As for the food, now, you might be right," he said, biting into the wedge roughly.

Violeta, too, had noticed the change in her father, the disappearance of his usual good humor. She started emulating Margarita's efforts to please him. She ran straight home from school in the afternoons to do extra chores "to lighten Papi's load." She filled their living room with the sounds of her piano practicing without complaint. She assumed full responsibility for the puppy, who she had named Pastor because he looked like "one of those shepherd dogs." She worked on his house-training and tied him outside each morning before she left for school.

Still, one night as Margarita tucked her into bed, she whispered, "What's the matter with Papi?"

"Nothing, sweetheart," said Margarita. "He must still be tired from his work."

"But it's been days now," whined Violeta. "When is he going to stop being tired?"

Margarita smoothed Violeta's hair off her forehead. "I don't know, querida. Soon, I hope."

Thirteen days after Jorge's return, the second vegetable seed shipment arrived.

"The seeds are here, Jorge," Margarita called as soon as the delivery man had left.

"Mmm-hmm," said Jorge from the attic loft.

"Don't you want to open them with me like always?" Her voice came out a little too high.

"No, you can do it."

Margarita pried open the wooden crates with the claw of a hammer. Silently, she unpacked the anticipated seeds and sorted them into two piles: one for commercial growing and the other for the family garden. Seeing the piles grow cheered her, the first high with alfalfa, cotton, barley, and half of the corn seeds, and the second smaller with corn for feed, three varieties of tomatoes, squashes, beans, and shelling peas. She straightened up and rolled her shoulders back.

Just then, Jorge called Margarita to come up to the attic, where her seedlings were growing. Her heart jumped at the edge to his voice, unsure whether he was angry or excited. She passed through the open door and climbed the steep steps to the loft where silver trays of broccoli, greens, and onions covered the floor. Even though it was still early spring, the skylight let in warmth and light almost all day. The little seedlings were now several inches high, and Margarita expected to be able to plant them before the end of the month.

"What is it, querido?"

"Look over here," Jorge said, pointing to an open space on the floor. "I think we can put the tomato starts right here. You have more soil?"

Margarita searched his face, then smiled. Maybe it was going to be a good day. "Yes, in the sack." She indicated a slouching burlap bag in the corner. "I kept it out of the shed so that it wouldn't freeze."

Her husband squeezed past her without touching even the hem of her dress. Margarita stepped aside. "Don't let me get in your way," she mumbled.

"What's that?" he asked, poised to go down the steps.

"Nothing. Never mind," she said, feeling her face turn hot.

In a moment Jorge returned with the packets of tomato seeds and a sprinkling can of water. They spent the afternoon side by side, tending to their new little sprouts and planting seeds for cherry tomatoes, beefsteak tomatoes, and tomatillos.

After over an hour bent to her work, Margarita stood up and pressed her hands into her lower back, her head coming to rest against the sloped ceiling above. She squinted her eyes slightly, enabling her to see the attic floor as a miniature farm. The trays became fields, the inches became acres. Row upon row of light green stems topped with twin leaves stretched out before her to the horizon. She imagined the stems stretching upward, cotyledons giving way to true leaves, spiky, darker, and spread out below the sun's rays. Blinking, she smiled at the miracle of regeneration.

It was a miracle they had seen play out on their own farm. Only seven years ago, shortly after Margarita had inherited the homestead after her parents passed away, her hopes for a good growing season were smothered under thirteen inches of silt. The flood of 1929 had come as a shock to the people of the valley, since it came in mid-August, rather than with the spring runoff. The Rio overflowed its banks and spilled into the low-lying farmland along its shores. In its haste to find its level, the water had raced around the stone foundation of Margarita and Jorge's wooden house built on a small incline, splashes invading the house via the small space under their wooden door.

It was a few seconds before Margarita realized that Jorge was staring at her from his crouch among the seedlings on their attic floor. "What are you thinking about *now*?"

Margarita blinked and looked down at her husband. "Oh, just how far we've come."

"Since when, the floods?"

"Yes. Remember how you always used to know what I was thinking? You still do, I guess."

Jorge's eyes shifted to the left. "That's because you're always thinking about the floods. I've told you I don't want to talk about them anymore. Not since you started getting all … upset." He said the last word as if it was an insult.

She took a breath, let it out, and tried again. "That hasn't happened in a long time."

After the rains had stopped, they opened their door and found themselves isolated inside their house on what was a tiny island. The only other land visible was the rise above the river, with their three cows huddled together under Margarita's favorite mesquite tree on top. There was no sign of their chicken coop. The view out their door was bleak and crushing, but Jorge reminded her that they had plenty of food inside the house and that they simply needed to care for their baby and wait for the waters to recede.

However, when the waters receded, they exposed an even bleaker landscape than they had feared. Their small farm was covered in sticky silt that belched when Jorge stepped into it in his work boots. All the cotton plants were bent in half and buried in mud and it was clear that the crop had no chance of survival. The vegetables they had been growing for themselves were not even visible. That was the only time in her life that Margarita felt she could not go on without her strong mother or her practical father still there to bolster her.

Margarita looked over her miniature field in the attic, trying to usher Jorge into the memory with her. "Remember when we lived in town, though? It seemed like it lasted for so long."

"I guess so. Nine months." Jorge kept working, not meeting her eyes.

After the flood, the family had had no choice but to temporarily relocate, since they were completely cut off from supplies and transportation, with no prospect of growing food that year. The day that Margarita left the only home she had ever known was devastating. Tears filled her eyes as she watched her husband carry their baby on his right shoulder and their tan duffle bag, bulging with clothing, baby bottles, bibs, and a few kitchen essentials, on his left. He armed her with a walking stick to pick her way through the muck, which had surpassed the tops of her lace-up boots by the time she reached the road. There, the layer of silt was thinner, packed down by the few tractors and trucks that had passed by since the waters receded. The walking became easier and she squared her shoulders, tossed her walking stick, and caught up to her husband and baby. They had stridden into town together, side by side.

The family adjusted well to its temporary new life in town. They shared the full-sized bed in the room that they had rented, and used a single propane burner for heat and for warming canned beans and chili. Margarita had use of the house's kitchen for washing up and cooking. Mother and baby enjoyed more frequent social visits now that they were in the center of town. Margarita also began cleaning and helping at the mission church and school while the baby napped, in exchange for a ration of rice and canned vegetables.

Meanwhile, every morning at dawn Jorge walked back to the farm and spent long days cleaning and making repairs. Once the land became more easily traversable, he began to sleep in their house so that he could dedicate all of his time and energy to restoring his family to their home. He patched the concrete in the stone foundation, repaired the door, raised the jamb, and tacked a strip of thick felt weatherproofing around the entire door.

"Oh yes, it was nine months. Because that's when—" Margarita began.

"—the second flood hit," Jorge completed her thought. He met her eyes for a second, then flushed and turned away.

At the time of the second flood, Jorge had just completed two full days clearing muck from the road that cut across their property to the house. The region's regular seasonal cloudbursts turned ravaging, and on September 21, floodwaters barreled down the Rio Grande. This time, the waters broke through all remaining dykes, swept away railroad tracks, and covered the only highway, leaving Socorro completely stranded.

In town, rumors abounded of villages to the north that were hit harder still, one completely destroyed by a wall of water eight feet high that rushed down its main street. Margarita tried to shield her panic from her baby daughter as she awaited Jorge's return that day. The flood occurred before noon and by nightfall, he still wasn't back.

Fortunately, when the flood hit, Jorge was in town buying supplies to rebuild the chicken coop. Once the streets in town were passable, he went directly to the rented room and stayed until the flood waters receded farther. When he was finally able to return to the farm, he again started his repairs from scratch, uncomplaining.

Margarita scowled, both at Jorge's embarrassment and at the memories of the worst year of their lives. They had had to wait for federal relief money all year. "You had to take the mining job."

"Right." A silence hung between them for a few moments.

Margarita remembered the uncertainty of the wait, neither knowing if the money was ever going to come. The US Army Corps of Engineers came to Socorro long before any federal relief funds, and they worked up and down the Rio Grande. With their aid, it wasn't long before rail and road travel, along with the hopes of the people of Socorro, was restored. Residents were relieved to know that supplies for survival and reconstruction would arrive regularly. The Corps also restored communication, bringing confirmation of the rumors of damage farther upstream. During the months that followed, hundreds of families relocated to other towns and states, and many businesses never reopened.

"Uh-huh. It was a rough time," continued Jorge. "But it's over."

Margarita smiled and reached toward his arm.

"We made it through."

"Yup," said Jorge, moving his arm away as he turned back to work on the seedlings.

Margarita dropped her hand to her side. "And you've supported us with mining for six years. Maybe that's enough."

"Why do you have to push me about that all the time?" Jorge asked, standing so that his stature matched his vocal volume. "Just get off my back about it, would you?" He stormed to the steps and descended them in two jumps. "And stop worrying about the floods!" he called back.

Margarita loomed over her helpless seedlings like an awkward giant alone in a foreign land. She watched her miniature farm blur below her. Then she lifted her right foot and sank it squarely in the middle of the broccoli patch, twisting the heel of her boot on top of the healthiest blue-green sprouts until they lay flat and withered, caked with dirt and pinned to the bottom of the tray.

14

That night, Silvia simply had to escape from the house. Even Melinda's bristly indifference would better than Lucy's rage. And there was a chance that maybe she could fix things with Mel tonight. Silvia really needed her friend back.

Leaving Lucy in charge with some hesitation, she met up with Melinda at the ice cream shop. They sat outside Texas State's Theater Center, the campus's most iconic setting. The building was perched like a recently landed UFO in the middle of a lagoon that glowed blue in the late-evening light. Man-made islands and bridges, many with tall trees on them to shade the walkways beneath, crisscrossed the shallow waters in several places. The abundant water seemed to ensure that there was always a breeze on the little islands, and the girls chose their usual bench on the fountain side to view the underwater lights that would soon turn on.

"Have you talked to your mother?"

Silvia was surprised and encouraged that her friend had asked. "Yes," she beamed, relieved that she had some good news to share for once. "We FaceTime with her every Wednesday afternoon. She's with my aunts and uncles in Conchos. She's fine. But she's trying to make a plan. She wants to borrow some money from our relatives and then come back up to the border to file her papers to enter legally. I keep telling her not to. I'm so scared that she's going to end up in jail."

"Your mother and her plans. This one sounds crazier than most of them."

Silvia stiffened. Somehow Melinda's comment was akin to speaking ill of the dead.

"At least where she is, you can talk to her and even FaceTime her." Melinda took a mouthful of strawberry-Nutella ice cream, tossing back her blond hair.

"Yeah. At least we have that." Silvia looked down, then took a breath and tried again. "FaceTiming makes Sebastián really happy because she can play with him on the screen, but he's always extra sad after."

"I'm sure. And how's Lucy?"

It sounded like Melinda was running through a list of obligatory questions, not asking out of care or interest. Nevertheless, Silvia confessed, "I wish I knew. But right now I'm trying to keep an eye on *what* she's doing."

"What do you mean?"

"Well, remember I told you at the beginning of the semester that she was acting strange and being secretive?"

"Yeah. And you said you were going to talk to her about it. I remember." Melinda paused, then sighed as she pushed a strand of hair out of her eyes with the back of her hand. "So, how did it go?"

Silvia tried not to register her friend's just-tolerant tone. She took a moment and a spoonful of avocado-and-coconut ice cream, then tried one last time. "Well, she's thirteen. She was pretty resentful. I think with Mami gone … I don't know. She just doesn't want to talk to me about anything. She's being mean to Sebastián, and he's just a little kid, you know?" She glanced at Melinda, who didn't respond. "He's going through stuff, too."

"Yeah." Melinda pressed the button on the side of her phone in her lap, glanced at the screen, then looked back at her ice cream. "Well? Did things get any better after you talked?"

Silvia hesitated at her friend's impatient tone. Her eye was caught by movement on the other side of the fountain. A police car was slowly entering the traffic circle. Silvia swallowed hard, sat up straighter, and angled herself slightly away from the road. She felt her cheeks get hot but she tried to talk normally.

"Um, well, Lucy and Seba are interacting less these days, which is sad, but at least she's not hitting him. She's interacting less with me, too, but I guess that's because I'm now keeping an eye on her and she doesn't appreciate it." Her eyes darted toward the traffic circle. The cruiser was moving on.

Melinda said, "Because she's being secretive? I mean, she's always been like that. What's the big deal?"

Silvia blinked and turned her body back to face the fountain. "It is a big deal, Mel. When they were fighting one day, Sebastián caught sight of a box she has, filled with little baggies, in her backpack. So of course I had to confront her about it." Silvia could feel her heart rate climbing as she glared at Melinda.

Melinda slurped audibly from her ice cream cup. She looked at Silvia and raised her eyebrows over the cup. "What? Why are you looking at me like that?"

Silvia slammed her dish down on the bench beside her harder than she had intended to. "Because," she said, "I'm telling you huge stuff here and you're not even listening!"

"Sure I am. The kids are fighting. Lucy has a box." Melinda placed her cup in her lap and made a show of turning her head to look directly into Silvia's eyes. "Okay. So what happened?"

Silvia swallowed hard and took a deep breath before she was able to continue. "Nothing. She denied that she even had it! She let me look in her bag, but of course there was only her makeup case."

"No baggies?"

"Nope. Only the ones she keeps her Q-tips and eye-shadow in. After we talked, I told her that, because of her behavior, I have no choice but to watch her. I said I have to know where she's going, who she'll be with, what time she'll be back." Silvia ticked off the rules on her fingers. "I have to be allowed to check her backpack. I hate being in this position. I wasn't supposed to be her mom."

"Yeah, I bet she's getting sick of it. What has it been, three months?"

"No! More than five! Since before graduation. You know that!" Silvia stood up. "What's going on with you today? If you don't want to be here, just say so."

"Wow." Melinda licked her spoon and walked slowly over to the trash can to toss out her cup, shaking her head as she went. When she returned, she stayed standing. "You know, you really need to get out."

Silvia laughed coldly. "Yeah, right."

"No, I'm serious. You've been playing mommy all this time and Lucy's sick of it and I'm sick of it." Melinda stopped when she looked at Silvia's face. "Look, I just don't want to see you miss out on your college experience, too. Remember, we always said college would be the best time of our lives?"

Silvia was silent, her jaw set tightly, teeth clenched.

"Hey." Melinda took a step toward Silvia. "Bill and some of the guys from high school who stayed local have been asking about you. They'll be at a party tomorrow night at the apartment of a guy from my film class. Why don't you just go with me?"

Silvia didn't respond. She stood staring at her friend, her eyes burning. Then she pulled her lip gloss out of her pocket and pretended to read the label. It was her favorite red, the one she wore to feel more confident. She took the cap off and looked at the waxy round inside. Clenching her jaw, she capped the tube and returned it to her pocket.

"Look. It's a Thursday night, almost the end of the week, you could relax a bit before the weekend. Just be a student, not a … *mother*." Melinda spat out the word like an insult.

Silvia broke her eye contact with Melinda and instead stared at the fountain. "I don't know, Mel. I mean, thanks for the invitation."

"You're going to say 'but,' aren't you?" Melinda shifted her voice to a whiny pitch. "'*But* I can't go. *But* I have to cook dinner. *But* I have two kids now.' Come on, Silvia." Melinda folded her arms. "Just be cool for once."

Now Silvia's whole face was burning, either with anger or guilt. Or maybe shame. "Let's see how tomorrow goes," she muttered.

"Yeah, sure. We'll see how it goes." Melinda took her first few steps backward, widening the gap between her and Silvia.

"No, really, Mel," Silvia said in a louder voice. "Text me at five and maybe I'll try to get out."

"Okay, text you at five." Melinda was nearly across the fountain from Silvia now.

Silvia could feel them being pulled apart like particles in a centrifuge. She gave her friend a wave, anyway, trying to restore normalcy. "Have a good night. See you again!" she called overbrightly.

"Of course." Melinda finally waved back. "Maybe tomorrow." Then she burst out laughing and jogged away, her blond hair bouncing on her shoulders as she ran.

Silvia turned toward home. *Yeah, maybe,* she thought.

15

Silvia came down the hall wearing her short jeans skirt, a black lace blouse with a matching satin camisole underneath, and high-heeled black pumps. Her unruly dark hair was slicked back into a tight chignon and the wisps were sprayed to keep them in order.

Where he sat playing with his trucks on the living room floor, Sebastián's mouth fell open. "Wooooooooow, hermanota, you look beautiful!" he breathed.

"Thanks, buddy." She kissed the top of his sandy head. A strand of his hair stuck to her glossy lips. "I'll see you in the morning, okay?"

"Okay," he said, his gaze falling to the floor. "But I'll really miss you, you know."

"I'll miss you, too, hermanito. But you're with Lucy. You'll be fine."

Silvia wished she felt as convinced as she sounded. But she blinked away her doubts. Lucy was a good girl. And it was only one evening. She stepped into the kitchen, where Lucy was finishing up the dishes.

"Okay, Luce, I'm out."

Lucy didn't lift her gaze from the suds in the sink. "Bye. Have fun."

"You have everything you need?"

"What do I need? We already ate. I have milk and cookies for Seba and then he's going to bed. We're fine."

Silvia hesitated. "Okay, then. I've got my phone if you need anything."

"I told you we're fine!" Lucy raised her voice, turning to glare at her sister. Her eyebrows rose when she saw Silvia's outfit, but she didn't comment on it. Finally, she said in a softer voice, "Just go. I'll see you later." And she turned on the faucet to rinse the last of the plates.

Passing through the living room on her way to the door, Silvia blew a kiss at Sebastián, and then she was out.

Out! She could hardly believe it. Her heart pounded in her chest. She had been worried about saying goodbye to the kids, worried that Sebastián would cry or Lucy would make a scene. None of that had happened. Still, her thoughts raced. What would Melinda be like with her new friends? Would her high school friends be different than they used to be? She glanced down at her shoes as she walked. Did anyone even dress like this for college parties?

Given the height of her heels, Silvia decided to take the Bobcat Shuttle to campus. Melinda had texted that they could meet at the fountain if Silvia wasn't too late. She glanced at the time on her phone and jogged a little to make sure that she'd arrive at the shuttle stop in time.

A few minutes later she was at the fountain just a little bit late, looking around for Melinda. She checked her phone. No texts since the ones they had exchanged at dinner time, confirming their plans. Heart pounding, she paced around the fountain to give Melinda a few more moments.

Twenty minutes later, she decided to text.

Mel, are you almost here?

I'm already here.

Where? I've been at the fountain for half an hour.

Her phone registered two minutes' passing while she awaited a response.

Hold on. I'll be right there.

Silvia breathed a sigh and sank onto a bench.

Four minutes later, her friend arrived, dressed in tight jeans and a burgundy tank top. Melinda's pale, bare arms were adorned with a stack of bracelets that gleamed under the street lights. Her strappy black sandals clicked on the brick walkway as she approached the fountain.

"Come on!" she called. "Don't make me walk all the way over there!"

Silvia got up from the bench, pulling her denim skirt down as she stood, wishing it could hide her scuffed patent-leather pumps. She walked quickly to meet her friend at the north side of the fountain.

"Thanks for coming to meet me."

"Sure." Melinda smelled of beer. "I didn't know you still wanted to meet here."

Silvia thought again of their recent texts. *How could Melinda make such a mistake?*

By then they were turning onto a street of large, slightly run-down homes. Melinda led the way to a dark green one in the middle of the block. Both light and people spilled out of its double front door onto the wide porch. Silvia could hear the din and smell the beer all the way from the sidewalk. She swallowed and smoothed back her hair out of habit.

"Come on," Melinda said. "I'll introduce you to my friends."

Silvia stood up straighter and put on a smile, following Melinda up the six steps and through the crowd into the house. Inside, deafening music pounded from the speakers hooked up to somebody's phone, which was balanced on a dusty mantel. The fireplace beneath held a metal trash can brimming with plastic cups and empty oversized cans. Several people were dancing in the middle of the room, liquid from their cups splashing out onto their shoes and the floor as they moved. The room was humid with beery exhalations and Silvia coughed, wrinkling her nose.

Melinda led her through the old galley kitchen, where the crowd was even denser. Most kids stood close together, yelling to be heard in their conversations. A couple was making out in the corner, leaning against the spot where two counters came together. As Silvia tried to pass, the man lifted the black-haired girl up onto the countertop and she threw her bare legs out to wrap them around him. As she did, one of her spiky heels stabbed Silvia in the thigh and she leaned down to rub it, thinking with a shudder how the girl looked a lot like Lucy. When she straightened up again, Melinda was out of sight.

Pushing past the protruding heels, Silvia managed to squeeze through the doorway into what must have been the dining room of the old house. Now it was packed with college kids talking at high volume, trying to be heard over the pounding music and the shouting of the others. Silvia squeezed her hands over her ears and kept walking.

She made the full circle of the first floor and found herself back in the living room with the blaring rap music. *God, Sebastián would hate this,* she thought, remembering her brother's penchant for classical music. Kids were rapping along with the song, shouting out profanity-laden lyrics. A guy came up to Silvia with a sloshing cup in his hand and blocked her path. Bending backward so that his denim crotch contacted her thigh, he enclosed her between his spread legs and bumped against her repeatedly while a group of four or five of his friends laughed. Silvia laughed along, hoping that he would stop. When he straightened up, she yelled, "Hi. I'm looking for Melinda."

"Who?"

She struggled to project against the music and shouting. "Me-lin-da. Melinda Carel."

He shrugged. "Don't know her." He returned to his friends.

Silvia circled the house one more time, asking a few people on her way. No one knew Melinda. Silvia was beer-splattered, half-deafened, and near tears when she decided to just leave. Pushing her way through the front door, she burst out into the night air and took in a couple of deep breaths. But as she moved toward the stairs, she caught a glimpse of burgundy near the porch railing. The sound of her pumps on the wooden floorboards stopped suddenly, and the girl in burgundy turned around to look over her shoulder. The guy she was with had his hands on her waist, and as she twisted, he slid them up to hold her breasts.

Silvia froze as she saw her friend's face. Her eyes moved to Melinda's chest and back up to her face.

"Where are you going?" Melinda asked, laughing and putting her hands over the guy's hands, not to move them, but to squeeze them tighter.

"Um …" said Silvia loudly, "I thought you were inside. I …" She looked down at Melinda's chest again. "I'm not doing this." Silvia took two steps toward the stairs. "I'll see you, I guess."

Melinda didn't answer. She gave Silvia a disgusted look, one side of her lip curled up, then turned back to the guy.

"What's her problem?" Silvia heard him ask as she went down the steps, his voice muffled in Melinda's hair.

"Who knows?" said Melinda. "Now, where were we?"

* * *

Silvia opted against the shuttle and began the twenty-minute walk to their apartment on North LBJ Drive. Still trembling from seeing Melinda like that, Silvia thought about her mother and how she never had any close friends. Mami had even cautioned Silvia early in high school when it was clear that Melinda was becoming a close friend:

"I'm glad you have someone to talk to, Silvi. Just don't let any one person know everything. You don't want anyone to ever be too close."

Silvia had scowled at her mother. "I don't get it. Too close for what?"

Her mother had turned back to the dishes she was washing in the sink. Silvia remembered hearing the clank of a fork dropping too hard into the bottom of a sauce pan. "It's just what we do in this family. We keep a safe distance and keep a low profile. It's how we get along so well."

Maybe Mami was right about keeping our distance, Silvia thought as she walked. *If you don't get too close, you don't get hurt.*

She tried to distract herself by focusing on the clicking of her heels on the sidewalk. At first it was fast, mechanical, as she stormed away from the party house. But after a few blocks, as her right shoe started to rub a sore spot on her heel, the rhythm changed from *clack-clack* to *kuhclack-clack* as she dragged her right foot a little. *Kuhclack-clack.* Then slower, and she relaxed her breathing as well.

A few blocks later and she was able to look at her surroundings and shift her thoughts from Melinda. She walked on brick-and-concrete pedestrian pathways as she passed between the strangely deserted university buildings and the gently hissing fountains. She started when a shrub picked at her sweater, then quickened her step.

I wish I had never tried to go out, she thought. Then, *I wish I had gone away to school and never had to deal with any of this!* She imagined what her campus in the East would have been like. It probably wouldn't have had Spanish tiles like the buildings at Texas State, but certainly the requisite trees, bricks, and fountains. Maybe she would have been enjoying a walk back from the library right now with some cosmopolitan new friends from places that bespoke ownership and belonging: Martha's Vineyard, Toms River. Her friends would all have sun-bleached hair and freckled skin and have names that sounded lighthearted no matter the tone you used: Emily, Molly, and Kerri. They'd be laughing about the boys in their classes and heading back to the dorm together. She'd be far from the border in the Northeast, like Dr. Cisneros.

Instead, she was leaving an uncomfortable party and going home to take care of children! Silvia laughed bitterly and turned along the circle that marked the end of the pedestrian portion of LBJ Drive. She abruptly left the university section and began passing the minimalist student apartment buildings. She crossed a few silent intersections, trying to stop thinking.

WALNUT STREET. Silvia smiled at the irony of the street sign that she used to so look forward to seeing with Melinda as they would walk to Spring Lake. On warm Saturdays when they were in high school, the two friends used to pack a picnic lunch and hike in through the preservation, dipping their feet in the cool water when they finally reached the lake, or sometimes heading down to Spring Lake Falls to cannonball into the churning pool beneath with other high schoolers who would gather there.

Well, I guess that's all over now, too, along with everything else, she thought, shaking off the memories and quickening her pace as LBJ Drive inclined slightly. Only six more blocks to home.

The trees thickened and the shadows of the trees loomed. Silvia tried to remind herself that the live oaks of Texas were among her favorites, by day, anyway. Just this morning she had been studying trees again in botany and had learned that live oaks were considered a perennial tree, sort of like an evergreen in the literal sense of the word, since they don't drop their leaves in the fall, but rather replace them as needed throughout the year, giving the appearance of keeping them year-round. Glancing at their hulking, shadowy forms, Silvia reminded herself that they'd been considered a symbol of strength and shelter since colonial times. *Strength and shelter,* she repeated, glancing around out of the corner of her eye. *Strength and shelter.*

Three blocks farther on, Silvia's shoulders relaxed as the road elevated a bit more, and she found herself at eye level with the canopy of the trees, instead of dwarfed by it. A touch of light, gold from lamps or blue from screens, shone through the windows of the little houses tucked among the oak trunks, giving them a fairy-tale mystique. *Almost home*, she thought. *Where I belong.*

At last she spied the white of the motion-activated security lamps outside their own low, three-building complex. Illuminated under them like ghosts were two white sedans with government plates.

16

The shades were drawn on many of the neighbors' windows, an ominous sign. Usually she could see light emanating from the television in most apartments, but tonight there was nothing. With a knot in her stomach and her heart pounding, Silvia made her way to the front door, keys in hand, trying not to run, endeavoring to appear normal.

She opened the door to the living room to find Sebastián in his firetruck pajamas, not in bed, but instead playing on the floor with a stranger who was driving Sebastián's bulldozer into a pile of Lincoln Logs. The red-haired man was reclining on one hip, awkwardly, and Silvia noticed a clipboard lying on the floor next to him. He looked to be in his early twenties, not much older than Silvia, and he smiled and nodded at her as she entered.

Sebastián grinned up at his sister. 'We're playing demolition site!"

"I bet," replied Silvia without a smile. She pulled her skirt down as far as it would go. "Who's your playmate?"

"Oh, this is Agent Randolph. He loves trucks."

"I'm sure he does. Sebastián, didn't I tell you not to open the door when I'm not home?"

"I—" began Sebastián.

The agent interrupted, getting to his feet. "I can answer that, Silvia. It's Silvia, right?"

"Right," said Silvia, hands on her hips.

"I'm from the Department of Social Services. I just came by to see how everyone is doing in your house, especially your little sister and brother. We had reason to be concerned that they were on their own."

Silvia's mind raced. She shouldn't have gone out tonight. Did she smell like beer? Had she done everything she needed to do to take care of the family before leaving? She had fed them, made sure their homework was done. Everything was in order. She smoothed her hair back, tucking an unruly wave into the chignon. "Well, they're not. Thank you."

"Your brother said that it was just you kids living here, so I decided to spend some time playing with him while I waited to see who came home."

"We're not kids. That is, Lucy and Sebastián are kids, but I'm an adult." Silvia drew herself up a little taller and squared her shoulders.

"I see. And your parents?"

"I'm sure the agency knows perfectly well where my mother is, and she left me in charge."

"Sure, Silvia, I'm glad to hear it." The agent ran a hand through his wavy hair. "Just doing my job."

"And is it also your job to check up on Lucy at her school?" Silvia demanded.

Lucy emerged in the kitchen doorway at the sound of her name, arms crossed over her sweatshirt, trembling. Silvia threw her a warning glance to be quiet.

"Yes, Miss, it is," said the agent. "It's part of my job to make sure that the kids who are left behind when someone is detained are still being taken care of, that they're safe, fed, going to school, and so on."

"Thank you, Officer ... Randolph, was it?"

"Agent. Agent Randolph."

Silvia blinked. "Well, Agent Randolph, if you see anything here of concern, please say so. But my kids ... I mean, *these* kids are never late for school, always clean and fed, and happy, as you can see."

"Right!" chimed in Sebastián, picking up a truck, eager to get back to his playing.

"Lucy, you agree?" asked the social worker, turning to look her in the eye.

"Yeah, sure," mumbled Lucy, looking at the floor.

"Okay, then, we'll get out of your way. I'm sure you have homework to do." Agent Randolph opened the front door. Across the parking lot, Silvia could see a woman dressed in a pants suit and holding a clipboard that matched Agent Randolph's closing an apartment door behind her. She could hear muffled crying from a neighboring unit.

"Actually," Silvia said, trying not to glance at the diario and stack of notebooks on her desk across the room, "all of their homework is done."

"Very well, then," said the agent, nodding respectfully to Silvia. "Sebastián, thank you for playing with me. Y'all have a good night. And stay out of trouble." Silvia stiffened as the officer glanced at Lucy with his last line.

As the door closed behind him, Silvia collapsed on the recliner, trembling. Her brother and sister rushed over and piled on her with hugs. For once, Lucy had shed the hard set of her jaw and actually had tears in her eyes.

"I was scared, sis," she said, burying her face in Silvia's lap.

"Me too," admitted Silvia. "Scared that something would happen to you two, but also scared that I wouldn't be able to control what I said. Silvia smoothed back her hair with shaky hands, trying to calm down.

"Well, you handled it pretty well," said Lucy.

"You did great." said Sebastián. "You kept us safe. But now I have a problem."

"What is it?" asked Silvia, stroking his blond hair.

"I need someone to play with me! Agent Randolph wasn't really that good with the bulldozer."

Lucy and Silvia laughed, releasing some of the tension hanging in the room. "Look, hermanito," said Lucy. "It's way past bedtime, but I'll drive down the hall with you. Which truck is mine?"

Silvia watched as they slid off the recliner and down to the demolition site to grab trucks, then she went to the kitchen to make some coffee. There was no way she was going to sleep anytime soon, and she was behind on her classes, anyway. She instinctively started thumbing in a text to Melinda about what had just happened, but she hesitated over the keys. The last image of Melinda at the party, with that guy's hands all over her and the disgusted look on her face, stuck in her mind.

We just belong to two different worlds, she thought, deleting the letters. *Or she belongs and I don't.*

After Silvia made coffee and Lucy and Sebastián had gone to bed, she listened to her US Borders lecture on forced migration. It ended with a question: "If the law dictates that certain people belong in the country and others don't, is it morally right to uphold it? Do we work within unjust laws or work to change them? And what do we do in the meantime?"

Silvia jotted in her notes: *The law states that Mami belongs in Mexico and we belong here, as citizens born in this country. At least for now. Therefore, under the law, we don't belong with Mami.*

But she knew in her heart that that was a lie. Troubled Lucy and innocent Sebastián needed to be with their mother. "I need you, too, Mami," Silvia said through tears as she thought of the bills, her piled-up schoolwork, and finally Melinda. *I have no one else.* Clutching her pen like a dagger, she scribbled out notes through blurred eyes until the entire page was black and torn.

17

I'm trying to keep as busy and distracted as possible to avoid worrying about our marriage, about my dreams, about my panic. During the day, it's easy. There's plenty of work to do on the farm and in the house. Jorge and I do it all almost without talking. Once Violeta comes home, overseeing her chores and homework while cooking dinner lightens the mood and keeps me occupied. In the evening, we sit with the puppy (it's funny we still call him that, even though he's big now) and Jorge and I listen to Violeta practice. Yes, the days are easy. It's the nights that I fear.

Margarita stilled her pen and listened. Silence blanketed the house and farm and stifled her breath. Seeking distraction, her glance landed on the pile of newspapers that she had heaped beside the woodstove for starting fires. While Jorge read most of them right away, Margarita had found herself too busy or tired to keep up with the weekly news.

Shrugging, she decided to begin catching up, even though the papers were weeks or in some cases even months out of date. She reached for one from the bottom of the pile and read in her wooden rocking chair by lamplight until she was certain that she was exhausted enough to fall straight to sleep when she got to her room.

During the next week, Margarita read one or even two weekly newspapers per night, while Jorge snored softly from the bedroom and Violeta's dim light glowed down the hall. Compressing the events of three months by reading them in close succession highlighted a disturbing trend. She noticed that every issue of the paper contained at least one report of unfair treatment or outright discrimination against people of Mexican descent. As she read, her heart sank and that familiar ache under her collarbones returned.

One article told of a mob in Colorado chasing Mexican mine workers off of company land, yelling at them to "go back where they belonged." The Mexican workers' jobs were promptly taken by formerly unemployed white men. The next week's paper, which Margarita read the same night, contained an article describing the dilapidated condition of a "Mexican school" in California. It contrasted the crumbling walls, rodent infestations, and concrete schoolyard for Mexican kids with the pristine, well-appointed facilities and grassy schoolyard for white children. Until then, Margarita had no idea that such differences existed among public schools.

The following night she read of the varied methods of repatriation employed so far in 1936. The Border Patrol had sent Mexicans and people of Mexican descent across the border by train, automobile, and foot. It received authority from the President to deport not just workers who had crossed the border illegally, but entire families who had been living in the United States for years. One officer boasted that the agency had repatriated more people than in any previous year.

The stories that Margarita read in the papers each evening echoed the news she heard in town, where more than half the population was of Mexican descent. One Thursday, she accompanied Violeta on her walk to school, then stayed to do the week's shopping and sell a few bunches of onions, some early broccoli, and the box of soap that she had made that week. Standing at the counter of Carlton's store, she overheard several men discussing the recent cases of discrimination in the Southwest.

"And did you read about the schools? How awful they are for the Mexican kids?"

"Sure did. They say that people think us Mexicans are not as smart as everybody else." The men laughed.

Margarita stepped toward the group, all of whom she had known since her school days. "It seems laughable to us, but imagine how it feels to the children, to be told you're not smart enough, that you don't deserve a clean school with a grassy schoolyard like other children have. Imagine if that had happened when we were kids here."

The men nodded. Then one of them said, "Yeah, there'd have been one school for all of us, and a nicer one just for Willy!"

Willy, whose full name was Guillermo, laughed and pinched his own freckled cheeks. Born in Mexico, Willy was always teased for being lighter-skinned than his friends in Socorro. "Just the way it should be," he said. "But seriously, amigos. This whole thing has got to stop. I read that Border Patrol took sick people from a hospital in San Diego and dumped them over the border in Mexico. That just ain't right."

"None of it is," said Margarita. "I worry about our safety here, sometimes." She scanned her friends' faces. "We're so close to the border, and near the mines and other jobs that people are desperate for. These things could happen here any time."

"That's true," said Willy's wife, who had joined the circle. "Look at the Rivera family."

"Well, now," said Willy, "nobody knows what really happened to them. They just moved away suddenly is all."

"But they weren't citizens," said his wife. "And neither were the Mejías, who left around the same time."

"All I know is we'd all better have our papers in order in case Border Patrol comes knocking," said one of the men.

Margarita had heard enough. She politely excused herself, bought the newspaper, and walked home with a renewed conviction to protect her family. And a burgeoning plan.

18

Silvia awoke with a weight on her chest. In a flash, she remembered the events of the previous evening, from the nightmarish party to the visit from Social Services. But it was Friday and she had two kids to get on the bus. She lay for a while, listening to the radio crackling out the alarm to get up. Before she was able to gather the strength to move, it was nearly leaving time.

"Lucy, Seba! Get moving; it's late!" she called into their rooms as she passed each one on the way to the kitchen. She pulled their brown bags out of the refrigerator, stuffed Sebastián's into his backpack, and glanced into Lucy's.

"Get out of there!" Lucy snapped, walking into the kitchen. "Just leave my stuff alone, okay? I don't feel like fighting today."

"Me neither. Just do the right thing, okay?"

Lucy rolled her eyes.

"And please stop rolling your eyes at me. I'm tired, Lucy."

"Oh, now you're going to police my facial expressions, too? Anything else, oh mighty sister?"

Sebastián came into the room, stopping their argument before it could start. "I have a tummy ache, Silvi," he whined. "I can't go to school."

Silvia placed her hands on his shoulders. "Seba, I need you to go to school today. I have so much work to do." She glanced in the direction of her desk, where work for all three of her classes lay piled up. "When did it start?"

"Last night, after Agent Randolph left."

Silvia tightened her jaw. She rubbed her brother's round stomach with her left hand. "Okay, kiddo. Just see how it feels today. I bet you'll feel better when you're with your friends."

Sebastián looked unconvinced. "I guess so. Love you, Silvi."

Silvia could tell that Sebastián, like Lucy, was low energy today. The constant stress was taking a lot out of them all. "I love you, too, hermanito. Now go! The bus is coming!"

The two kids hurried toward the door with Silvia close behind. She closed the door softly after waving to Sebastián, who kept looking back. *Poor kid*, she thought. *He's probably getting an ulcer or something from all this stress.*

Silvia turned away from the door to confront the coursework on her desk.

The next several days passed the same way, with the exception of Sebastian's stomach ache, which seemed to have improved. All three siblings were quieter than usual, and Silvia felt that something had changed the night of Agent Randolph's visit. Their little sanctuary, the place where they could "keep a low profile," had been violated. There was no longer any way to pretend that things were all right and that Mami would be home sometime soon.

The only thing that Silvia was able to get done during those days was reading. She became engrossed in the diario, studying the pictures, deciphering the loopy handwriting, and researching every item that was unfamiliar. In a sense, she escaped into the world painted for her, sometimes in Spanish, sometimes in English, sometimes in charcoal, in the little book.

She also took meticulous notes. Although her Borders questions still sat unanswered and her botany take-home test remained unopened, her Memoirs notebook bulged with observations. But she was puzzled by some words that the book's author highlighted in very specific ways. Taking a green- or yellow- or blue-colored pencil, or sometimes all three, she—Silvia knew from the Spanish that the author was female—traced four words each time they appeared: *"Coyote ... acequia ... mesquite ... soap."* Silvia often spoke them, trying to decipher the significance of the words to the writer. Maybe their embellishment was accidental, just the product of mindless doodling. But what if it wasn't?

The next Wednesday, she decided to find out.

"Aló?" Mami's voice sounded before her face appeared on the screen. "Mis hijos?"

"Mami!" cried Sebastián and Lucy in unison, grinning into the webcam.

"How are you?" Silvia asked, staring in alarm at her mother's sunken eyes and red nose.

"I'm fine, bebés. Just a little under the weather. How are you? Everyone looks great!" Their mother simultaneously beamed and brushed tears from her eyes.

Lucy pulled the hood of her favorite black sweater over her hair before answering. "Thanks, Mami. You look great, too."

Silvia glanced sideways at her sister, then back at the screen. "We're fine, Ma. Happy to see you. So what's going on?"

"Not too much, mija. Your tíos are fine, the tomatoes are growing, your mother is missing you." She blew her nose.

"Same here, Mami," replied Lucy quietly.

"Lucy, things are going well? You're listening to your sister and being good to your brother?"

Lucy looked sheepish and scratched at a pimple she had covered with a heavy layer of concealer. "Yeah, I'm trying."

"She's doing fine," added Silvia, watching her sister out of the corner of her eye. "Just a little quiet today."

Lucy looked down.

"Mami, look!" announced Sebastián, brandishing a Pokémon card. "I got it in a trade from Josiah today."

Their mother screwed up her face and peered out from the screen, then adopted a suitably impressed look. "Wow, that's great, Seba. It looks really cool. Do you have homework?"

"Just my sight words." Sebastián pulled out his index cards and held them up to the camera. "Wanna help me practice?"

"Sure, hijito."

While their mother quizzed Sebastián on his new words, Silvia turned away from the camera to lean toward Lucy. "Can I have a minute alone with Mami?" she whispered to her sister.

Lucy looked downcast, but nodded. "Is it about me?"

Silvia sat back away from her sister and crossed her arms. "No, Lucy, not everything is about you."

"It was that other time," grumbled Lucy under her breath. Then she stood and waved at the camera. "Bye, Mami. I'm going to go start my homework. I have so much reading. See you next week."

"Adiós, Lucy. Te quiero," answered Rosa, following Lucy's departure with her eyes, then raising her eyebrows at Silvia. Silvia shrugged and looked back at Sebastián, who was still reading the words from his flash cards. She exchanged smiles of pride with her mother as he finished going over his vocabulary.

When he got to the end of the pile, Sebastián jumped up from his stool and blew a kiss toward the camera. "Adios, Mami," he said. "I'm getting a snack!" He ran off to the kitchen and Silvia assumed the spot in front of the camera.

"So, Mami, I have to ask you something. And I don't want you to be disappointed or mad."

Her mother smiled sadly. "I couldn't be mad at you, Silvi. Not now. What is it?"

"Well, I found a box under your bed while I was looking for ... while I was looking for something." Silvia swallowed, not wanting to dwell on the financial problems this time. "It had a book in it, and I've been using it for my Memoirs class." Silvia stretched over to her desk, grabbed the small volume, and held it in front of the camera.

Mami leaned toward her screen, squinting her swollen eyes. "My bisabuela's diary? I didn't think that was still around!"

Silvia's mouth dropped open. "Is that whose it is? Wait, which great-grandmother?"

"Margarita, la abuela de mi mamá," said Mami. "I think she lived in Socorro."

Silvia jumped in her seat. To think her own great-great-grandmother was the author of the diary! "Yes! There are lots of drawings of Socorro in there. So can I use it?"

"It sounds like you already are." Mami smiled. "Anyway, Mamá always said her abuelita had a gift for escritura. You'll have it, too, probably."

"I don't know about that," Silvia said. "I haven't been able to get any writing done lately." She frowned.

"For Memoirs?"

"For anything." Silvia's eyes burned. "It's just too much, with the kids and the housework. And then the other night, a federal agent came to the house."

Her mother jumped up from the table where she was sitting, knocking over the wooden chair behind her and sending it clattering to the hard tile floor. "What? Why didn't you tell me? Where was he from?" She grabbed a Kleenex from an ornate Talavera box on the table behind her and began wiping at her eyes.

"No, Mami, don't cry. We're all fine." Silvia wished she could reach through the screen to her mother. "We're fine. He was from DSS. I got home right away and told him that I'm in charge."

"Home from where? Didn't you say it was night?"

Silvia swallowed. "I was out with Melinda. I had a really bad time and I'll never do it again, but the important thing is that I got home."

Mami had righted the chair and sat down. She was staring at the screen, jaw set.

"Mami, did you hear me? I said everything's all fine."

"Not for me, it's not." She spoke in a quiet voice. "This settles it. I'm not going to just sit around here any longer."

Now it was Silvia's turn to cry. "No, Mami. Stay where you are. Here I can see you, Seba can play with you. If you get caught—"

"I won't get caught. I've got a plan."

Silvia felt the panic rise in her chest. She heard Melinda's ridicule of her mother echo in her ears. *Your mother and her plans.* "A plan?"

"Yes. I'm going to come across. In time for Christmas." Mami rubbed her Kleenex underneath her dark-rimmed eyes. "Silvia, get a pen."

"No, Mami." Silvia wiped at her eyes, willing them away.

"Trust me, Silvia. I can do this. I have no choice. They can't keep a mother from her babies when they need her. Do you have the pen?"

Silvia was alarmed by her mother's deadly calm. She reached behind her to her desk once again and grabbed a pen and spiral-bound notebook from her homework pile. She held up the black ballpoint toward the camera, reassuming the role of obedient oldest child. "Yes, I have it."

"I have inheritance money from your abuelo that I will use for the expenses. I can't tell you too many details but you need to write this down: December tenth, ten a.m., Brownsville."

Silvia wrote in her notebook.

"Got it?" her mother asked.

Silvia nodded. December tenth was about six weeks away.

"Show me," her mother ordered.

Dutifully Silvia held her notebook up to the webcam.

"Good." Mami nodded.

Just then, Sebastián passed through the room, bringing his snack bowl back to the kitchen. Immediately Mami changed the subject and brightened her tone. "Okay, mi hija, I've got to go make dinner, and you do, too. What are you having tonight?"

Silvia opened her mouth to speak but no sound came out. She held her hand to her mouth for a moment, glancing after her brother and hoping to look normal to him, despite her internal turmoil. She took a deep breath. "Spaghetti. One of Sebastián's favorites."

"Good. Cuídate, hija. Give big hugs to your brother and sister for me. I hope to be with you all before you know it."

"I hope so, too," said Silvia. But her stomach clenched even thinking of the danger her mother would face trying to cross the border illegally. And if she were caught and incarcerated on either side of the border, they might never get to see her again. Silvia tried to brush away her fatalistic thoughts and turned to say goodbye to her mother but she had already clicked to disconnect. Heart pounding, Silvia closed up the laptop and dropped it off on her desk on her way to the kitchen to start boiling water.

Taking the bag of meatballs out of the freezer, she thought about the timing of her mother's plan. It was the first week in November now, and her mother aimed to cross on December tenth. She would have to be at the border and looking for her opportunity at least a couple of weeks earlier, so by the end of the month she would already be on the road from Conchos. That gave Silvia only a couple of weeks to find a reason compelling enough to convince her mother not to take the risk.

She sank into a kitchen chair and put her head in her hands. *This is all my fault*, she thought. *Mami said it: she's only coming because she thinks we need her. If I could have kept Lucy out of trouble, we wouldn't have ICE and CPS after us. Maybe I can get a job to pay the bills and get some more cash for food. But first I have to catch up on my work.* And what about Seba and his stomachaches? Why couldn't everyone just have followed Mami's low-profile plan?

The pasta water boiled over, its sudden hiss startling Silvia out of her anxious worry. "Shit!" she screamed, turning off the heat as the smell of burning starchy water filled the room. Turning around, she saw her brother and sister in the doorway, staring at her open-mouthed. She burst into tears and ran out of the room to escape into the diario.

19

Today I'm feeling grateful. Grateful for the incredible growing season we've had. It's August and our corn cribs are already half-filled with feed for the animals this winter. Our cotton, barley, and alfalfa are thriving and have been contracted for sale. I've never seen our vegetable garden so robust! It's already provided Violeta and me with entire days in the kitchen, pickling cucumbers and early onions, peeling and canning tomatoes, and simmering plump berries into our delicious jam. One wall of our wooden pantry is already neatly lined with colorful jars. Sometimes I go in there just to gaze at them. They make me feel safe and hopeful. Hopeful that Jorge will stay.

Margarita smiled at Socorro's good fortune. All the talk in town was about how great a growing season it was, the best in decades.

"My corn is already up to my shoulders," said one farmer in early July when Margarita went to the market to sell some of their vegetables.

"You should see Tito's," said Mrs. Blanco, who sold produce from a variety of farms in her stand. "It's up to his head!"

"But Tito is two feet shorter than me!" said the farmer, laughing.

Everyone in town was in good spirits. There was plenty of food to go around and no more drought than was usual for summer. The men were home. And economic problems, much like the Border Patrol, seemed to be staying away from Socorro for now.

Even Jorge's dark mood seemed to have lifted slightly. He'd spent the long, hot growing days of July and August watering the plants and watching them grow. He carved a channel from the acequia that ran through their land to divert some of the water directly up the middle of their field. From there, he used a team of cows to carry buckets up and down the rows of crops, spilling water onto the cracking soil.

Violeta followed along behind him, hauling a heavy tin watering can and sprinkling the plants that he missed. She was his shadow all season, chattering to him about music and birds and flowers and rocks while he uttered small grunts of agreement. Sometimes the two of them would take a rest in the shade of the mesquite tree on top of the rise overlooking the river. From her kitchen window or her flower garden near the house, Margarita would see Jorge's mouth moving much more than it ever did with her. Violeta's peals of laughter floated on the breeze to the little cottage.

That spot under the mesquite had always been Margarita's favorite place on their property, too. As a child, she would so often walk from the house to the top of the rise that she could do it with her eyes closed against the bright sun. Even now, she knew it was exactly seventy-five steps to the tree. In spring, she would still climb the hill to inhale the aroma of the mesquite's yellow fluffy blossoms and peer among the dark bark and thorns for signs of newly budding leaves.

But summer was her favorite time under the tree, for then she truly appreciated the dense shade that the spreading canopy provided. She had spent several afternoons that summer sitting on a rock beside the new rose bush, facing away from the farm and gazing at the Rio Grande below as she contemplated the wideness of the earth and the vastness of the sky. Or she would find a clear spot between the yuccas, facing home, and watch her husband work, her cows graze, and her daughter alternate between helping and frolicking. At those times, she would remember to relax her knitted brow and breathe deeply.

One late summer afternoon, Margarita looked over the red-stained pots she was scrubbing in the sink and out the kitchen window. The mesquite shade was inviting her to come, to cool off after a long morning of preserving berries. Even with all the windows open, the heat of the wood fire was trapped inside their square house.

She let the pots sink deep into the pink soapy water, shed her apron, and stepped outside. As always when she entered her kitchen garden, she inhaled deeply and recited each flower's scientific name in her mind. That day, the *Gaillardia aristata* and *Rudbeckia hirta* were in bloom, spreading their soft petals to the side as they reached their stubbly centers toward the sun. At the edges of the garden, her mother's cherished hedge of *Rosa floribuna* created a barrier for invading herbivores, and they were blooming in deep purple, or yellow edged with red, their beauty and aroma concealing the thorny stems beneath. Interspersed with the flowers, Margarita grew basil, parsley, thyme, and sage—*Ocimum basilicum, Petroselinum crispum, Thymus,* and *Salvia.* The summer dryness made the herbs constantly send up flowering stalks like emergency flares into the sky, and Margarita pinched a few off as she walked, to encourage them to keep producing fragrant leaves.

At the far edge of the garden, she turned to face the house. She felt her stiff shoulders relax as she regarded the curve of the garden plot with the kitchen window centered at its base. She had carefully chosen that location on the pretense that the proximity of the house might keep pests away, and that the cooking herbs would be easily accessible. But the truth was that she wanted to hear the hum of the honey bees and smell the rich fragrance of the *Lavandula* and the gentle whiff of the *Viola odorata* even while she worked in the house.

She glanced down at her feet, where tiny wild violets grew in the shade of the rosebushes. She loved her violetas, the flowers of protection, connection, and love. Margarita had learned about flower nomenclature and symbolism from her grandmother when she was a child, and later from a small volume that her father had bought her for her birthday. The heart-shaped petals of the violet clearly connoted love, while the embellished part of the flower, hidden deep in the center, symbolized the secrets of the soul that one must nurture, far from the eyes of the outside world. It had been an easy choice for her daughter's name, as its qualities were precisely what Margarita wished for her baby girl: love easily given, inner life rich and protected.

She turned to count her steps and climb the hill, eager to catch the little breeze off the river that she knew would be swirling around the mesquite tree. Down on the field where she walked, not a breath of air circulated among the fluffy cornstalks and reaching bean vines. Yet even on the hottest days, the cool waters of the Rio Grande caused a light wind to swoop up the rise like an eagle gliding to roost. Atop the rise, the breeze would be strong enough to billow a skirt or ruffle a head of hair. It always seemed somehow magical.

Reaching the crest of the hill, Margarita undid the top three buttons of her shirtdress, flapping the lapels a little to encourage the air in. She turned around, spotting Jorge and Violeta at the far end of the field by the shed. Violeta's black hair gleamed in the sun as she was petting the nose of one of their cows. The little girl looked so tiny at this distance, just a fragile speck that could blow away like a wind-borne seed.

Margarita turned around to face the river and then it happened again. Her eye was caught by a gnarly cedar tree washing downstream, its twisted branches reaching for a hold on the shore. Instantly she saw the water filled with flotsam: branches and trees and boards from people's barns. A dog, screeching, struggled against the current, its eyes wild. The water swirled brown and rose up, foaming and frothing like a crazed horse. She shook her head—"No, no, no"—and pressed the heels of her hands against her eyes.

Still she saw it. The water was more than halfway up the rise now, and it suddenly split in two channels, one on either side of the hill. The south stream raced toward their little house, carving a path through the beans as it charged straight for the stone foundation. But Margarita turned frantically toward the north branch, the one plowing through the corn in its drive toward her husband and little daughter. They were facing away, Violeta still stroking the cow. How could they not hear? Margarita tried to scream, but no sound came out. She began to sob.

She opened her eyes when her knees hit something hard. She put her hands out to catch herself and saw them, cracked and trembling, on dusty soil. The breeze told her that her face was drenched with tears, while her body shook with cold sweat. The sun was hot on her back and the sounds of the gently flowing river and chirping birds filled her ears in a crescendo, replacing the pounding of her heart. She pivoted to sit, rubbing the dirt from her hands on her dress before wiping her face. Her eyes, no longer traitorous, confirmed what her ears suggested: the Rio flowed softly, summer-shallow, more than thirty feet below her. Overhead, a golden eagle circled.

She jumped to her feet. *Violeta!* Yet there she was across the field, now walking toward the house with her papi. Margarita pressed a hand to her chest, surprised to feel her bare skin. She fastened her buttons, breathing a prayer. *Dios, send me socorro. Help me keep her safe from all the danger I see.*

20

The following Monday, Silvia turned the last page of her great-great-grandmother's diary and looked down at the thick notebook she had filled with her reflections on the book, which had turned out to be a snapshot of her bisabuela's life from spring 1936 to spring 1937. Silvia's Memoirs professor had approved her proposal to write her final paper on the stylistic devices of the diary, and she was making progress in that class. But only in that class.

Trying to stay focused, she thumbed through her notes she had taken on her bisabuela's descriptive techniques, her use of emotion, and the ways in which she interwove maps, newspaper clippings, and sketches into her writing. She turned the page to review the list she had made of the townspeople of Socorro, Texas, the secondary characters in Margarita's book. Some were farmers-turned-miners leaving on the train in the fall, not to return until planting season. Others were shop owners, or schoolchildren who carried their books tied together with brown twine on their way home to do their chores in the afternoons. Through her vibrant word choices, Bisabuela had brought Socorro during the Great Depression to life for Silvia.

Bisabuela had also brought herself, with her joys and pains, to life for her descendant reader. While Silvia immersed herself in the important events of that transformative year, the writer transformed into a beloved character, a friend with whom Silvia had laughed and cried, and to whom Silvia related as a person. That person was Margarita, brave and passionate about her land and her family, and Silvia was proud to know about her life.

But like Silvia, Margarita was also a woman at the border, on the margins of society, feeling the screw tightening on the press of racism and prejudice. At times, Margarita's experiences were almost too familiar for Silvia, and as she read, she'd feel a trembling potentiality just below the surface like a simmering pot about to boil over. They both shared the same love of plants and nature, yet also the same fear of deportation and instability. They both missed a loved one away at the border and feared that their tenuous hold on life would escape their tight control. How could she connect so well with a woman she never met and barely ever heard of? And how could eighty years have passed yet nothing have changed for Mexican Americans?

Somehow, spending time with her bisabuela's writing also made Silvia feel closer to her mother. She looked down at her legs stretched out on the bed in front of her. Today she wore one of Mami's T-shirts tucked into her sweatpants and sealed under a zipped-up pink hoodie. Since Wednesday's video chat, she found that keeping Mami close and escaping into the diario were the best ways for her to stave off panic about losing her.

Today was a good day and Silvia was able to channel her nervous energy into analysis of the text, shoving the pain of Margarita's story and her own into a box like the one in which she had discovered the diario. Or like Lucy's black box.

She flipped through her notes and again puzzled over the pattern of decorated words in the diario. She imagined Margarita gazing out the window of her cabin, or perhaps sitting under her tree as she traced over the words *coyote, acequia, mesquite,* and *soap* with layers of color. It was funny how the commonplace words were the ones most decorated, the ones most repeated in the book. But why?

Silvia flopped back onto her pillow, resting the back of her hand over her eyes, and thought. She really wished she could talk the puzzle through with Melinda, who was quite talented at interpreting symbolism in literature. She reached for her phone. Why not? It had been nearly two weeks since their night at the party and Silvia wondered what would happen if she reached out.

"Hey, what's up?" Melinda's voice was dry on the phone.

"Hi, Mel. Do you have a sec?"

"I guess, sure. I don't have class for a few minutes." Melinda was chewing.

"Okay, thanks. It's … academic." The image of light-haired Melinda on the front porch at the party flashed into her mind for a moment, but she pushed it away.

"Okay …" Melinda sounded unsure.

"So, I'm working on a project for my Memoirs class, and I know you're good at interpreting stuff. It's from my great-great-grandmother's diary."

"Yeah. Okay?" The rising tone of Melinda's voice made her at least sound interested.

Silvia took a deep breath, heart ticking a little faster. "So, when she writes, she highlights certain words, like they're really important. But I can't figure out what they have in common or why they're highlighted."

"Okay, what are they?"

Silvia recited them: "*Coyote, acequia, mesquite,* and *soap.*"

"Soap?" Melinda actually laughed.

"Yeah. It's a weird combination, but I can't help but feel like they fit together somehow."

"Well, let's see," said Melinda. "I know *coyote* has several meanings. There's the coyote who helps families sneak across the border, but I don't know how old that term is. When was she writing, again?"

"In the thirties."

"Okay, so there's that. And of course there's the animal."

"Yeah. Hang on." Silvia had moved to her computer desk in the living room and was keying the word into a search engine. "Okay, in Mexican slang, a coyote is also a sneaky person, a person who moves at the margins of society."

"Right, and that fits with the role of the coyote in myths and fables as sneaky and crafty. Think Little Red Riding Hood."

"That was a wolf!" Silvia laughed. This was good. They were actually talking like the old days.

"Close enough. What's next?" Melinda asked.

"Um … *acequia,*" said Silvia, reviewing her notes. That one was clearer. Irrigation ditches were not uncommon in San Marcos, and she remembered seeing the acequias historic site when her high school class took a field trip to San Antonio. There, ditches were excavated and restored around the Mission area, and historical signage highlighted their importance to the survival of the Spanish colonial residents of the town. Clearly, the irrigation system would have still been important in her great-great-grandmother's time, when many homes did not have running water. Indeed, Margarita had repeatedly mentioned that her own cabin was just steps from the nearest acequia. "I think that one must be literal: the irrigation ditch by Margarita's cabin."

"Okay, moving on," said Melinda. "I have like four minutes."

Silvia swallowed. "Okay, then. *Mesquite.* Obviously a tree. But why would it be important enough for Margarita to color and highlight in her book and include on her maps all the time?" Silvia wondered.

"Well, Uncle Phil uses it …"

"The one in Arizona?"

"Yeah. He heats his whole house with it in the winter."

"Winter in Arizona?"

"He lives in ski country. Flagstaff. I can't believe you don't remember that."

"Sorry. I've had a few things on my mind." Silvia blinked. "So then maybe Margarita used mesquite wood for heat, too." Silvia keyed in the word on the computer and up popped a picture of a dark-barked, spreading tree that matched the drawing that Margarita had done in the diary. She quickly skimmed the History and Uses section of the wiki and confirmed what Melinda had said about the dense wood's long burn for heating houses and for cooking. "Looks right, from what I can see online. Margarita drew one in her book, too, and often wrote about the one on her property on a rise overlooking the Rio Grande."

"Okay, so she likes trees," said Melinda. "I've got to start walking, but we can still talk for a sec."

"Okay. Then *soap* is the last one," Silvia said. "Every time she writes it, she draws flowery lines around it or colors it with green or yellow pencil."

"I don't know, Silvi, I guess she liked soap," said Melinda.

"Or she really needed a bath!" laughed Silvia. "All right, Mel. Thanks for talking this through with me."

"Sure," said Melinda.

"It was nice to talk to you." Silvia was looking for something more, maybe a space to start over.

"Yeah, you too. I gotta go."

"Okay, bye," Silvia said, but Melinda had already clicked off.

Silvia closed her notes, trying to determine if that had been a good conversation or not.

21

Silvia had just settled in the recliner to finally face her botany reading that had been waiting for three weeks, when she heard a knock. She got up and peered through the peephole, recognizing Agent Randolph. Tightening her lips, she gathered her wavy dark hair into a bun and smoothed back the pieces that always tried to escape containment. Glancing down to make sure that her sweatshirt was zipped and completely covering her mother's shirt, she set her jaw and opened the door.

"Hello, Silvia. Could I come in, please?"

She wondered if she had a choice. She reluctantly accepted the hand he held out to shake hers and gestured the agent in. "What can I do for you?"

"I'm just checking in. May I please sit down?"

"I guess so," Silvia said, leading the way to the couch, heart pounding. "How can I help you?" She sat at one end with her hip pressed against the arm of the gold sofa. The agent lowered himself onto the front edge of the cushion at the other end.

"I was in the neighborhood and just wanted to stop in and see how you are all doing."

"Well, my siblings are at school, as always," she said curtly. "I'm doing my college work and we're all fine. Thank you for asking."

"What are you studying?"

Silvia sighed. "I'm attending Penn State online. It's a really good program. Are you here to talk about college?"

The agent smiled and shook his head. "No, I wanted to tell you something while the kids are out. The other day I was over in Blanco Gardens and I saw your sister."

Silvia scowled, then quickly rearranged her face into a neutral expression. Blanco Gardens was all the way across town. "Did you talk to her? Are you sure it was her?"

"I didn't talk to her, but I'm sure it was her. It's pretty far from home and, as you probably know, some areas on the outskirts there can be pretty rough. "I wanted to be sure that you knew she was over there."

"Oh yes, of course I knew she was there. She …" Silvia hesitated, "has a friend over there. Which day was it, again?"

"Sunday. But as long as you know, it's fine. I just wanted to be sure." The tall agent got up off the couch and began to walk toward the door.

Silvia stayed sitting. "How can you live with yourself and what you do for a living?" she asked quietly.

"Excuse me?" he asked politely, turning back to face Silvia.

"How can you separate children and parents? And then follow children to school and across town? How can you live with having everybody afraid of you all the time?"

"Silvia, I'm from the Department of Social Services. We help families and children."

"I've heard the kids crying when you guys come around. The windows and blinds close. People are afraid of you." Silvia stared up into his eyes.

"Federal agencies are not all bad, you know, Miss. We all work together to try to keep families, children, and the American public in general safe in an area and a time that can be pretty uncertain. We aim to protect."

"Well, a federal agency deported my mother. How did that protect her *or* me?" Silvia demanded. She clenched her teeth, feeling her face growing hot. She was conscious on some level that she was not keeping a low profile in that moment, but she couldn't seem to stop herself.

The agent sighed. "To some extent, you're right, Silvia. But removing illegal aliens allows the government to catch and remove dangerous criminals from our country. ICE, if that's who you're referring to, is casting a wide net right now because exactly who poses a threat to our nation is not always clear until it's too late, such as after a terror attack."

"Well, I would say it's pretty clear who is *not* a threat, like a single mother. Or a middle-school girl. Or the house painter and his wife and baby son across the parking lot."

"This isn't exactly my department, Miss, but I'll do my best to explain." Agent Randolph sat back down on the far end of the couch. "The president's orders are to remove everyone who's here illegally, regardless of family or other circumstances, and then as a nation we can start fresh, with a better, more humane system of immigration and homeland security that will keep us all safe."

Silvia hesitated. But then she scowled and got to her feet. "Well, I hope it works. And I sincerely hope you and all the other agents can sleep at night. Because a lot of families and children are suffering because of your 'orders.'"

Officer Randolph stood and nodded politely to Silvia on his way to the door. "I think you're misdirecting your aggression, Miss. I'm here to help you. As are all the federal agencies."

Silvia held the door open, staring at the floor and shaking her head. The inside corners of her eyes burned.

"You have a good day, Miss."

"Right," Silvia said. "You too." She closed the door behind him, then peeked out the living room window to watch him get into his white Suburban with the federal seal on the side.

She shook her head, hoping to dismiss the entire incident.

But the book trembled before her eyes as if in an earthquake when she sat down to study.

22

Silvia found herself unable to focus on her work after Agent Randolph's visit. Troubled by the information she had learned about Lucy's unauthorized trip across town, her immediate instinct was to try to call her mother. But then she remembered her mother's risky plan and the urgency in her face during their video call. She knew that Lucy's erratic behavior and Agent Randolph's first visit had catalyzed that urgency, and she resolved not to worry Mami any further.

Instead, she composed an email to Dr. Cisneros, telling her about her mother's timeframe for crossing and inquiring whether there was a legal way to bring her back into the country. Although she tried to keep the email professional, she ended up in tears, listing all the things that were going wrong—finances, missed coursework, Lucy, ICE. *It's my fault, it's all my fault,* she wrote. *If only I had been able to keep everything under control, she wouldn't be in danger.*

As she finished writing, Silvia's stomach fluttered with the nervousness of vulnerability. Yet her advisor's experience at the border was the only lead she had for aborting her mother's plan and finding a safer way to reunite. She hit Send.

Hands trembling, she looked around for something to help her pass the time while she awaited her advisor's response. Her guilty gaze landed on the pile of school books at her left. "Maybe I'll finally try Borders," she said, sighing and pulling that textbook out of the bottom of the stack where it had sat for days.

She logged in to the course's distance learning platform and settled in to watch the lecture, a case study on the extended border issues between Texas and Mexico. *How timely,* thought Silvia, as she pressed Play on the lecture video and tried to focus on the professor's explication of the Chazimal region between Ciudad Juárez and El Paso.

It was a fascinating story. In Chazimal, the Rio Grande formed the border as defined by agreement between the Mexico and the United States. However, over time, the border was found to be literally fluid, as the Rio changed course not insignificantly after floods and storms. At times, considerable amounts of land moved from north of the border to south, or vice versa. As a result, the people of the Chazimal area easily lived biculturally and bilingually, with families moving freely across the border to do their shopping, visit friends, and so on.

But property conflicts involving the governments, taxation, laws, and businesses of the two countries were not so easily resolved. Disputes over land at in Chazimal continued into the 1960s, complicated by deserved propaganda against the United States as a greedy grabber of land in Latin America. Ultimately, as it seemed to Silvia was always the case, Mexico and the U.S. reached an agreement that displaced hundreds of Mexican families from their lands. It seemed to her that Mexicans had been moving out of the way of Americans since the foundations of the two countries. And now her mother was one of them.

She checked her email. Nothing from Dr. Cisneros yet.

Silvia glanced at her great-great-grandmother's diario. The lecture she just watched called to mind Margarita's descriptions of Socorro's setting along the Rio Grande, just outside of the Chazimal between Texas and Mexico. Indeed, Margarita had described two historic floods that had impacted her town. Silvia almost reached for the book to reread those passages, so heart-wrenchingly described in her great-great-grandmother's prose.

"Not yet," she said, knowing that she had botany reading to do first. She pushed away her Borders book, still unopened, and checked her botany syllabus. "Okay, where was I?" As her eyes scanned the course calendar, she realized just how far behind she was in her work. On the entry for three weeks ago, she finally found the title of the chapter where she had left off: "Trees of the American Southwest."

Although she loved botany, studying leaves and bark while a federal agent was watching her sister and while her mother was packing to sneak across the border felt ridiculously irrelevant. Nevertheless, she grabbed her botany text and settled down on the recliner with a cup of coffee. After nearly an hour of reading the descriptive introductory material, she was finally engrossed. At last, she came to her favorite chapter section: the identification tables, with photos of each plant's silhouette, bark, leaves, and flowers.

Making her way through the alphabetized entries, she smiled in recognition as she came to *M* and the *mesquite tree*. She learned that the tree was very important to the native inhabitants of the Southwest, for fuel as well as for food, since the mesquite bean was a high-energy desert food source. The tree's adaptations to the harsh, dry climate of the region were fascinating. It had evolved thorns along its branches to discourage damage by herbivores, waxy leaves to minimize evaporation, and the deepest documented root systems to reach ground water well below the dry surface. Its yellow clusters of frothy flowers attracted pollinators, but Silvia thought they also brought beauty to the desert, as they must have done on her great-great-grandmother's land.

A few pages later, the text shifted to oasis trees, those that flourish alongside rivers and streams in the Southwest. *Like in West Texas*, she thought, getting up to refill her cup and returning to her chair. She ignored the computer as she passed it both times, determined to stay focused and finally get her reading done, even though she was anxious for her advisor's reply.

Featured in the oasis section of the text were wide varieties of willows, whose fast-growing networks of roots safeguarded riverbanks from erosion and served as a filter for flowing water. After reading about desert willow and black willow, Silvia paused at coyote willow. *First mesquite, now coyote*, she thought. *Huh.*

She continued reading. This small tree or large shrub with smooth bark and silvery hairy leaves and twigs was common along the Rio Grande and many other rivers throughout the West. Looking at the images of the plant, Silvia wondered whether the common name had come from the fact that the tree provided shelter for animals such as the coyote, or whether it was due to its resemblance to the furry animal itself.

She grabbed her laptop to look up more information on the willow's name, when she saw that an email had come through from Dr. Cisneros. Abandoning her studies, she clicked to open it. Inside the sympathetic response, the professor had mentioned a few local organizations that might be starting places for Silvia's research into possible legal channels for her mother's return. She offered little hope, however, especially considering the compressed timeline that her mother had laid out.

The only deportation cases that have been overturned within a timeframe like your mother's, her advisor wrote, *are those for which the family was able to produce documentation proving that the deported was in fact a US citizen and had been falsely charged. If there is any way I can help, I will. I will try not to fail again.*

Silvia clicked to reply and wrote a brief response, ending with: *Professor, I know you will try to help us and I am so grateful for your background at the border, even if it was painful for you. Will keep you posted.*

Then she reread the part of the message about documentation. Mami had entered illegally with her parents, so no such document existed. Sighing, Silvia took a moment to look up the three agencies that Dr. Cisneros had referenced.

One of them was the Refugee and Immigrant Center for Education and Legal Services, and Silvia quickly found the listing for a contact in San Marcos. She glanced at the corner of her screen. She still had three hours until the kids came home, just enough time to go visit the RAICES office. Silvia quickly brushed her hair back into a tight ponytail and applied the red lip gloss that always made her feel confident. She grabbed her purse and headed out to walk several blocks to catch the number 5 bus across town.

Forty minutes later she was knocking on the door of an older white mobile home set in the middle of a trailer park. The door buzzed and Silvia heard the lock click for her to enter. She found herself in a tiny waiting area with a wooden chair right next to the door, a brown plaid love seat with lacquered wooden arms, and a wobbly coffee table in front of it. The entire space was no more than six by eight feet. Silvia sat down on the love seat to wait for assistance, her knees practically touching the edge of the coffee table. She set her purse on the couch beside her, first pulling out a small red notebook and a pen.

When Dolores Hernández, who presented herself simply as an ally in immigrants' issues, came out of a back room, it became clear that this was not a waiting space but rather the entire office. Evidently Dolores lived in the rest of the trailer, because the smell of beans followed her out as she slipped through the door, pulling it quickly closed behind her.

Dolores tried to make Silvia comfortable right away, but the nature of the subject matter they were discussing meant that both women were on guard. Silvia knew that they were each most likely under scrutiny by federal agencies. After exchanging some pleasantries, Silvia explained in generic terms what her mother's situation was, omitting her name and any specifics about her plans. Her Spanish comprehension was better than her speaking, so they agreed that Silvia would talk in English and Dolores in Spanish.

"So there's no way to bring someone back into the country legally who was already deported for being here illegally?"

Dolores paused as a siren sounded in the distance. She glanced at the automatically locked trailer door. After a moment, she took a breath. "No, señorita, ya no." Dolores explained that there used to be some possibility of deportation reversals under previous administrations, especially when there were children left behind. However, such cases were now virtually nonexistent.

"I see," said Silvia, looking down at her hands in her lap.

Dolores then echoed Dr. Cisneros's information about the exceptions that have been made for people who produced documentation of citizenship—not legal residency—after having been deported.

"Okay, so there's basically no way." Silvia's shoulders slumped, and she avoided Dolores's eyes.

"No, señorita. Sólo en casos en los cuales se produjo algún título, alguna escritura legal …" Dolores continued, but Silvia's mind froze around two words she had just heard: *título* and *escritura*. Strangely, they were two words that appeared together multiple times in her great-great-grandmother's diary. Silvia had read them at face value, as the literary terms for *title* and *writing*. But could they be legal terms as well?

"Could you say that again, please?"

"Seguro." Dolores paused, trying to simplify her language. "Solamente cuando existe algún documento legal, un título, una escritura—"

Hearing those words, Silvia suddenly couldn't wait to get home to the diario. "Disculpe, señora, but I just remembered an assignment I have to finish. I'm so sorry but I have to run. Muchísimas gracias," she said, gathering her things and getting up quickly. "I'll be back if I need more help but this has been great!"

"Pero señorita … no hemos terminado," called Dolores, but Silvia was already up and heading out the door for the approaching bus.

When Silvia heard the plastic door slam shut, she was already at the street.

23

Jorge is gone, back to the mines, nearly a month already. Violeta and I are getting into our fall routines, as if everything were fine and normal, even though we both know it's not … I've returned to selling herbs and vegetables at the market. Violeta is practicing her piano and doing her chores. We never speak of the relief we feel now that Jorge's gloomy temper is no longer hanging over us. Nor of the guilt we feel about our relief, like a shadow in the room that we're afraid to shine a light on.

Talking of light and shadows, it's been weeks since I've had one of my episodes. Tonight I actually feel good. That's because in the morning I begin the next stage of my plan to protect my family. At the same time, I get to enjoy one of a mother's greatest pleasures: giving my daughter a wonderful surprise. The next time I write, we'll be in the big city. Good night!

At dawn, Margarita surprised Violeta with an announcement.

"Pack a bag! We're going to the city!"

"You mean, no school?"

"No school. Get packed!"

Violeta was off like a shot, and within twenty minutes, the two met at the door to their little house, duffle bags in hand. Violeta's bulged with day and night clothes for both her and her porcelain doll, who was absolutely not going to miss a trip to the bustling city. Margarita tied Pastor out with a big bowl of food and water, locked the door to the house, and headed down the road across the browning field. Violeta skipped by her side, clutching her overnight bag in one hand and her doll in the other.

They arrived at Socorro station and Margarita was surprised to see Willy and his son waiting on the platform.

"Willy," she said, giving him a quick hug. "Where are you off to?"

"Hello, Margarita, Miss Violeta. I'm not leaving. I'm just picking up a shipment from Albuquerque." He glanced at their bags and scowled. "But don't tell me you two are leaving town like the others."

Margarita grabbed Violeta's hand, laughing a little as she looked down at her daughter, hoping she wasn't listening to the conversation. "Of course not! We're just going on a little trip."

"Well, now, Miss Vi. Where are you going?"

"El Paso," said Violeta, rocking onto her toes and swinging her porcelain doll.

Willy straightened up. "Why, the big city! That's exciting!" He raised his eyebrows at Margarita.

She swallowed. "We're just going to have a look around, maybe see some of the sights."

His eyebrows were still raised. "Well, that's great. And in the middle of the week, too. You're one lucky girl, Miss Vi."

The train whistle blew a short distance up the track, echoing off the hills.

"Here she comes!" said Willy. "You all have a safe trip now. Let me know if you need anything." He looked pointedly at Margarita.

She smiled. "Of course we will. We'll be back in a couple of days. Violeta, grab your bag. The train's pulling in."

They waved as Willy walked to the end of the platform to pick up his packages. Then they boarded the train to El Paso, right on time at 9:45.

Violeta passed the time during the ride with her face pressed to the glass, pulling her eyes away only to take bites of the cheese sandwich her mother had packed for her. Margarita chatted quietly with the women across the aisle from them or wrote in her journal. By midafternoon, they were pulling into the "big city."

Violeta's eyes were wide as she and Margarita emerged from the train into noisy Union Station. Passengers' heels clicked as they hurried across the tiled floor. The aroma of seafood and steaks wafted down from Harvey House on the second floor, the smoke and steam from the restaurant making "sun dust" in the light from the arched windows above. Inhaling deeply, Violeta looked hopefully up at her mother, who shook her head and smiled as they passed beneath the balustrade and stepped out onto the city streets.

The few blocks to the El Paso Public Library were filled with the sights, sounds, and smells of the city. Car horns beeped and streetcars clanged. Newsboys shouted headlines from the *Herald-Post* on the corners, competing with vendors offering fragrant roast corn on the cob or hot peanuts. A departing train huffed out of the station and down Franklin Avenue as smiling children waved it on its way toward Kansas City and Chicago. Men in shirt sleeves and vests waited in line for coffee or bread to take home for dinner.

Despite all the sensory stimulation on the ground, Violeta's face remained turned upward under the Texas afternoon sun. Margarita smiled as she saw her daughter gaping at the columns of the post office, the marble facades of the banks, the startling height of the Hilton Hotel.

Keeping her sights lower, Margarita noted that many of the storefronts were shuttered. On one corner, a bank's door was barred with a metal grate. Halfway down the same block, a jewelry store's sign was covered up with a torn cardboard scrawled with *Closed for Business*. Other vacant storefronts appeared to have had recent lives as lunch counters, department stores, or drug stores. Glancing up a side street as they crossed, Margarita saw a line of men in suits and hats outside of what must have been a city or county government building. She had seen many pictures of lines of jobless men in the newspaper, but never in person. She tightened her grip on Violeta as they crossed Franklin Avenue and entered the city park that surrounded the library.

The sounds of urban life instantly faded as they stepped into the shade of the live oaks and pecan trees that lined the walkways through the park and up the small rise to the library. After a brief rest and snack in the grass, they climbed the granite steps, passed between the stately columns, and entered the Greek Revival building. Margarita deeply inhaled the smells of paper and glue that reminded her of the books her father and grandmother had given her as a child: *Shakespeare's Sonnets*,

Little Women, Webster's Practical Dictionary. A spot she couldn't quite identify in her brain tingled with the excitement of knowledge and the safety that she hoped it would afford her family.

Margarita had spent the time since the concerning conversation in the Socorro shop making a plan to protect herself and her family from the outside forces that seemed to be organizing against them. On one front there was Jorge and his emotional distance from her and Violeta. If the summer had made anything clear, it was that she couldn't count on him for support and protection the way she used to. After all, she was the one alone with Violeta more than half the year. It was her responsibility to safeguard their child. On a more forbidding front, cultural and political elements threatened the security of Socorro and its residents. These attacks from within and without had caused a dangerous chemical reaction in Margarita, one that she was sure was compromising her emotional and mental stability. Now their little wooden house felt isolated, over-remote, vulnerable. And Margarita felt the same.

So she had to take control. She organized a plan and began its first stage, which she named Escritura: gathering documentation of her legal rights and possessions. She started by going to the mission church and securing a copy of her marriage license and her and Violeta's birth registrations. She also procured copies of the records of her parents' and grandparents' marriages and births. She listed every document she found neatly in her notebook.

She passed the evenings graphing her family's genealogy, first by memory, then by checking it against the record in her mother's family Bible, and finally by memory once again. By lamplight, she studied the tiny script inside the Bible's cover, watching it become curvier and more ornate with each preceding generation. At the very top of the page was the name of the first ancestor to settle on this land, Enrique de Riveras Salazar.

She knew from family lore that he had been party to the land grant in 1816 that guaranteed US citizenship to all residents, and their heirs, of the parcels contained therein. Since her three times great-grandfather had only daughters, he had originated the family tradition of passing the land to the eldest daughter, and so it had continued down to Margarita.

Coincidentally or not, most of the families listed in the genealogy had birthed only girls or at least had more girls than boys. In the six generations since the formation of the land grant, twenty-two daughters were born and only nine sons.

With the marriage and birth records in place to confirm the genealogy information, Margarita expected to feel secure in the documentation of her citizenship against any inquiries by the Border Patrol. But she did not. So she determined to gather all of the legal records possible about the land grant in Socorro to round out her personal escritura archive. When she took Violeta out of school, it was because her peace of mind couldn't withstand delaying the project. She had to protect her daughter now.

Taking Violeta's hand, she approached the reference desk.

"Good afternoon. My name is Margarita and this is my daughter, Violeta. We have traveled some distance today to see if we can find information about the land our family has lived on for generations. Would you be able to help us?"

"Sure, ma'am," replied the woman at the desk, wearing a navy-blue short-sleeved shirtdress with brass buttons that caught Margarita's eye. "What kind of information are you looking for?"

"Thank you. I need to know which government offices to contact for certain types of records, such as deeds, land grants, and so on. But my family's history on our property dates to before the Southwest was part of the United States, so I wonder where I could find copies of the agreements between America and Mexico and that kind of thing." Margarita suddenly felt unqualified to be making requests that she was having trouble even articulating.

The clerk, whose nametag read ELEANOR, brightened visibly with the mention of treaties. "I recently filled a similar request for a patron interested in Mexican history, and I think I can show you what you're looking for." She led Margarita and Violeta to a wide wooden table with four glass-shaded lamps and plenty of space to work. "I'll be right back."

"These are so pretty, Mami," said Violeta, fingering the bumpy molded-glass shades.

"Shhhh," said Margarita. "And don't touch. Be really careful here."

Margarita reached into her handbag and pulled out her journal. She ripped a blank page out and gave it to her daughter with a pencil to draw. When Eleanor returned, she brought two volumes of an encyclopedia and placed them in front of Violeta. She held an oversized volume bound in red leather and a smaller light brown tome for Margarita.

"Young lady, you might want to get started reading about the Louisiana Purchase and the Spanish-American war for your mother. Both affected this area."

Violeta looked up at Eleanor's face for a moment, then nodded, accepting her task. She sat down to work, pencil poised over her blank sheet of paper while she flipped through the *L* volume to begin her assignment.

"For you," smiled the clerk, turning to Margarita, "I have some heavier lifting. Do you read Spanish?"

"I do," said Margarita, feeling her face warm and brushing a hair away from her eye as casually as she could.

"Good. Then I have two books for you." She opened the large volume, which turned out to be an annotated atlas of the Spanish land grants from the seventeenth to the nineteenth centuries. Then she showed her the small book, a facsimile reproduction of the Treaty of Guadalupe Hidalgo with all of its addenda.

Margarita took a deep breath. "Thank you. I guess I have my work cut out for me!" She grinned across the table at Violeta.

"Mami, what is all this for?" asked the little girl.

"Shhhh." Margarita leaned in, swallowing, her eyes scanning the book in front of Violeta. "I just thought you might like to do a little research for school. You'll be learning about the Louisiana Purchase soon." She smiled, meeting her daughter's eyes.

"Swell," Violeta said, smiling back.

And mother and daughter settled into what Margarita hoped would be the completion of Stage One of her plan: gathering la escritura, the documents that would protect them.

24

Silvia was buzzing with excitement to continue her research on the words *título* and *escritura* in her bisabuela's diary. She got off the bus one stop past home so that she could cautiously approach the apartment complex. Ever since she'd come home to find Agent Randolph with her brother on the floor of their home, she could no longer think of their home as a sanctuary. She now always approached it on foot from a distance so that she could see the parking lot clearly before she was near enough to the complex to be noticed. She scowled, resenting the undercurrent of insecurity and the delay of her research necessitated by the detour.

Today, she was approaching home from the north. She could see the back of their building first, before getting a view of the parking lot that was nestled among the complex's three apartment buildings arranged in a U-shape. Next, she'd have to cross the street to see into the parking lot from a safe distance.

All clear. Silvia hurried back across the street and opened the door into their living room, hoping to arrive before her brother and sister got home so she could get straight to work. But Lucy was already slumped on the couch watching a video on her phone, which meant Seba was also home. Lucy turned serious eyes up at her sister.

"We heard about the raid in San Antonio on the bus today," said Lucy without greeting her. "I was just watching the coverage."

Silvia dimly recalled that, while she had been puzzling over the words Dolores had used in their conversation and their connection to the diario, she had heard the bus radio repeating the words *San Antonio*.

"Give me one sec, Lucy," she said, dropping her bag in the kitchen and taking a quick moment to key in *San Antonio* and *raid* on her phone.

Immediately, headlines popped up telling of an immigration raid that day at an elementary school in the neighboring city. Silvia skimmed a few headlines and returned to the living room.

"Yeah, Luce, that's not around here. Don't worry," said Silvia, hoping to brush off the scary situation for now and get to her work on the diary.

"It's not that far. It could happen here any day." Lucy picked at a pimple on her forehead.

"That's why I'm glad you and Seba travel together every day, to take care of each other," said Silvia. "What did they say on the report you were watching?"

"That ICE arrived demanding to enter the classrooms, but the principal wouldn't let them."

"Good. See?"

"She said that they couldn't come in without warrants. She actually stepped outside the building to talk to them and wouldn't let them in the school." Lucy hazarded a smile.

"Good. All schools should be safe for kids." Silvia paused. "Where's Seba? Does he know, too?"

"He's in his room with another stomachache. Yeah, we were all listening. A couple of kids called their moms before they got off the bus to make sure that everything was okay. Everyone's scared."

"I know," Silvia said, sitting down on the couch next to her sister. "But the school did the right thing and maybe ICE learned its lesson."

Lucy laughed. "Yeah, right. Or maybe next time they'll come back with warrants."

"Kids are not criminals, Lucy. We are not criminals. There will be no warrants." Silvia's eyes blazed. "I'd better go see how Seba is feeling. Let me know if there are any more developments." Silvia stood up and headed to the hallway. Pausing and looking back over her shoulder, she said, "Thanks for telling me, Lucy. We're going to be okay."

Lucy shrugged.

Silvia walked slowly down the hallway, replacing titulo and escritura with words she could use to calm Sebastián. She entered his room and saw him facedown on the bed. She sighed, then immediately came back out to grab his water bottle. As she emerged into the hallway, she saw Lucy hurriedly zip her backpack shut and jump up off the couch.

"I'm going out for a little while!" she yelled.

"What?" Silvia paused at the entrance to the living room. "You've only been home a few minutes!"

"I know, but I've got to go out for a little bit," Lucy said. She was already beside the front door, pulling her tennis shoes on without untying them.

"What about your homework?" asked Silvia, grabbing Sebastián's water bottle from the counter just inside the kitchen, then turning around to face her sister directly.

"It's done," said Lucy with a cheerful smile. "I'll be back after dinner." She threw her backpack on her shoulders and burst out the front door, letting the screen slam behind her.

Silvia ran to the door and called after her, "Okay, Lucy, but where are you going?"

Lucy whirled around in the middle of the complex's parking lot, turning to face Silvia with her hands on her hips. Her smile was gone. "Just out, okay? I need to see someone. Just a friend. Get off my case, would you?"

Get off my case, Silvia thought as she closed and locked the front door. The same phrase Lucy used with her science teacher. The same phrase that made Mrs. Black think she was hiding a drug habit. Frowning, she went back down the hall with Sebastián's water.

He was still lying down, holding his blue stuffed elephant in one arm. His shoes were still on and his feet were hanging off his bed. Silvia loosened the Velcro closures and slipped the shoes off his feet, rubbing them gently as she sat next to him on the bed.
"Hey, buddy."

Sebastián grunted in response and rolled away from her onto his side. Silvia could tell that he'd been crying.

"Hey, Sebastián, come on." Silvia stretched out beside him and reached for his chubby hand, still dimpled like a baby's. "Listen, are you scared or sad?"

"Both," said Sebastián into the top of his elephant's head. "But mostly scared. My tummy hurts. And I want Mami."

"I know, hermanito." Silvia had to stay strong for her little brother. She fought down her feelings of panic at the thought of Mami preparing to cross the border.

"They're taking kids from schools now and sending them to jail."

"Wait a minute." Silvia sat up. "No, they're not. All the kids are fine and went home to their families."

Sebastián raised his head, still not turning toward Silvia. "Really?"

"Yeah. The school wouldn't let ICE in to get them, or even to talk to them. Schools are safe. You are safe."

Sebastián wiped his eyes on his elephant. "Are you sure?"

"Positive."

The little boy at last rolled over and looked Silvia in the eyes. "But ICE wanted to take the kids to jail."

"Well, ICE wants everyone out of here that they think doesn't belong here."

"Like Mami?"

Silvia paused. "Yes, like Mami."

"But she did belong here," he said defiantly, his little forehead furrowing. "With us."

"I know." Silvia struggled to keep her voice steady.

Sebastián didn't seem to notice. After a moment, he looked intently at Silvia's face and asked in a soft voice, "Do we belong here?"

"Of course we do," said Silvia, smoothing her hair back into its ponytail holder. "We were born here. This is our home."

"So, wait. Kids that weren't born here don't belong here?" he asked, sitting up cross-legged and pulling Blue Elephant onto his lap.

"No, that's not what I meant at all." Silvia could see that her brother, a loving little boy who got along with nearly everyone, was struggling to apply logic to the incomprehensible situation. "Look, Seba. The way I see it, anyone who wants to be in the United States and behaves according to the laws belongs here. In the past, many people have come here to escape problems or wars in their own countries. Others came because they thought there would be better opportunities for their families here."

"Like our abuelos when they brought Mami, right?"

"Exactly. And some families had to come here in a hurry, like for safety or something, and they sometimes didn't have time to fill out all the right papers and follow all the rules of getting in. Know what I mean?"

Sebastián nodded. "Yeah, but if they follow all the rules once they're here, then they can stay, right?"

"Well, that's what I believe, and what many people believe, that we should help our neighbors and that everyone should be allowed to live a safe, happy life wherever they choose."

Sebastián blew out his breath and put his hand in his sister's.

Silvia hesitated, but continued. "But some people don't agree. They think that if a child or his mom or his abuelo came in without the right papers, he has to leave. They all have to leave! Do you think that sounds fair?"

"No way! So that's why they were trying to get the kids, to make them leave because they are indocumentados?"

"I didn't know you knew that word."

Sebastián smiled proudly. "So is it?"

"Yes, that's basically why, because they don't have the right documents, or papers. But remember, the school did the right thing and protected the kids. Like I protect you and Lucy."

"And we protect you, right?"

Silvia felt tears prickle at the inside corners of her eyes. "Right, Seba."

The little boy's brow creased. "Are we indocumentados?"

Silvia's heart dropped, then started racing. "No, Seba. I mean, we're citizens so we don't need documents." She frowned, thinking. Their family had never planned to travel internationally, so their mother had not gotten them passports. Their birth certificates were in a safe-deposit box somewhere. And she didn't drive, so she didn't have a license. None of them really had any documentation at all. Silvia supposed they had social security cards, but couldn't anyone get a social security number? How could Mami not have thought of this?

Silvia swallowed hard and pushed her worries away. She stood up. "So we have a deal? We're going to keep protecting each other?"

"Mm-hmm."

She softened, and put her hand under Sebastián's chin. "And we're going to stop worrying for tonight. Does your tummy feel any better?"

Sebastián stretched his arms, arching his back. "Uh-huh. And Silvi, we've got to protect all the kids at my school, too, right? Because we all belong here?"

"Right." They high-fived and Silvia set him up to do his addition homework, crossing her fingers that what Sebastián said would turn out to be true, that they would all be able to protect each other even without documentation, and that they all did, in fact, belong here.

25

"The best night of her life." That's what Violeta told me right before falling asleep. That's what I'll hang on to. I'm taking steps to protect my family, and my little girl is having the time of her life. I never would have guessed that leaving our quiet little town and coming to the big city would make me feel safer, but it has! Thank you, El Paso. Thank you!

I wrote the above last night. Who could have guessed that such joy and gratitude could turn into such bitterness and discrimination in the course of one day?

Margarita closed her diary and stared out the train window into the blackness. She thought about the contrast between their two days in El Paso and wondered how things could have turned so fast.

They had finished their first day's research with pages of notes and a request for copies of several book pages to add to the archive of escritura. When Margarita noticed the streetlights shining through the library's tall windows, she decided it was time to take Violeta out on the town.

They had strolled together along El Paso's Great White Way. "Mami, look how bright the street lights are!"

Margarita smiled down at her. "They are!" she said. "Look at your shadow!"

Violeta tried jumping on her shadow as it grew black directly beneath a light and then fainter as they passed between lamps. "I'm tall! Now I'm short! I'm tall again!" she cried as she hopped, duffle bag bouncing into her leg at each landing.

They walked in silence for a moment, Violeta striding formally as they encountered two women walking in the opposite direction. Just after they had passed, Violeta half whispered, "Mami, did you see their dresses? Bright red with polka dots? And bright yellow?" Her eyes shone as she looked up.

"I did," said Margarita. "Beautiful." She smoothed her own floral dress, with its brown background and patch pockets trimmed with lace, thinking of the sleek profiles and satiny fabrics of the two women.

"Ooh!" Violeta said. "Here comes another one."

A lady in a shiny navy-blue dress and matching pillbox hat sauntered by, her black pumps clicking against the concrete. She carried a small beaded bag.

"Wasn't she magnificent, Mami?" Violeta asked.

Margarita grinned at her daughter's word. "Lovely, amor." She again glanced down, this time at her brown ankle-strap heels, a little scuffed at the toes.

They traveled south on Mesa Street and lingered in San Jacinto Plaza to watch a mariachi trio perform under the trees. Then they passed the bright marquis of the enormous Plaza Theater. They splurged on a single serving of Belgian-style mussels and frites while listening to a jazz band at Howard's in Union Station.

Margarita's eyes crinkled at the memory of her daughter playing the part of the cultured cosmopolitan lady by mirroring the actions of the glamorous young woman at the next table with a fur wrap buttoned at the throat. Yet despite Violeta's feigned formality, she couldn't help bursting into applause when each song finished with a squeal of horns or a crash of the cymbal. That had been "the best night" of her life.

Even this morning, Margarita thought, things started off perfectly. The two had awoken in the boarding house to the smell of strong coffee and fresh doughnuts. Then they had returned to the library to pick up the copies that Eleanor had left for them, and to finish their reading. At noon, Violeta sighed and leaned over Margarita's shoulder only to see that the newspaper she was reading was open to the entertainment section, the motion picture timetable for the Plaza blazing proudly from the page.

"Mami, are we going?" shouted Violeta.

"Shhhh!" Margarita looked sharply at her daughter. "Don't forget we're still in the library!"

"Sorry, Mami," said Violeta in a stage whisper. "But are we going?"

"Well, we still have five hours before the train, and there's a one o'clock show that—" Before Margarita could finish, Violeta gathered up both of their duffle bags and began dragging them toward the tall brass exit door.

"I guess we're going," said Margarita under her breath, smiling. She returned the newspaper to the wooden rack where she had found it, grabbed her notes and copies, and followed her daughter into the midday Texas sunlight.

At fifteen minutes before one, they arrived at the theater. In the light of day, the Plaza Theater's shiny marquis and towering stucco facade presided grandly over the short alley leading up to it. The mission-style roofline cut a fancy edge against the deep blue sky, which found its echo in some of the tiles of the mosaic false doorway near the facade's peak. Back on the ground and perfectly aligned with the center of the building stood the carnivalesque ticket booth, supported by four rope-like columns and crowned with a red-yellow-and-blue feather motif that suggested the headdress of a vaudeville dancer.

"Hey!" said a man who had approached them from behind while they were taking in the beauty of the theater. "Hey, I'm talking to you. You look at me when I'm talking to you."

His sharp words echoed in Margarita's memory. She knew that was the moment when everything had changed.

Margarita had turned around, placing a hand on Violeta's shoulder protectively. "May I help you?"

"Yeah, sweetie, you may help me by getting out of here. We don't serve jumping beans here."

"Excuse me, do you work here?" asked Margarita.

"I live here. As in, I live in the United States of America. You and your dirty daughter can go back where you belong. I see you've already packed your bags." The man kicked Margarita's duffle roughly with the toe of his work boot.

"Hey—" started Violeta, but Margarita silenced her with a firm squeeze of her shoulder.

"Sir," began Margarita with measured calm, "I'm sure we can work this out. Let me just speak to the manager." She began to shepherd Violeta under the marquis to see if there was an usher visible through the brass and glass doors.

The scruffy man grabbed her elbow, forcing Margarita to whirl around to face him again. He growled, "Don't turn your back on me, Mexican. If I said we don't serve jumping beans here, we don't serve jumping beans here."

By then a few couples had turned to watch the commotion, but no one moved to approach the increasingly loud man. Margarita turned away slowly, pulling Violeta between her body and the locked theater doors. Shortly, a slim manager in a red uniform approached the doors and unlocked one. He stepped out, hurriedly pulling the door closed behind him.

"May I help you, ma'am?"

"Yes sir. My daughter and I were waiting to see the film and that gentleman over there began harassing us. Would you please speak to him, or could we perhaps come in and wait inside?" She peered over the manager's shoulder at the red carpeted lobby within.

The manager eyed the rough-looking man in rolled-up sleeves and gray vest. Margarita could see him in the reflection, glaring at their backs, gesturing back and forth at Margarita and Violeta with one fat hand as if they were refuse that someone had neglected to pick up. The manager looked back at Margarita. "Uh, ma'am, I'm terribly sorry, but I think it would be best if you left."

Margarita's mouth dropped open. "Sir, we are paying customers and have every right to be here, no matter what he, or anyone else, thinks."

"I know, ma'am, but perhaps it would be best if you came back for one of our later showings, when there are more people around. Easier to blend in, you know? In the afternoons, with just a few people at the theater, well, there've been some incidents." He glanced nervously at the glowering man in the alley. "I wouldn't want you to get in trouble, you know?"

"You don't want *us* to get in trouble? We're only trying to watch a picture, sir. He's the one who should be in trouble for threatening us."

"Well, I'm just saying that's not the way it works, ma'am, if the authorities have to come here. They usually assume that the problem is the … er …"

"The what, sir?" demanded Margarita, standing up straighter.

"Look, ma'am, I'll give you tickets for tomorrow night. Just please go now." The manager tried an apologetic smile as he fumbled in his vest pocket.

"We'll go, but we are certainly not coming back here tomorrow night, nor any other. Have a pleasant day." Margarita turned on her heel, holding her head high as she stalked past their harasser and out of the alley, with Violeta by the hand.

Tears sprang to Margarita's eyes at the memory. She thought of Violeta's assessment of their trip while they waited on the platform to go back home. "I like the country better than the city," she had said. "Here there are fancy people and working people and mean people and indifferent people. But at home everyone's nice."

Margarita had smiled sadly at her daughter as they sat on the hard wooden bench.

Violeta continued, "Plus nobody cares what you look like. Most people at home are brown like you and me, or they get that way from working in the sun. Nobody minds. Here it's different."

Margarita sighed. "Maybe it's only different for now. These are hard times all around the country, hija. Maybe when there are more jobs and more money, people won't feel scared of people who look different than they do."

"Maybe," Violeta had said, tossing a peanut on the tracks for a lonely pigeon, the color of café con leche.

Margarita glanced down now at her diary, and at the paper underneath it on the small train desk in front of her. It was a list of government offices and addresses that Eleanor had left for her that morning.

It seemed like so long ago. She took out a stack of blank paper and, fighting against the rhythmic rocking of the train, she wrote letters to every government office on Eleanor's list, and with each stroke of the pen, hoped.

26

Silvia blinked back tears reading of her bisabuela's heartbreak, as the text notification chime sounded on her phone.

Silvia, please call me. It's urgent. It's not about school.

Her heart jumped as she read the brief message from Dr. Cisneros. Maybe her professor had found the loophole that would bring her mother back. She clicked to call her in her office at Penn State.

"I saw the coverage of the ICE raid in San Antonio," the professor began, after they'd said their greetings. "And I've been reading the backlash afterward, using it to take the pulse of the nation regarding the issue of the children of undocumented immigrants. I'm afraid it doesn't sound too good."

Silvia sank down into the armchair by the door, thinking of the anti-Mexican sentiment in El Paso in her bisabuela's time. She glanced at the door reflexively to make sure the lock was engaged. "What do you mean?"

"Well, the commentary on the news and on social media is heartless, increasingly isolationist. It seems that many people want immigrants of all sorts out of the country. Although many of those commenting are just bitter or uneducated people spouting off in any forum that will have them, some are people with money, people in the position to influence legislation."

"Hmm, I see," said Silvia.

"And it's not just San Antonio. Before that was the raid of the trailer community in New Mexico."

"Right, I followed that one, too. Las Cruces. Five or six people, right?"

"Yes, taken from their families, some even before anyone else was home to be with the kids."

"That's awful!" Silvia smoothed her hair back hard with her free hand.

"And dangerous," added Dr. Cisneros. "That leaves kids subject to custody by CPS, which I fear will result in their deportation, too, perhaps even without our government's knowledge of or concern for where the parents are."

Silvia was silent, remembering Agent Randolph's visits.

Her professor continued. "And did you hear that more than two thousand children in Las Cruces missed school for days afterward, afraid that either they'd be taken on their way or their parents would be gone when they got home?"

Silvia still couldn't answer; the memory of her own homecoming the day ICE took her mother was still too fresh. She was glad that she had confided in her advisor about her mother's deportation when she had started her online program at Penn State. She might not have the real college experience, but she at least had a trusted mentor. "Mm-hmm," she managed on the phone with Dr. Cisneros.

"I know, Silvia, I know what you must be feeling. But listen, I didn't call to upset you. I called to warn you."

"Warn me?" Silvia sat up in the chair.

"Yes. I've heard they're going to propose new legislation any day now in Congress that could allow children born here of undocumented parents to be deported. It may even be happening already in indirect ways, such as not letting them back in the country after an international trip."

"Oh, geez."

"What I'm saying is that you need to seek help now from those agencies that I told you about, not just for your mother, but for your-selves. You've got to be prepared to defend your right to be here." She paused, then said quietly, "I refuse to let this happen again."

Silvia let that sink in, remembering Dr. Cisneros's heartbreaking story. She felt responsible, somehow, for reassuring her professor. "Don't worry. We're okay. I actually visited one of the organizations already."

Dr. Cisneros's sigh rasped across the phone. "Great. Which one?"

"I met a lady from RAICES. It mostly was a dead end, but I did get a lead from her that could be promising." Silvia recounted Dolores's emphasis on the words *título* and *escritura*. She told Dr. Cisneros how she had finally gotten to her desk late that night, after settling Sebastián down. She had looked up the words first in her Spanish-English dictionary, then in the online dictionary of the Spanish Royal Academy, and finally in a glossary of Spanish legal terms. In addition to the familiar literary usages of the words, she had been thrilled to find that the two terms were closely related.

Escritura in the legal sense was a public document that was signed with witnesses and notarized. This excited Silvia, thinking of the possible types of documents her bisabuela could be referencing, from court records to military enlistments to patents.

The reference for the other term quickly narrowed those possibilities, since *título* meant, as it does in English, either possession of nobility or possession of property. While Silvia was intrigued by the prospect of being a descendant of a Spanish knight or duke, she found the second possibility much more promising for her mother's case.

"So if Mami actually owns land in the States that she would have inherited from her great-great-grandmother, maybe that will give her a way to argue for legal entry?"

"Well, Silvia," said Dr. Cisneros, "this might be promising for your Memoirs paper, but I wouldn't hang my hopes on an antique journal for fixing a very contemporary problem. Use your ingenuity and caution, above all, to keep yourself and your brother and sister safe."

"I'll try."

"You have to do more than try, Silvia. You must keep them safe. That's your first job right now. It may be your full-time job for a while."

The professor's words rang in Silvia's ears after they hung up, as did Mami's statement that school was her job. If staying safe was also a full-time obligation, that might explain why she was having so much trouble keeping up with schoolwork.

Silvia scowled. She wasn't convinced about her advisor's assessment of the diary's limited usefulness. If her US Borders course had taught her anything, despite her own reluctance, it was that the problems of Mexican Americans had been ongoing for centuries. Even her own great-great-grandmother experienced it just decades earlier. Maybe she was being overly optimistic, but she thought it was possible that the insight passed down from her strong female ancestor from the borderlands could aid her own family in twenty-first-century Texas.

Plus, hadn't she learned from her Memoirs course that the humanities were not just for final papers or personal enrichment? Its tools, like close reading, textual analysis, comparative study, and interdisciplinarity, could help her analyze the past to better understand the present. With her new suspicion that Bisabuela had hidden in her writings some sort of message regarding property—título and escritura—Silvia was not ready to give up on the diario yet.

27

"Botany next," said Silvia that afternoon, trying to focus.

She thought of how, despite the constant fear for their mother and of ICE that overshadowed them, her brother and sister managed to get through their days. Sebastián was into his geology club and was doing better in school than he had been earlier in the fall. Lucy stopped having trouble in science class once Mr. McCloskey had started leaving her alone. In fact, she brought her average to ninety-seven and had never missed another homework assignment.

"Now it's my turn to get caught up," Silvia mused.

Today's topic was yuccas. Silvia had long known the taste of the root, having grown up eating it mashed, fried, and stewed. Not surprisingly, her textbook revealed that Native Americans had depended on it as a food source as well. But Silvia was astounded by the variety of yuccas that grew in the desert. Some were named for their physical features: narrow-leaf, twist-leaf, and banana yuccas. Others were called by the people who had "discovered" them: Buckley's, Schott's, Torrey's, and Thompson's yuccas. Silvia studied them all in preparation for her makeup quiz next week, trying to distinguish their leaves, variegations, curling hairs, stalks, and flowers. Some even grew as trees: Joshua tree and soaptree yuccas.

Silvia paused to take a closer look at this last one. Other common names: palmilla, Spanish bayonet, soapweed. Habitat: grasslands, canyons, hillsides of Arizona, New Mexico, West Texas. Uses: basket weaving and soapmaking. Habits: slow-growing, may live two hundred to three hundred years! She raised her eyebrows. So the very soap plants that her bisabuela may have seen growing above the Rio Grande could still be there today? Margarita wrote about soap with surprising frequency, and would certainly have known about the plants' longevity.

Silvia hurriedly flipped back in her textbook to the identification pages for the mesquites. Mesquite trees could easily live more than one hundred years. Again, the same trees that her great-great-grandmother had described in 1930s Socorro could still be standing. She wondered about their history, too. Next, she checked the willows: these were also long-lived, having evolved to be resistant to traumatic events such as flooding, high winds, and pruning by wildlife. Their resilience, combined with their reproduction method via root cloning, meant that the continuity of a coyote willow stand was indefinite.

Thoroughly distracted from the assigned yuccas and newly energized about Bisabuela's writing, Silvia reached for the diary and flipped again to the first page she had tagged for an instance of *título* or *escritura*. She studied the Spanish on one page of text, then the next, beginning to flip faster and faster as her scanning proved fruitful. For every occurrence of either of the two key terms, there was a decorated everyday word on the same page, either *soap* (could she mean *soapweed*?), *coyote* (is it *coyote willow*?), *mesquite*, or *acequia*. In most instances, more than one of the illuminated words appeared in conjunction with *título* or *escritura*. It was curious.

Silvia skipped to one of Margarita's maps, the detailed drawing of Socorro from an aerial perspective. She remembered having noticed some place names on the map alongside labels of some of the doodled words. There they were in the map of Margarita's own property: *coyote* along the river; *soap* and *mesquite* on the flat top of the steep bank, seventy-five tick-marked steps from the stone and wood cabin. Only *acequia* seemed to be missing, but that was most likely the river itself, or perhaps a ditch that had been carved alongside it for irrigation, but not labeled. Silvia buzzed with possibility. The book contained several maps, but what if the *diario* itself were really a map, even a treasure map? What if the treasure, whether it was a court document or a title of nobility, could somehow help her family?

Silvia we still fired up about the day's discoveries when her siblings came home. But once homework, dinner, and cleanup were done, Dr. Cisneros's grave warning crept back into Silvia's consciousness.

You have to do more than try, Silvia. You must keep them safe.

Needing someone to talk to about Dr. Cisneros' warnings, and unwilling to burden her mother about them, Silvia reached out to Melinda that evening:

Need to talk. Ice cream?

Twenty minutes passed with no response.

She tried again. *Hi Mel. Ice cream and chat?*

Six more minutes. Then:

Sry not tonight

Silvia wondered if this was how their lifelong friendship was going to end, not even epitaphed by a full sentence.

After Lucy and Sebastián were in bed, Silvia went to her room and took off her long-sleeved shirt. She touched the soft jersey of her mother's tank top that she had worn all day underneath, tracing her fingers over the three hearts that Sebastián always said represented Mami's three babies. She flopped down onto her bed and pulled out her phone.

Glancing again at Melinda's curt rejection, she felt a weight on her chest. Looking down her text inbox, she reread Dr. Cisneros's urgent message before their call yesterday. Her heart sank further. *Mami,* thought Silvia with tears filling her eyes. *Mami, everything's going wrong. I'm losing control of everything.*

She thought of her mother, always so controlled. Until lately, that is, when Silvia had seen her eyes red from crying and her skin stretched over her bones as though she had been too grieved to eat. A tear ran down Silvia's cheek and she rolled onto her stomach to write her mother an email. Clearly, they needed each other.

> *Dear Mami,*
>
> *You look like I feel, stretched thin and sad. This was not how we planned it. Our plan was four or five weeks, five easy steps: pay the bills, clean the house, cook the food,*

do the shopping, and manage the kids' schools until you got home. Well, I've been doing all that, but it isn't keeping us safe and it isn't bringing you back. Once Lucy's school called and then Agent Randolph showed up, following your plan was like using a bucket to catch a flood. I've lost Melinda, ICE is watching Lucy, and my professor called to warn me about deportation. How am I supposed to handle all this with a five-step plan?

Tears ran down Silvia's face as she wrote what she knew she could never send. Mami couldn't know about Lucy's trip across town or Agent Randolph's second visit, or RAICES or even Melinda. Their mother already had enough to worry about, and Silvia knew that adding one more thing might push her to risk an even sooner crossing. Instead of sending the email to her mother, Silvia keyed in her own email address and sent herself the message, protecting her mother from the pain that her children were suffering without her.

Irrationally, when the notification came in, Silvia clicked to open the email she'd just written. She reread her words, pausing at the list of five steps. Schools, *check*. Shopping and cooking, *check*. Cleaning? She looked around at her room with clothes strewn on the bed, shoes not put away. Still, the living room and kitchen were neat and the kids helped with chores every week. *Check.*

Now the bills. She sat down at the computer to log in to the checking account that her mother had set up in both their names. One look at the screen confirmed what she already knew: they only had just over seven hundred dollars left, and the bill payments were due next week. For a moment she thought optimistically that Mami would be back soon, but then she remembered the dangers surrounding her crossing. There was absolutely no guarantee that Mami would be able to come home at all, let alone go back to work and get these bills paid.

Silvia clicked to open a new window for the credit card account. She had no choice; she was going to have to finally set up to pay the power bill on the credit card account, as well as take a cash advance from the credit card to keep the household running. She keyed in the credentials to log on. *Access Denied.* She must have mistyped. She tried again. *Access Denied.*

Silvia's hands were trembling and her mind raced through the passcodes that she had for their various accounts. She tried a different combination. *Access Denied.*

Banging on the keys now, she tried the first combination. Then a new one. Hot tears pooled in her eyes. Then a window popped up on her screen:

Suspicious Activity Detected.
To protect your account, further charges may be limited
until this issue is resolved.
Please contact Customer Service immediately.

Silvia slammed the lid of her laptop shut, collapsing over it in sobs that seemed as though they'd never cease.

28

I noticed today that we have barely spoken of Jorge since he left. Whenever we do, I try to keep the conversation light. I don't want to cry, and I don't want to cause Violeta any pain or worry. I don't want her to see me wonder why he left when our finances were good enough. He could have been brave, he could have chosen to take a risk and stay with us, if he had wanted to. Why hadn't he wanted to?

"I can't wait for next summer, Mami," Violeta interrupted.

"I know, mi amor, but that's a long way off," Margarita said, putting down her pen and closing her diary's warm leather cover. "But don't worry. We'll have lots of fun on our beautiful tierra all fall and winter."

"Like making scarecrows?"

Margarita rose from her writing spot at the table and took Violeta by the hand. "Of course," she said, as they began to walk toward Violeta's room.

"And ice-skating on the acequia if it gets cold enough?"

"Well, sure, but that hardly ever happens."

"No, but we can hope," said the little girl, climbing into bed and beaming up at Margarita. "Remember when Papi brought the skates home from Carlton's, just for the day?"

Margarita's smile didn't quite reach her eyes. "Yes, that was a wonderful surprise, wasn't it?"

"Yes! And we spent all afternoon gliding up and down the acequia. I never heard Papi laugh so much." The little girl's eyes clouded and she scowled.

Margarita leaned over the bed. "Lie down, now," she said, and settled her daughter back on the pillows. "That's enough talking. Time for sleep." She turned off the lamp and walked to the door.

"Why doesn't Papi laugh like that anymore?" said Violeta in a small voice.

Margarita paused with a hand on the door latch. She felt its textured iron under her thumb and the cool handle in her palm. She knew that her grandfather had made some of the latches himself, but she never knew which ones. So she chose to believe they were all his.

"I don't know, cariño. But you don't need to worry about that at this moment. I'm sure he's doing better already, back at the mine."

As she softly closed the door to Violeta's room, she glanced into her own bedroom, small, cold, and empty. She leaned her forehead against the doorway and laid her hand on her chest as if to counterbalance the ache she felt pressing up from just under her collarbones. Her palm vibrated with the thumping of her heart, and her breath against the doorframe was shallow and quick.

Margarita closed her eyes as the last conversation they had had about Jorge staying echoed in her mind. They had been sitting alone in the mission after church one Sunday, while Violeta played with her friends outside.

She had taken a deep breath and looked to the statue of the Virgin Mary for strength before beginning. "It's been a great season, Jorge. Everybody's been saying it. I can't believe it's the end already." Her voice resounded a little too loudly in the whitewashed church. She knew that Jorge would leave again soon, school would start for Violeta, and Margarita would be on her own again during the endless days.

Jorge had stiffened slightly in the pew as if he'd sat on a thistle. "Yes, it's gone fast."

"I wanted to tell you. I've been doing some extra work this summer."

He turned his head to the left to look at her under raised eyebrows. His whisper came out as a hiss. "Oh sí? Without my knowing?"

Margarita continued in a hushed voice. "Just a few things. I took in some sewing for the church, and I've been doing it during the little breaks in the day." She paused and looked at Jorge, who was staring unblinking toward the front of the church. She followed his gaze and then pointed in the same direction. "I did all those altar cloths, plus the new ones for the fall. And the altar boys' robes, too."

"Very nice," Jorge said. Margarita saw his gaze move to the embroidered flowers at the hem of the altar cloth. He breathed in and huffed out. "It's good to help the church, I guess." He put his hands on his knees to stand.

Margarita put her hand on his arm and held him in place. "I wasn't just helping. They paid me."

Jorge frowned, finally turning toward her in the pew. "Why? We have everything we need. That's why I work so hard."

Margarita's mind raced. The truth was that she had started trying to bring in extra money for a number of reasons. First, there was the constant threat of the sky and the river, the legacy of the floods of 1929 that haunted her mind. Since then, she never knew when everything could be wiped out again. Her work was helping her fight the panic.

Also, there was the instability of the nation's economy. She knew from the newspapers that shops were closing down throughout the Southwest and entire towns were emptying of their populations, as if someone had unplugged the drain beneath them. Crops had plummeted in value to less than half of what their worth was last decade. How long would it be until all of this happened in Socorro?

Plus, Jorge himself said that pay was dropping for mining work. Workers of Mexican descent were often the first to be let go. The worries echoed in her head so loudly that for a moment Margarita couldn't comprehend her husband's "Why?" She took a deep breath and settled on the least contentious answer. "I just want to do my part, too."

Jorge's face was immobile, so she continued. "I've also been making soap, not just for us to use, but to sell. I used my grandmother's technique with the soapweed yuccas that grow on top of the rise, you know?" She peeked under her eyebrows to look at Jorge, then down at her hands, twisted in her lap. "We now have plenty for the year, and I sold seven cases so far to families at Violeta's school. With that plus the money from the sewing, we have enough for her schoolbooks and shoes. We're doing so much better than last year!" she finished, yet her voice echoed emptily on the whitewashed adobe walls.

Jorge spoke in nearly a whisper. "You mean *you're* doing so much better."

Margarita blinked. She knew her husband was worried, too. Sometimes she would awaken past midnight and find him with a lamp lit beside the bed, working numbers on a scrap of paper. She pretended not to see, but Margarita knew he was calculating their safety against the threatening financial situation just outside Socorro. Maybe that was what was wrong between them all summer.

"No, Jorge, nosotros. Together. We're a family. We are all doing better." She took a moment to recover her courage, looking toward the statue of the Virgin Mary in the front of the church. She was holding the infant Jesus in her arms, gazing out calmly at the empty pews while her baby smiled up at her face. *A family*, Margarita thought.

She continued. "Anyway, at home our pantry shelves are all full, and I've even started stacking jars on the floor. They're nearly up to my knees now. We have more money than usual and plenty of food and that's why I want to ask you—"

"Don't, Margarita. Just stick to the plan."

"But plans can change! Surely that's how you operate at the mine. If you hit a new vein, you have to reevaluate your plan, no?" She looked at his hard face. "So this is your new vein," she finished weakly.

Jorge moved to stand, this time avoiding Margarita's interference. "You know nothing about what happens at the mine," he said in a fierce whisper with a hint of growl. "Nothing." He stepped out of the pew and walked to the back of the church. He paused at the wooden doors, his tall form framed in the harsh light from outside. "You coming?"

"En un momento," she managed to say around the lump in her throat.

As Margarita pored over the memory, she thought of what she had been writing in her diary and the ache in her chest began to burn. *Why had Jorge gone back, even though she had proven that they had enough food and money for the year? Why hadn't he wanted to try?*

Feeling the heat of her breath bounce off the doorframe at her face, Margarita thought that the hallway was altogether too narrow, quickly filling with her stale exhalations. She pressed the doorway away with her hands, turned her back on her bedroom, and walked toward the kitchen.

She had left only a dim lamp glowing on the dining table, so she was surprised to find that the entire room was illuminated. Stepping to the window over the kitchen sink, she saw the full moon, shining a blue beam onto the pine cutting board she had left on the counter.

The corn moon, she thought. *It has been a good year for corn. And for beans and squash and everything else. So why didn't he stay?*

The moonbeam was glinting off something metallic.

Was there someone else? With all those men in the boardinghouse, certainly women of ill repute came around. Perhaps Jorge had been tempted and didn't know how to tell her. Maybe he was going "home" to her, to them!

Margarita slowly approached the counter and saw that the metallic object was her everyday knife, which she had left there after sharpening it on the honing stone that evening. She glanced at the rosebud knife that Jorge had made for her, sitting at the far edge of the cutting board. "No!" she growled, and shoved the carved handle away, scarcely hearing it clatter on the enamel countertop. Then she saw her other hand reach out, run her thumbnail down the blade, shaving off a papery sliver of nail. Through blurred eyes, she saw the sliver curl onto the cutting board, heard the whisper as it landed on the wood.

"Mami?"

Margarita jumped, feeling a sharp jab in her thumb as she reflexively grabbed the whetted edge.

"Violeta, what are you doing out of bed?" She whirled around to face her daughter, squeezing her thumb in a fold of her apron both to hide it from sight and to stanch the blood that she felt bubbling up from the slice.

"Nothing, Mami," Violeta said in a small voice. "I just saw the moonlight and couldn't sleep."

Margarita frowned uncharacteristically at her daughter, but then softened and took her hand to walk her back to bed. She settled into the rocking chair by the bedside, moving forward and back ever so slightly so that the tapping of the rockers on the floor created a rhythm that soothed them both. Once the little girl was again drifting off to sleep, Margarita closed her eyes and inhaled fully. She held her thumb tightly tucked into her fist as she let out the breath with a soft blow.

When she opened her eyes, she could see Violeta in the golden glow just before dawn. She arched her back to stretch out the stiffness from spending the night in the rocking chair. Peering out the window over her daughter's bed, Margarita was relieved to see that the sun was not yet above the horizon, and she'd have at least a few minutes to change her bloodstained apron and neaten her hair before Violeta came out for breakfast and school.

Straightening up, she tiptoed out into the growing light.

29

"Can you come in right away?" Mrs. Black's words echoed in Silvia's head as she took the city bus to Goodnight Middle School.

"Lucy had another fight with the same girl. Both girls have bruises, and Lucy's very upset. Can your mom come in right away?"

"She's away again, Mrs. Black, but I can come."

The counselor hesitated. "Okay, but get here as soon as you can."

Silvia quickly changed out of her pajama pants. She chose dark blue jeans and an olive twill blazer to help her look more grown up and legitimate as Lucy's guardian. Within thirty minutes, she was rushing into the school. She checked in at the security desk, nostrils flaring at the forgotten aroma of her past: whiteboard markers and locker room sweat layered with cleaning products and the distant hint of pool chlorine.

Silvia's heart thumped as the security guard scrutinized her identification. "Do you know where you're going?" he asked in a rough voice.

She nodded and tried to smile, glancing at the officer's badge and reminding herself that this was normal procedure for anyone visiting the school. Still, as she walked down the hall to the counselor's office, she could feel his eyes on her. She smoothed her wavy hair and put on a fresh layer of red lip gloss for confidence.

Entering the room, Silvia was surprised to see not only Lucy and Mrs. Black, but also the other girl and her parents.

"I'm Mr. Harding, and this is Libby," the girl's father said, ignoring his wife's silent presence on the couch. His white shirtsleeves stretched over his bulging biceps. "She's the one your ... daughter ... has been bullying." He looked back and forth from Silvia to Lucy and back to Silvia again.

Lucy stood up, eyes flashing. "Silvia's my sister, and Libby's the one who has been bullying me!"

"Okay, let's all just sit down for a moment," said Mrs. Black, gesturing toward the black vinyl couches arranged around a coffee table spread with college brochures and a bowl of Hershey's Kisses.

Mr. Harding wedged himself between Libby and his wife, who remained silent with her eyes downcast. Silvia assumed a seat beside Lucy on the smaller sofa.

Mrs. Black sank into a rolling office chair that held her at least two heads above everyone else. "Let's start with the facts. Lucy and Libby had to be physically separated today after lunch, when they were caught throwing punches at each other. A few weeks ago, as you all know, they had an altercation in the locker room. Who's going to calmly explain what this is all about?"

Libby was staring at the floor, avoiding eye contact with everyone, so Lucy was the first to speak. "Every time I turn around, she's there. In the lunchroom, she's there. In the locker room, she's there. We're not even friends, so why is she always on my back? That's what happened in gym last month. I asked her to step off, and she pinned me against the lockers."

"Is that all?" asked Mrs. Black, raising her eyebrows.

Lucy scratched at a pimple on her chin. "Well, so then I shoved her. I needed her out of my space."

"And what happened today at lunch?"

Libby's father jumped up. "Wait a minute here. Why is she the only one who gets to talk?"

"Please sit down, Mr. Harding. Libby will get her chance to speak." Mrs. Black turned back to Lucy. "So? Today at lunch?"

"The same thing happened. She was looking over my shoulder while I put things in my backpack at lunch, and I just couldn't take it anymore. I need to be left alone!"

Mrs. Black paused and turned slowly toward the other couch, letting Lucy's words settle. "Libby, how does this sound to you?"

Libby glanced at her parents. "Like someone who's trying to hide something. It's not my problem that Lucy needs her privacy. I have as much right to be in the locker room or in the cafeteria as she does."

"She certainly does," added Mr. Harding, standing up. "I think it's clear that Lucy is the problem here. And don't worry. We'll take care of disciplining Libby at home." He drew himself up taller as Libby shrank down on the couch.

Lucy uncrossed her legs impatiently. "But it's not just 'being' in the locker room or in the cafeteria. Libby goes out of her way to look over my shoulder at my business."

Mrs. Black took a breath. "Okay, so can we agree that you two girls will give each other space for the next few weeks? We'll let your teachers know so that they are aware as well."

"Fine with me," said Mr. Harding. "But if there's another incident, we're filing charges." He glared at Lucy and then Silvia while he let a beat pass for emphasis. Then he pivoted his pointy black alligator shoes toward the door and walked out. Mrs. Harding tightened her lips at the counselor in a poor imitation of a smile, then she and her daughter dutifully stood and followed out the door, eyes on the floor.

Silvia rose to leave, but Mrs. Black stopped her. "One moment, ladies. I just want to make sure we've got this all straightened out. Lucy, is there anything else you want to talk about? What is this need for privacy?"

"I don't know. I just was raised to keep to myself and lately it seems like everyone is on my case." She glanced accusatorily at Silvia. "I just need everyone to leave me alone and let me do my thing."

"We'll all be able to do that once you've shown that you can be trusted not to do this kind of thing at school or at home," Silvia said, eyes flashing. With some effort to remain calm in public, she turned to Mrs. Black. "Don't worry. We've got a system in place now to make sure that Lucy's work is done. You've seen the difference in her science grade, I'm sure."

"Yes, I have. Good work, Lucy. Keep it up. But you have to stay out of trouble."

"I will." Lucy pulled her backpack close to her chest, a gesture that did not escape Silvia's notice.

"We have a system for that, too," Silvia said, making sure that Lucy saw her pointed glance at the backpack. Then she held out her hand to the counselor. "Thank you for your time. I hope we won't be taking any more of it in the future."

"I'm always here for whatever you need. You know that. But Lucy, your mom and sister and I will all be checking on your behavior for a while here. Just remember that we're on your team." Mrs. Black stood up and shook both girls' hands.

Lucy and Silvia walked in silence through the glass hallway, into the lobby, and out the door. It was dismissal time and the buses were stationed in the semicircular drive with the elementary school kids already on board.

"How about we grab Seba off his bus and walk home?" suggested Silvia. "I think we could all use some air and exercise."

Without a word, Lucy headed over to bus 25, knocked on Sebastián's window, and gestured to him to come out. As he climbed down the bus's big steps, his little face showed worry at the disruption of routine. But Silvia's hug reassured him and soon he was chattering about his day, breaking through the tension like stones skipping cheerfully on a dark, stagnant pond.

"And the best part?" he said, building the suspense. "We had pizza as a special treat for being good listeners all month!"

Silvia and Lucy finally softened at his enthusiasm. "That's awesome," said Lucy. "Great job."

After that, their walk home was more lighthearted. They chatted about the houses they passed, dreaming of someday owning a big one. They talked about the good parts of their days and left the bad behind. Lucy was just finishing describing an Impressionist painting they had looked at in her morning art class as they rounded the last bend in the road before their apartment. Lucy and Silvia were both peering ahead to make sure the coast was clear, when their steps froze.

"What?" asked Sebastián, looking up at his sisters.

"ICE," said Lucy.

30

In the apartment complex three down from theirs were two black pickup trucks, like the ones they saw on news reports of Border Patrol activity. But this time they were joined by two white vans with federal seals on the sides, a sure sign of impending detentions.

"Come on!" said Silvia, and they turned sharply left into the trees by the side of the road. "We'll go around back."

The three ran as quietly as they could along the tree line, then turned north, keeping to the trees that ran behind the apartment complexes up to theirs. Sweating from the late fall heat and the weight of their backpacks, they arrived behind their own building. Silvia peered from behind a large live oak to confirm that there were no ICE vehicles in the parking lot of their complex. She gestured her brother and sister on.

They all scuttled over to their door and slipped in. Silvia immediately locked the door and drew the blinds.

Silvia whispered to her siblings, "Grab only what you need for a few days: underwear, socks, shirts, power bars. I'll get everything else."

"But, Silvi," said Sebastián, "can't we call Agent Randolph to help us? He's so nice!"

"Absolutely not, hermanito. We don't know if his agency is working with ICE. But on the plus side, looks like we're going on a trip!"

"Yaaaaaay!" Sebastián whisper-shouted and ran off to get some of his things.

"I'll be right back," Silvia called as she crept out the back door off the laundry room and over to the storage shed shared by the residents of the apartment complex. Unlike the residential buildings' brown wooden siding, the shed was gray concrete block. It had three doors that corresponded to the three apartment buildings. Half-crouched, she walked to the far-right door and unlocked it with her key.

Inside, each family had a closet made of a pine frame and chicken wire, secured with a padlock. Silvia had to jimmy the key a bit in the rusted lock of her family's bin, but shortly it yielded and she pushed past old bikes and scooters to reach the plastic storage containers of holiday decorations and sporting equipment. The bottommost container held her father's old camping equipment, which their mother had kept out of inertia and because the kids used to like to play with it.

Silvia slid the container out of its spot and dragged it to the middle of the floor. She pulled out a green nylon tent bag and worked to untie the thin closure. "Come on …" she said through clenched teeth as she struggled with the knot. Once she got it untied, she quickly checked to make sure that the set was complete with poles, stakes, and tarp, and that there were no mice or bugs inside. Then she locked the storage cage and peered out of the cracked door toward the parking lot. Seeing it all clear, she again scurried across the parking lot and slipped into the house through the back door.

"Are you ready yet?" she called softly as she passed her brother's and sister's rooms on her way to their mother's.

"Almost," came Sebastián's muffled reply. Silvia imagined him on his knees with his face under the bed, probably dragging out his travel backpack.

In her mother's room, she raided the closet for any other supplies they'd need for survival, tossing them into a large black trash bag that she found in the back of the closet. Conscious of the weight they'd be carrying, she grabbed three hand towels, the one sleeping bag she found, and two fleece throws. On her way out of the room, she paused in the doorway. Then she opened her mother's dresser drawer and pulled out a T-shirt.

She stopped in her room to get socks and underwear for herself, plus a sweater and a pair of sweatpants that would have to do for both daytime and pajamas. She stripped off her blazer and threw it on the bed. She grabbed the credit card from the dresser and stuffed it in her pocket, wondering if it would work after last night's security message.

"Come on, you two!" she said as she again passed her siblings' rooms. "We're out of time."

Silvia ran to the kitchen and threw a few more items into the bag: a cooking fork and spoon, plastic utensils, newspaper from the recycling bin for fire starting, matches, aluminum foil, soap, and a sponge. Finally, she gathered all the money she had in the house, her laptop, her phone, their water bottles, and Bisabuela's diary before moving to the living room. Disturbing the blinds as little as possible, she peeked out to make sure that there were no vans or pickup trucks in sight.

Sebastián burst into the living room with his backpack bulging.

"What do you have in there?" asked Silvia, pulling open the zipper. She rifled through it and saw, along with socks and underwear, Sebastián's favorite outer space pajamas, his United States atlas, a compass, his minerals box and a trowel ("for digging rocks!"), and his blue elephant. She was about to take the elephant out but thought better of it. If there was ever a time that Sebastián was going to need some comforting, it was now.

"Seba, could you leave your book, please? It's too heavy."

"But those are my maps, Silvi. I'm going to need them when we're away. And I'll carry everything myself. Promise."

"Okay, fine. What about you, Lucy?" she called softly. "Hurry!"

Lucy ran into the room, clean black jeans on and tennis shoes untied. Her school backpack was slung over one shoulder. "I'm ready. Let's get out of here."

Silvia thought about checking her sister's bag, both to make sure that she had everything she needed and to be certain that it didn't contain any of Lucy's contraband. But she decided they had no time for either policing or the inevitable drama. "Then let's go. We'll run back to the trees like before, but we'll keep heading north this time, until we get to the bus stop. We'll take the bus to the Greyhound station, and then get out of town for a while. Hope you won't mind missing a few days of school." Silvia grinned at Sebastián, keeping her terror in check for his benefit.

"Yay!" shouted Sebastián, which caused both Lucy and Silvia to shush him. Pouting, Sebastián glanced around. "Bye, casita," he said.

"Yeah, bye." Silvia took in more than a glance as the three slipped out the door. Memories of her mother and even of her father threatened her with tears, but she shut them down, telling herself that they'd be back and safe—maybe with Mami—before long.

As they carried their heavy loads down the parking lot and under the cover of the trees, Silvia stole a glance toward the road. The ICE vehicles were now in the next apartment complex closer, only two parking lots away from their own. *Thank God we came home when we did,* she thought. *And thank God Lucy and Seba didn't take the school bus! And all because Lucy got in trouble!*

Silvia turned to follow her brother and sister through the trees behind several more buildings. Once they were safely out of sight, she steered them toward the street and the nearest bus stop.

Thirty-five minutes later, they were at the Guadalupe Street Greyhound station with tickets to El Paso on the 7:15 p.m. bus. Silvia left Lucy in charge of Sebastián while she walked four blocks to an ATM. First she tried the credit card, to see if she could get the cash advance before the account was shut down. To her horror, the screen lit up with the message: *Please Contact Customer Service* and her card was not returned. She repeatedly pressed the cancel button, glancing at her image in the reflective glass over the security camera, hoping that her panic didn't show on her face. When the card still did not eject, she turned and left, crossing the street to a different bank. There, she withdrew all but twenty dollars from the family's checking account, using her debit card.

Looking around the street, she spotted a variety store and went in to buy a rolling cooler. She stocked it with ice, snacks, and waters, then stopped to pick up barbecue for dinner across the street from the station. When she at last made it back with her purchases, she found her hungry brother and sister finishing up Sebastián's homework so that he would be free to "explore new lands" during their trip.

"Seba, you brought your homework?" Silvia laughed.

"Of course. Miss D. said it was due tomorrow."

"Well, then, I'm glad it's done. I don't think you'll have homework again for a while."

Sebastián jumped off the bench and did a little dance.

"No hooooomework, no hoooooomework!" he chanted.

Finally, the three hours were up and the siblings were safely settled on the bus. Sebastián leaned his head on Silvia's shoulder and Lucy sank into the seat across the aisle, plugging her headphones into her phone and putting her feet up on the empty seat beside her.

"Where are we going, anyway?" her brother asked her.

"I bought tickets to El Paso, all the way in West Texas," Silvia said, finally giving a full exhalation. She felt for the rectangular form of the diario inside her computer bag on her lap. "I've been reading a book about our family, and it turns out one of our relatives was from near there."

"Oh, cool," Sebastián mumbled, already getting sleepy. He snuggled into Silvia's shoulder again.

After a few moments, Silvia relaxed slightly, and even allowed the smile of relief that was welling up within her to materialize, realizing that they were headed to their family's homeland. She thought about the name of the town, Socorro, meaning "assistance, relief, aid." From Margarita's diary, Silvia knew that the town had represented all of those things to her ancestors.

Now, Socorro would offer assistance, relief, and aid to three of Margarita's great-great-grandchildren, at least temporarily. It would assist them in their escape from cruel immigration practices. It would relieve them of fear for a while. And it would hopefully aid Silvia in her mission to get their mother back—safely. Silvia realized that it was time to talk to her siblings about the diary.

31

Mexicans or Americans? Mexican Americans? Which are we and why does it matter? Why does what language we speak or whether we eat rice or french-fried potatoes matter to anyone else? Why does the color of our skin determine who belongs and who doesn't? Who has rights and who doesn't?

Margarita glanced toward the door. She was looking for the mail as she did every day since returning from El Paso. Over the last two weeks, letters had started arriving from Washington, Albuquerque, Austin, and Mexico City. A few were apologetic: *No, we can't help you. Try your local title office.* But then thicker envelopes arrived, and Margarita amassed a respectable sheaf of papers to complement the copies she made in El Paso and her own notes. A great victory was the delivery of a certified copy of the original Spanish land grant from 1816 drawn up just before Mexico gained its independence. But still no title to her family's own parcel arrived. She couldn't declare her archive complete without that título to complete her file.

With anxiety picking at the edges of her consciousness for two weeks now, the best Margarita could do was try to fend off the desperation and panic. She'd spent the shorter days out working in the field, beginning the process of closing up for the end of the season. With the help of their team of cows, she turned the remaining alfalfa stalks into the soil to fertilize the field for next year's plants. She put the winter windows on the chicken coop and checked the hay supply with satisfaction. She clipped the rosemary, lavender, sage, oregano, and parsley plants down to the ground, leaving only the woody stems, which she tucked in with some dry leaves to serve as their winter blanket. She bundled the cut herbs and hung them to dry from the wooden beams in the kitchen. She strung up slices of tomato, apple, and pear on strands of twine that crisscrossed their living space.

Margarita turned her eyes up to the drying fruits and herbs in a little prayer. Sighing, she laid a hand on her belly. She was just over two months pregnant, too soon to show. As she reckoned it, the baby should arrive in June, well after Jorge's return. She swallowed, pushing away the doubts that always came when she thought of Jorge.

"Next year, baby, your papi will stay." She hoped that saying it would dispel the worry, but as soon as she spoke, she felt a chill. She pulled her sweater tighter around her, thoughts caravanning through her mind like car after car of the train from Albuquerque that she could hear blowing its whistle up the track. Would the baby arrive well and healthy? Would Jorge really stay next time? Would she get all the documents? Would they keep them safe from deportation?

She sank onto her dining chair and again reached for her diary that always lay in the middle of the table. She slid it toward her but kept it closed, laying her head on the table for a few moments, feeling the coolness of the wood against her forehead. When she sat up, she opened the diary to the back and tore out a blank page, leaving a jagged edge protruding from the binding. It was time. She had to write to Jorge about the baby.

Violeta came singing up the path to the house, her notes breaking through Margarita's writing. She burst in the door breathless, waving a letter from the Kelly Mine in her right hand while her bundle of books dangled from her left.

"Mami! ¡Una carta de papá!"

Margarita hugged her girl, then the two stepped out into the sun and sat on the stone steps to read the letter together. Violeta proved too excited to sit, however, so Margarita read her the highlights.

"He says the work is good, that they found a new vein, so there will be mining work for the rest of the season."

"That's good, I guess, right, Mami?" Violeta was breathless, hopping on one foot while she spoke.

"Yes. It's always good for the men to have work. He says they've even been hiring some new miners."

"Great!" shouted Violeta, now running in circles in the dry grass.

"Let's see … He says the first day they put out the ad for workers they had a line of men all the way down the road. They all came with their bags packed to move right into the boarding houses. They had so many spots to fill and the hiring took so long that those waiting sat down and ate their lunches right there in line."

"Wow. That must have been a lot of men," said Violeta. "A whole ton!" Violeta opened her arms wide and twirled in a circle.

Margarita looked up from the letter smiling, but then her smile faded. She thought about the photographs in the newspaper every day: hundreds of dark suits and hats lined up in cities across the country to apply for a handful of jobs. Shuttered storefronts. Piles of furniture at the curb after mass evictions. Men and children sleeping on sidewalks. Lines of men before signs reading FREE COFFEE AND DOUGHNUTS FOR THE UNEMPLOYED. And in the background of some of those photos, hand-written bills that read No SPANISH, No MEXICANS or No DOGS OR MEXICANS ALLOWED. Margarita felt at once ashamed that she sometimes resented her husband's job and distance, when she should have been grateful that he even had paying work.

"You know, Violeta, it's like we saw in El Paso on our trip. There are so many men out of work right now. Wages are down and people are having trouble feeding their families."

"Why are wages down?"

"When lots of people need jobs, companies can afford to offer them low pay. People will take anything. In the past, a job that paid thirty dollars per week might only pay twenty dollars now. But people will take it, because twenty dollars is better than nothing."

"It sure is! I wish I had twenty dollars! I'd …"

While Violeta talked and jumped around, Margarita listened to the wind rustling through the mesquite leaves at the top of the rise. She turned her head to look at the tree, watching the leaves tremble, knowing they wouldn't hold on much longer. Soon they would fall and insulate the delicate roots of the new *Rosa floribunda* that marked the site of the Uneeda Biscuit tin. She sighed but then shivered and buttoned her sweater closer up to the neck.

"Don't you want to hear the rest of the letter?" she asked.

"Of course!" shouted Violeta, still hopping.

"So … he says the boarding houses started to fill up and the mine was getting ready to turn away the rest of the men when—" Margarita's voice cut off suddenly.

Violeta stopped hopping. "When what, Mami?"

"Oh, nothing, amor. I just couldn't read papi's writing for a second."

"Let me see," said Violeta, sidling up to her mother.

"Oh, that's all right. I've got it now." Margarita stood, keeping the letter out of her daughter's line of sight. "He says that the boarding houses are all full now, and he has lots of new friends at work. And he misses us and sends you a big hug and kiss."

"Great. I'm going to go give the chickens *their* great big hug and kiss!" announced Violeta, running off across the field toward the coop.

Margarita sat back down on the steps and read the text with more care. Jorge informed her that, when the boarding houses and the work roster were full, some of the men in line started complaining that the mine was picking "Mexicans" before "Americans." When the mine managers responded that the men were simply taken first come, first served and on the basis of prior mining experience, the protesters raised their voices, asserting that mining was an "American" profession and that "real Americans" needed those jobs. Everyone else should go back to Mexico to get jobs.

At the sound of raised voices, Jorge himself stepped out of the office to see if he could help. Margarita imagined him, small of stature but built like a brick house, casting an imposing figure in the doorway of the wooden mining office. Nevertheless, the group of men, which now numbered more than ten, continued to press forward.

One of them pointed at Jorge. "There's another one! You have them working inside, too?"

"I guess bean eaters can be bean counters just as well," another jeered.

"Yeah, but watch out for jumping beans. Sometimes they jump right out the door, taking your money with them!" shouted another. Then in a lower voice to the manager, "Seriously, mister. Everyone knows they're all thieves. Hire some real Americans like us if you want to avoid trouble."

"Seems to me you're the only ones causing trouble here, gentlemen," said the manager. "Come on, now, get outta here. There will be more work another day, but you gotta come early if you want it."

At that, four of the largest mine workers materialized from behind the manager and escorted all of the hopefuls, including the ruffians, off of the property, closing the barrier gate behind them.

Jorge, who wisely did not participate in their removal, wrote that he now shared Margarita's concerns about the sentiment toward Mexicans in the country. He suggested that she and Violeta keep to themselves as much as possible, and that they avoid strangers until his return. "The hard times have made everybody crazy," he wrote.

Violeta returned from across the field, skipping.

Margarita forced a smile. "How are the chickens?"

"Great," said Violeta. "But I forgot to ask how our little egg is doing today." She rested her ear on her mother's belly.

"She's perfect, amor. Just like her big sister. My perfect little chicks on our perfect little farm. Come on, let's go inside and wash up."

Mother and daughter stepped through the door, hand in hand. With her other hand, Margarita folded up the letter and tucked it into the pocket of her dress.

32

Around midnight, Lucy and Sebastián woke up, their sleep schedules thrown off by the rocking movement of the bus and their subsequent early bedtime. Both were hungry, so they all shared a sandwich that Silvia had ordered at the barbecue restaurant and had kept on ice in their cooler.

While her siblings were napping, Silvia had been studying the diary, rereading the many entries that dealt with discrimination. By the end, she found herself with the opposite problem from her siblings: she was utterly unable to fall asleep. Once they awoke, then, she passed her brother and sister their sandwiches and filled them in on the new mission of their trip. They knew that Silvia was working with a diary for her class project. Sebastián had even picked up the book once or twice from Silvia's desk and spent some time looking at the maps Margarita had drawn in the yellowed pages. But this was the first time that either was learning that it was a family book.

"That's so cool, Silvi," said Sebastián. "It's like talking to a really, really old grandmother, but she's already dead."

Silvia made a face at her little brother's concept of the book. "Yeah, kind of like that." She glanced at Lucy, who looked uninterested.

"But there's more. This book seems to have a little secret in it. I've talked to my professor about it. And even to Melinda, a bit." Her heart clenched at the memory of her last phone call with her friend before Melinda had cut her off with the dismissive text.

"A secret? Cool! What is it?"

"Well, I don't know yet. But there are some words that Bisabuela uses all the time in the book, and I think she's using them to try to tell us something about Socorro, where she lived."

"Ooh, like a hidden message? I have activity books like that! Where there's like a word you have to unscramble or a code you have to follow to find the hidden message."

"It might be kind of like that, Seba." Silvia turned to Lucy, looking for some kind of reaction.

Lucy raised her eyebrows. "Well? What are the words?"

Silvia explained the repeated and embellished everyday words from the diary: *coyote, soap, mesquite, acequia,* alongside *título* and *escritura.* As she spoke, she showed examples of the decorated words in the book.

Sebastián was intrigued. "I get it now. This is a scavenger hunt. We have to find the clues in the book and then the clues on the ground to find Bisabuela's hidden message."

"I think so," said Silvia, smiling. "I've already got the clues from the book, so now it's time to hit the ground. That's why we're going to El Paso."

"I thought she was from Socorro," said Lucy drily.

Silvia blinked in annoyance. "She was, and Socorro's right next to El Paso." She refrained from adding an insulting tag to her sentence, although she could certainly think of a few that fit her sister at that moment. Instead, she took a deep breath and looked out the bus window at the dry landscape passing by.

"Okay, so let me get this straight," said Lucy. "We're going to look at old trees by a ditch in a town that's now part of another city, as research for your paper. Seriously?"

"Well, hermanita," said Silvia, trying to hide her annoyance with her sister, "that's the last part of the puzzle, the part I just figured out while you two were asleep. And it turns out there's a lot in it for you."

"Why? What do you mean? Like a prize?" Sebastián leaned forward eagerly.

"Yeah, kind of like a treasure. All we've got to do is find it."

Sebastián's eyes grew wide and Silvia knew he must be imagining pirates' chests of gold coins or pearls.

"All right, I'm on it," he said. "But first, I've got to go to the bathroom."

Silvia moved to let him squeeze out and watched him sidle down the narrow aisle. Then she turned to Lucy. "Look, I'm not going to talk to Sebastián about this yet, but there's more to this than I've told you."

"Good," said Lucy grumpily. "Because I'm not into camping and I'm certainly not into doing your homework for you."

"Just listen, Lucy, and quit being so judgmental. Mira, I've known for a while that a título is a type of escritura, right? That is, a title of nobility or the title to a house is a legal document, an official paper."

"Yeah, sure." Lucy yawned without covering her mouth. "You already told us that."

"And the diary is full of references to both *título* and *escritura*, always alongside those everyday words I showed you."

"Yeah. I was listening, you know."

"Well, sometimes it's hard to tell." Silvia paused. "But while you guys were sleeping, I found something else. Something huge." She couldn't help beaming.

"You're such a nerd," started Lucy, but then she looked at Silvia's excited face and modified her insult into a complement. "It's nice to see your nerdiness again."

Silvia nodded, surprised that her sister had even noticed the lack of spark in her over recent months. "Thanks, sis."

"Yeah, sure. So, what is it?"

"There's a poem in the diario that I was ignoring because it was so emotional. Margarita wrote it when she was leaving Socorro, and I didn't like reading it because it reminded me of … everything."

"Uh-huh. Hurry up and tell me before he comes back." Lucy glanced down the aisle.

"Well, I spent the last two hours studying it because it contains the final instance of *título*. Turns out all the other key words are in the poem, too, so I read it carefully for the first time."

"And?"

"And it tells me that our great-great-grandmother hid her most precious possession, her título, on her property by the river, so that someday her children could return and claim their land. It's a *land* title, Lucy. And it's in West Texas!"

Lucy processed this for a moment. "I doubt it could still be there.

That was like, what, a hundred years ago?"

"Only eighty-something," Silvia said. "I don't know. It's possible. And right now it's the only chance we've got to prove that Mami belongs here. If she's a landowner, I don't know, maybe that will help."

"Yeah, but the house has to belong to someone else now, right? I mean, places don't just wait for people to come back to them."

Silvia's eyes flashed. "Lucy, don't take this away from me right now. I need something to believe in. Could you just support me on this?"

"Fine. Anything else?" Lucy had flopped back in her seat again.

"Two more quick things."

"One," Lucy counted.

"The poem tells how many steps to take from the house to where the título is hidden, and it matches the maps Bisabuela drew of her property. As long as the house is still there, counting the steps from the house toward the river will get us to the title!"

"Okay. And two?"

"Toward the end of the diary, Margarita wrote that she was afraid that she and her family might be deported. Even though their land deed guaranteed them citizenship dating from the Treaty of Guadalupe Hidalgo!" Silvia finished with a grin.

"Wait, when the US took like half of Mexico?"

"Exactly. If it's true," Silvia twisted in her seat and saw the bathroom door open. She lowered her voice, "and if we can find it, it guarantees us—and Mami—proof of citizenship! And property! But shhh. For now, it's just going to be a treasure hunt, okay? I don't want Sebastián heartbroken again if we can't get her back."

Lucy grabbed her little brother as he came down the aisle. "So we're gonna treasure-seek, huh?" Pulling him onto her lap, she tickled him.

Sebastián giggled, surprised at her playful mood. "I've got my maps. And Blue Elephant wants to be an archaeologist when he grows up, so this digging around old places will be good practice for him."

Silvia sat back in her seat, yawning. The relief and excitement were tangible, made visual by her sister and brother playing in the seat across the aisle. She smiled and closed her eyes. *Please, Bisabuela, please,* she thought, almost like a prayer.

33

They arrived in El Paso at 6:10 the next morning. Silvia opened her eyes and stared out into the dawn as the bus slowed and exited Interstate 10. She strained to see any signs of the old "Great White Way" that her great-great-grandmother had described during her trip to the big city. She saw office buildings, hotels, and shops. Some of the lights were still on in the gray of morning. A fountain glowed blue in the middle of a tree-lined square park, but it all fell short of any greatness or even whiteness. A moment later, though, Silvia briefly spotted the marquis of the old Plaza Theater tucked away down an alley as they rounded a corner. Her heart jumped, and then sank in echo of Bisabuela's two days in town.

A few minutes later, they pulled into the bus station and Silvia started to wake her brother and sister up. They staggered with their stuff into a waiting taxi and Silvia directed the driver to Mission RV Park just outside Socorro. She had called ahead and had learned that, despite its name, the park allowed tent camping and would permit them an exceptionally early check-in. She was hopeful that they could set up camp and get a bit more rest.

The RV park turned out to be more of a depressing mobile home parking lot than a wilderness adventure. It sat in the middle of a dusty field, and even that early in the morning Silvia could tell that the merciless rays of the Texas sun would soon be baking the metal-and-vinyl trailers, heating them up inside like ovens. Evidently it had rained somewhat recently; most of the houses were splattered with dried-on mud-puddle filth nearly up to their windows. The few vacant sites that were not occupied were sandwiched between the homes, cutting off any breeze that might otherwise have circulated through the area.

Silvia asked the driver to drop them and their belongings at the site closest to the bathhouse, where at least they'd have convenience, if not adventure.

"This is … different than I imagined when you said we were going camping," said Sebastián, looking dubiously around the dusty site. He walked over to the metal fire pit and shuffled his foot through the ashes of a past campfire. He looked back at Silvia, brightening. "At least we can toast marshmallows, though!"

Silvia smiled at her brother's optimism. "We will, don't worry," she assured him. "This is only the base for our real excursions, hermanito. We're not even going to be at the site very much."

It was almost eleven by the time they had figured out how to open the tent and gotten settled. They snacked on some fruit and nuts that Silvia had bought in San Marcos, and showered using the coin-operated machines in the bathhouse. Seeing that no one was able to sleep any more, Silvia laid out the plan for the day: They would use Margarita's maps to explore the town of Socorro, aiming to see what had changed and what remained the same in the eighty years that had passed since the diary's composition. They would take along Sebastián's Texas map for comparison and eventually end up at the river. Silvia was determined to make this feel like fun, like vacation meets scavenger hunt, despite their dreary surroundings and even though she and Lucy knew that the stakes were potentially much higher.

Walking the few blocks to Gateway Boulevard, the three siblings caught a local bus into Socorro. Silvia looked out the window as they rolled slowly toward town. The land was flat and dry, and the view was similar to the one of their own street in San Marcos: houses sitting just below the slightly elevated roadway, scrubby treetops almost even with the bus. Contrary to the impressions she carried from the diary, the terrain was exceedingly flat, although Silvia caught a glimpse of some hills on the horizon. She breathed deeply, trying to feel the presence of her ancestors in what must have been the place her own grandmother had been dreaming of when she took her little girl north to "nuestra tierra."

They passed familiar-looking single-story businesses: mechanics, warehouses, taquerías. Finally, the bus coasted into the residential part of town, and Silvia felt the excitement grip her stomach. *Where had Bisabuela lived?* she wondered, peering out at the single-story stucco homes along Socorro Road. Most houses had gates and a small tree in the front yard that Silvia tried to identify. A few were evergreens, and here and there she saw a live oak. *No mesquites yet. We must need to get closer to the river.*

Sebastián followed along with his finger on the map as they rolled toward the Rio Grande. With the river almost in sight, they crossed over a large ditch with a fair amount of water snaking through it.

"Look, an acequia!" Silvia said to her brother, and his eyes gleamed up at her. But turning back to the window, she frowned. Even nearing the riverside, she still couldn't see any hills. Eighty years was a long time. Maybe Socorro's planners had done some significant engineering to combat flooding in this area so close to the Chazimal.

Then Silvia saw the Socorro Mission out the bus's left window.

"The mission! Let's go!" she said, pulling the cord to signal the driver to stop. The bus lurched to a stop and the three hurried off with their backpacks. "I don't know how we got here so soon. I don't even see the river from here," said Silvia, puzzled. "But anyway, let's check it out."

The unassuming whitewashed adobe structure sat in the middle of an arid dirt parking lot. Silvia smiled at the church's unfailing symmetry, a hallmark of the Southwest's mission style. The two extremes of the facade were raised, and then stepped down to a lower roofline that paralleled the ground. From there, four stairs up invited the eye to climb the central bell tower, topped with a tiny white cross. The smooth adobe face of the building was broken by exactly five arched openings: one empty statuary recess on either end, and the double oak door, four-paned window, and belfry stacked in the center.

The church lot was separated from the road at one end by an adobe arch. As they passed through the archway and crossed the gravel parking field, Silvia guessed that at times the church complex must be quite crowded. At noon on a Friday, though, there appeared to be very few other visitors.

Entering the building, all three siblings were silent except for their footsteps on the stone floor. As they observed the beautiful herringbone ceiling, the delicately painted beams, the gold altarpiece, the celestial blue around the statues of the saints, and the simple choir loft, Silvia thought about Margarita, and how often she must have entered here to attend mass, to baptize her daughter, perhaps to pray for salvation when she knew that their existence in Texas was being threatened. The old wood held the smells of incense and ceremony from decades, indeed, centuries past, and Silvia closed her eyes to imagine her great-great-grandmother sitting in the second row, infant on her lap, husband by her side. She pictured her attending weddings and funerals here, crying after the devastation of the floods and the news of having to leave. For the first time since their mother had been deported, Silvia felt connected to someone older than she. She felt like someone's daughter, granddaughter, great-granddaughter. She felt like she belonged.

After a few moments, Lucy stepped out of the building to wait outside. Silvia held Sebastián's hand and they paused to read the sign detailing the history of the site. The mission was situated on what used to be the longest highway in North America, the Camino Real de Tierra Adentro. This road linked Mexico City with Santa Fe, New Mexico, since the early seventeenth century and was used primarily for the silver trade by the Spanish colonizers. Missions were founded along the route, including the Franciscan's Socorro Mission, which housed displaced Spanish colonizers and the Piros after the Pueblo Revolt in New Mexico in 1680. While the spot was occupied and run as a church and mission continually since then, the church structure in front of them was built around 1840, replacing earlier structures that were destroyed in the Rio Grande's historic floods. Silvia summarized the sign for Sebastián, and then the two stepped out of the mission and into the bright Texas sun.

Shielding her eyes, Silvia looked around. She wasn't worried until she heard Sebastián say, "Hey! Lucy's gone."

34

"I'm sure she's right around here," Silvia said as much to herself as to her brother. She fought a rising panic in her chest. The two walked the entire perimeter of the mission complex, always expecting to see Lucy around the next corner.

"Come on, Lucy!" Sebastián called. "I want to hunt for treasure!"

Five minutes passed. Then ten.

Finally, rounding the last side of the building, they spotted a group of teenagers in the driveway of a low vinyl-sided house across the street. Two boys and a girl were shooting baskets. The girl was wearing shorts and a sports bra, her long blond hair curling around her shoulders. As she turned toward them before taking a shot, Silvia could see that she was heavily made-up, her bright red lips parted with exertion, extended lashes narrowed in focus. One of the boys, shirtless and muscular, played serious defense, continually reaching in front of her and around her from the back pretending that he cared about stealing the ball. The other boy hopped around at a distance waving his arms, hoping someone would remember he was there.

On a junked blue Chevy in the yard, two girls reclined, their tops rolled up so that they could tan their stomachs. Three more boys sat on the house's crumbling porch, drinking from bottles inside brown paper bags. They were chatting as they watched the sunbathers openly.

On the floor of the porch, facing the road, sat Lucy. Her denim shorts were rolled up to her upper-thighs and she was leaning against the knees of one of the boys.

"Wait here, Seba. Have some water," Silvia said through gritted teeth as they entered the yard.

She handed him his water and strode toward the porch. Sebastián gave a low wave to the kids playing basketball as he sat down on an upside-down recycle bin at the end of the driveway.

Ignoring the boys, Silvia directed her gaze only at Lucy. "Lucy, what are you doing here?"

Lucy sat up straight, leaning away from the knees of the boy behind her. Her eyes grew large with teenage horror as she tried to will Silvia to not embarrass her. "I'm just having a drink with my new friends." She indicated the coke can sitting by her hip.

"We have been looking for you. You can't just wander off like that." Silvia's heart was racing and she closed her hands into fists inside her pockets.

"I didn't wander. I came here on purpose," Lucy said defiantly.

The boys behind her snickered.

"Next time, you can tell me where you're going 'on purpose,' then," said Silvia. "Come on. It's time to go."

"Your mom's hot," said one of the boys, and they all laughed.

Silvia smirked at them. "Funny. And where are *your* parents?"

The boy took a long drink from his paper bag. "Do we look like we want parents here right now? We already have all the mamas we need." He gestured to the girls on the car hood, one of whom had pulled her shirt all the way up and was lying facedown on the car, sunning her back with her bra strap unfastened.

The rest of the boys laughed, and one whistled.

"Yeah, very nice," said Silvia sarcastically. Then, with clenched teeth, "Lucy, we're going now."

"Okay, okay," Lucy said, getting up with the aid of her hand on the knee of the boy behind her. "Thanks, everyone, for your hospitality. Sorry for my sister."

Silvia was already down the driveway, pulling Sebastián up from his makeshift bench. As they left the yard, the kids cranked up the music on the car radio to a blast, the bass line thundering through the speakers.

Silvia marched down the street, dragging Sebastián with her at a pace too fast for the boy's short legs.

"Silvi, carry me?"

"Carry him, Lucy," Silvia ordered.

Lucy switched her backpack to her front, then squatted down to let Sebastián climb onto her back. Huffing to keep with up her sister, she had little breath to argue.

"What in the world were you thinking?" Silvia shouted, glaring toward her sister but not slowing her pace. "You don't know who those kids are! They could be into all kinds of things that aren't safe for you. And we don't even know this place! We literally just got off the bus! What could you possibly have been thinking?"

"I came out … of the church … and there they were," puffed Lucy, trotting with Sebastián on her back to keep up with Silvia. "They invited me … so I went. I thought you … wouldn't mind if I had friends … but clearly I was wrong."

"Those aren't friends, Lucy!" shouted Silvia. "They're strangers. And you took drinks from them and were sitting there like you'd known them all your life! And did you see those girls? Practically naked, all three of them! Is that the kind of girl you want to be? Is that how Mami raised you?"

Lucy stopped walking and dumped Sebastián off her back. She took a few quick steps to get in front of Silvia and whirled around to face her, hands on her hips. "Well, Mami's not here, is she? So I guess I'll do what I want. And I can't believe you embarrassed me like that in front of my friends!"

"Again, they're not your friends. They are strangers!" Silvia enunciated her sentence as if Lucy needed to read her lips to understand. "Let's get out of the middle of the road."

The three siblings crossed back over to the front of the mission. Silvia allowed the few beats of their crossing to calm her just a little. She unclenched her fists.

"Where are we going?" asked Sebastián in a little voice once they had crossed the street.

Silvia had nearly forgotten that he was there. She bent and pulled him in for a hug. "I'm sorry, kiddo. How about we have lunch and then decide where to treasure hunt next."

Sebastián pulled back to smile at her, and squeezed her hand. He and Lucy waited while Silvia bought them all tacos from a food truck across Socorro Road and worked on releasing the stress in her jaw. When she returned, the siblings ate sitting in the dry grass alongside one of the irrigation ditches, the Socorro Lateral.

Once she was calm enough to resume their day as planned, Silvia pointed to the ditch. "See, the acequias are everywhere here. We just have to find which one Margarita lived near. That's where her clue words are going to help us. We have to find the acequia that has all of her favorite trees growing nearby."

"Well, there's nothing growing at this one," said Lucy sourly.

"Yes, I can see that. Hmm …" Silvia opened her laptop and looked at the map she'd downloaded of downtown Socorro, trying to find the historic area of town. She toggled over to a map from 1940 that she had found during her research. The correspondences were not clear. It seemed that the shifting course of the Rio Grande had made Socorro into a town of only a few hundred people while Margarita had been living there. Earlier maps showed that it had been larger, but when the railroad was routed to El Paso instead of Socorro in 1881, families, local enterprises, and small farmers were forced out of business. Those remaining clustered near the mission, where Silvia hadn't seen any promising signs of Margarita's home.

Silvia looked up from her computer. "Well, I had wanted to see the historic sites, but there aren't too many. Just the mission, the Casa Ortiz, which is a house from the 1700s, and the Rio Vista Farm. There doesn't seem to be a real old section of town here."

"The farm sounds cool," said Sebastián. "I'd like to see some animals."

"All right, let's do that, but first let's check out the riverbank. Looks like there's a park along it now. I feel like if we can just see the willows and yuccas, we'll know we're on the right track."

"Actually, sis, I think we should go to the farm first." Sebastián was studying his atlas. "Look behind you."

Silvia craned her head around to see a vast dusty field and a historic place registry sign. The siblings gathered up their belongings to cross the street, where they learned that the site had recently been designated a national historic treasure and was slated for restoration. It had been a working farm for poor families during the Great Depression, when Margarita had been in Socorro, and then the point of entry for the Bracero Program, which brought Mexican men into the United States to work in agriculture during the 1950s and 60s.

Exploring the site, the siblings saw several long mission-style buildings in disrepair, their stucco flaking off and wooden roof shingles crumbling. A silence pervaded the compound, despite the fact that several of Socorro's public administration offices appeared to be housed there. Anxious to avoid any government entities, the three left the dusty field.

They decided that, because of the heat, Silvia would continue alone to the riverfront park to scout it out, while Lucy and Sebastián would take the bus back to the campsite to rest and start dinner. They parted company at the bus stop on the corner of Socorro and Winn Roads.

"No detours!" Silvia admonished Lucy, getting a dirty look in return.

Determined not to be distracted from her goal on the trip, notwithstanding Lucy's problems, Silvia began walking the two miles to the Rio Grande. Her mind raced with anger at her sister. But she had to focus; surely by the river she would find some traces of the items Margarita had so attentively described. There were bound to be trees both big and small on the river's oasis-like banks, and at least she could get the lay of the land before returning there to hunt in earnest with her siblings tomorrow.

Yet echoes of earlier with Lucy continued to roil her thoughts. She simply could not believe the way her sister was acting and her complete lack of judgment. A quintessential good girl all her life, Silvia felt utterly unequipped to deal in any constructive way with Lucy's behavior. She was going to have to get a counselor or something for her once this was all over and they got home. But how would they ever afford it?

Focus, she reminded herself. She shook her head, forced out a deep breath, and marched on toward the river.

35

Silvia walked alone. On her way, she strolled along the Socorro Lateral, crossed the Franklin Drain, then the Southside Feeder, all acequias.

I guess we've got that keyword covered, she thought, yawning to release her jaw.

At last arriving in Rio Bosque Park, Silvia inhaled a breeze that had just kicked up, thick with damp wood and wildflowers. She paused at the sign welcoming her to the wetlands park, and her heart jumped to find among the listings of plants both the mesquite and the coyote willow. She studied the map on the sign. There were over five miles of trails in the park; how was she to know which to follow?

She chose the two-and-a-half-mile wetlands trail, since it was the one that headed directly to the river. During her walk, she scrutinized stands of willow, looked for mesquite, and tried to feel her bisabuela's presence. However, the truth was that walking along the manicured trails and well-maintained boardwalks she could not imagine Margarita here. The park's twenty-first century accessibility and preservationist intent seemed so far removed from the rough everyday experiences that her bisabuela had described in 1930s Socorro.

Exhausted and discouraged, Silvia emerged once again at the visitors' center and read the history of the park before leaving. Nor did she find anything hopeful there. On the contrary, she learned that the wetlands trail she just hiked had led her along the former bed of the river, before the Rio Grande was rerouted farther to the south, in the mid-1930s. So most of the land that Silvia was exploring had been on the other side of the Rio Grande, in Mexico, and not where her bisabuela could have lived at all!

Disheartened by this news, Silvia could no longer imagine how to proceed. Only dinner and a good night's sleep might clear her head and allow her to formulate a plan. She needed to talk to an expert planner: Mami! Even though it wasn't Wednesday and her mother probably was not in a spot with service, Silvia decided to try calling.

She pulled out her phone, hoping that her mother's clear thinking could encourage her on the long walk back to the Socorro Road bus. Plus, she really should tell her where they were.

She dialed her mother's cell phone but of course there was no answer. Then she tried again. Near tears, she opened her contacts and selected her aunt's number in Mexico. After seven rings, she got through, only to learn that her mother was already gone.

"Ha salido, mi amor. Se fue para el norte," said her tía.

"But she wasn't supposed to leave until December! She wasn't going to arrive until three weeks from now!" said Silvia, fear mounting in her chest.

"Sí, Silvi, pero ya está en la frontera."

She's at the border already? Silvia began to shiver at the thought of her mother preparing to cross the border illegally again. This time a fugitive. And she didn't even know that her children were away nor that they were frustratingly close to finding her a legal way in. She felt her eyes prick with panicky tears, but managed to hold them back while she finished talking to her aunt.

After disconnecting the call, Silvia desperately sent her thoughts toward her mother: *We're right here in West Texas, Mami. We're right here, maybe just across the border from you, trying to get you some socorro: help, aid. Be patient,* she willed her mother. *Just a little longer.*

Rounding the corner onto Socorro Road, Silvia scanned for the nearest bus stop. She would be heading north, but as she turned her head right to check for traffic, she caught sight of the southbound bus shelter. There, an ICE van was pulled to the shoulder and two officers in black vests were questioning the waiting passengers. They had clipboards and tablets and were talking to a mother with a baby on her back and a little girl at her side, clutching her hand. A few passengers had apparently seen danger coming and were escaping down the roadside, hurrying along more than one hundred yards away already. But six or seven people were waiting to be questioned, some ready with documents in hand, submissive as puppies.

Despite the heat, Silvia wrapped her flannel shirt tighter around her chest and walked in the opposite direction, heading for a distant bus stop and safety.

36

Shaken, Silvia arrived at the campsite twenty-five minutes later. Her eyes anxiously scanned the campsite for Lucy. Thankfully, her brother and sister were bent over the fire, warming hot dogs and canned rice and beans. Lucy began scooping the food onto paper plates when they saw her walking up the lane. She sank down onto the picnic bench and unloaded her backpack. She couldn't meet her siblings' eyes, instead laying her head down on her arms on the tabletop.

"What's wrong, hermanota?" asked Sebastián, sitting beside her and rubbing her back. Silvia had noticed that he had become much more empathetic lately. He seemed to be getting past his tummy aches and emotional turmoil and settling in to be a very caring, if a little sad, boy.

Silvia sighed and resolved not to ruin their dinner. "Nothing, really, Seba. We'll talk about it after we eat."

But when they were done eating, it quickly became apparent that a thunderstorm was rolling in, so they efficiently washed up the cooking utensils, saving the water to put out the fire; stowed all of their belongings in the tent; and spread a tarp over the top. Before they were finished, thunder was rumbling closer. They sat by the dying fire to await the storm's arrival.

"So what happened out there?" asked Lucy.

"Nothing. Absolutely nothing." Silvia was uncharacteristically despairing. "What did we find today at the mission? Nothing. How about the farm? Nothing. In town? There isn't a town! So why did I think I would find something at the river?"

"Don't worry, Silvi," said Sebastián. "We don't need treasure. We can just have fun on our trip." He looked around at the dusty campsite, walled on two sides by dingy mobile homes. "I mean, it's not exactly the wilderness, but it's still vacation."

"But that's just the thing. It wasn't supposed to be vacation. Socorro was going to change—"

"Don't, Silvia," warned Lucy. "We'll figure it out."

Just then, a shockingly strong gust of wind swirled around the campground, stirring up the dust into a blinding cloud. They all jumped up from the picnic bench.

"Cover your nose and eyes," yelled Silvia over the sound of the wind. She pulled the neck of her T-shirt up over her mouth and flinched as little bits of gravel stung her legs.

"Get in the tent!" shouted Sebastián.

"No!" yelled Silvia, spotting the one big tree nearby, whose branches were flailing in the wind. "It's not safe under the tree. Over there!" She pointed toward the shower building.

Silvia hurriedly doused the embers of the fire, then joined her brother and sister running to the bathhouse. The three ducked under the overhang just as the sky opened up and rain began pelting the dusty ground. Just then, there was a flash of lightning accompanied almost instantaneously by a crack of thunder. Even the stoic Lucy jumped, and all three burst through the door into the concrete building. Inside, the noise of the rain and thunder against the tin rooftop was almost deafening, but it was dry and solid inside.

After they caught their breath, Lucy said, "It looks like this is going to last for a while. So tell us what happened today."

Silvia recounted her afternoon of dead ends, starting with her hike at the riverside park. She tried to give them some hope, being sure to emphasize the presence of acequias, coyote willow, and mesquite trees, but even she wasn't convinced.

When she came to the part of her story about the calls to Mexico, she realized that there was more that she hadn't told her brother and sister, dating back to her confidential FaceTime chat with their mother and her own alarming phone conversation with Dr. Cisneros about the unlikelihood of a legal return for their mother. "That day on FaceTime, Mami told me that she was determined not to stay away from us, that she was going to try coming across the border again." Silvia's face crumpled. "Because we need her."

Sebastián jumped with excitement, but then looked at his big sister's face. "What's wrong, Silvi? Aren't you happy that we're going to see her again?"

Silvia spoke through tears. "It's very dangerous, what she plans to do. She could get caught and we'd—"

"You mean, she's going to sneak across?" Sebastián asked, lip trembling.

"Yeah, Seba. I mean, she'd have help, but it's not safe."

Sebastián's eyes filled with tears. "Will she be sent to jail?"

"I don't know, Seba. I mean, no, not if she doesn't get caught." Silvia held her head in her hands. "This is all my fault. If I just could have followed Mami's plan …" She cried into her hands for a moment, then realized that Lucy had stepped away. She looked up to see Lucy standing in the entryway, watching through the screen door as the rain poured down outside.

Silvia pulled Sebastián close to her, as if to compensate for Lucy's distance. "Look, hermanito. We're going to figure out a way to help Mami."

"How?" asked the little boy.

"Well, I'm not sure exactly, but I'll know when we're done with the treasure hunt. That's why I need your help. You're so good with maps and puzzles." Silvia wiped her eyes on her T-shirt hem.

"That's true, I am," said Sebastián. "We'll go back to the river tomorrow. I'm sure I can find the clues."

Silvia nodded. "We're just going to have to hurry. Now that I can't reach Mami on the phone, I'm afraid we may be running out of time. I mean, she might be trying to come over earlier than she said."

"Well, then," said Sebastián resolutely, "we'll find it tomorrow. After that we'll figure out how to use it to help Mami."

"Perfect." Silvia smiled through her tears. "And we have to be extra careful, you know, like Mami always said, to keep a low profile. Even here."

Lucy turned and eyed Silvia suspiciously over her shoulder. "Why?

What else happened out there today?"

Silvia hesitantly told them about the ICE van she had seen at the bus stop, interrogating families as they tried to travel home at dinner time. Ironically, despite her own reminders about secrecy and not being noticed, Silvia had to yell out her story in full voice in order for her brother and sister to hear her above the thunder, rain, and wind.

Throughout the description, Lucy had been growing visibly agitated, and by the end of the story, she was ready to burst. "You mean we're in danger here, too? We're in danger and we're on vacation? Our lives are in danger and we're *camping*? And going on treasure hunts that are all dead ends? And living outside in lightning storms? Boy, Silvia, you have some really bad instincts! And your bad instincts are going to get us *and* Mami killed." She slammed out the door into the downpour, but the next crack of thunder brought her crashing back into the bathhouse. She let the door slam and threw herself down in the corner by the shower stall, hugging her knees in close to her body and dropping her head onto them.

Silvia absorbed Lucy's words, hanging in the humid, stormy air, thick as cobwebs. Miserable, she crawled over to the opposite corner, slipping her backpack under her head for a pillow. A moment later, she felt Sebastián slide himself onto her shoulder and wrap her arm around him like a blanket.

"I'm scared, Silvi."

"It's just a storm," Silvia told him brusquely, out of reserves to comfort anyone but herself.

"Not that. Everything else. ICE. Mami. Is she really going to get killed?"

Silvia sat up and glared toward Lucy's corner. "No. No, she's not. Sometimes your sister says—and does—things for drama, but they're not real."

"You sure?" asked Sebastián.

"Yes, I'm sure. Let's not talk about that ever again."

They lay in silence for a few moments. Then Sebastián spoke. "I missed naturalists' club today."

Silvia was slow to answer. "I'm so sorry. I'll make it up to you. And maybe we'll find some cool rocks out here."

Sebastián dubiously scanned the concrete floor. "I feel like we're lost."

"We're not lost, Sebastián," Silvia mumbled, sleep threatening to overtake her despite the noise and stress, or maybe because of them. "We have maps. We have each other."

Sebastián moved closer. "Okay, Silvi. I believe you. I believe in Socorro."

As Silvia drifted off, Sebastián's words rang in her head. *I believe in socorro, too,* she thought. *Help, relief. I need some relief right now.* Just then, she felt her sister slide in behind her for warmth, or maybe forgiveness. Moving gently so as to not to disturb their tenuous balance, Silvia grabbed Sebastián's little hand in her left hand and placed her right gently on Lucy's hip, forming a sad but tender tableau on the bathroom floor. Socorro. *I believe in socorro, too.*

37

We have settled into our winter patterns, and I must confess that they are homey and enjoyable, as long as I keep busy and keep from thinking. I've been busy, too, letting out the hems on Violeta's skirts, mending the knees of Jorge's summer work pants, knitting a yellow blanket for the baby. Violeta is progressing on her reading, figures, piano, and sewing. She plays Brahms's Lullaby to her baby sister every night before bed (she just knows it's a girl!) and is sewing her a dress using the fabric from one that she outgrew over the summer.

Margarita looked around her cozy kitchen. Using the stores they had for the off season, they had been eating well every night: turkey pot pies, bean chili, chicken stewed in canned tomatoes and onions. On the weekends, the two baked bread or pie to make their life a bit more festive and to fill the house with the aromas of joy and family.

She glanced at the clock. Before long, the seeds would arrive, and there would be a flurry of preparation and planting in the loft. Margarita knew that then they would begin to talk of their hopes for summer and for Jorge's return. "Let's not get ahead of ourselves," she always told Violeta when the little girl wanted to dream of how wonderful life would be when Papi came back. "Not yet." Now was the time for practicality, function, and focus; for keeping hopes tucked quietly inside like a swaddled baby.

Margarita's gaze landed on the notes and family records that she had amassed through her research. She tightened her lips. No matter how big the stack grew, she couldn't forget the fact that Jorge had no documents with him to prove his citizenship. He didn't drive and had no license. His family had always lived in the Southwest, so he had no immigration documents. In Socorro they had tax records and their bankbook, but even if he had them with him, neither would prove his citizenship status.

Margarita was well aware from her reading and from gossip in town that many of the people that Border Patrol or local agencies deported to Mexico were in fact citizens of the United States, yet they were not allowed the opportunity to prove it. Once President Hoover's speeches and writings had started labeling Mexicans as "criminals," truth and proof no longer seemed to matter. Physical appearance, name, language, or perceived threat to "American" jobs were enough to pull entire families and even whole neighborhoods cruelly up by the roots.

When several weeks would pass between letters from Jorge, her worries compounded. So she stifled the fears and the phantoms that tormented her and continued with her sewing, baking, and homemaking.

Violeta, though, always reminded her of what she was trying to forget. The clock chimed three and Violeta burst through the door. "Any letters from Papi?" she asked, her eyes scanning the newspaper basket and the table.

"Not yet, mi hija," Margarita said. When Jorge was at the mine, he sometimes would miss one or two weeks of writing, but now it had been five weeks. His previous letter had not even acknowledged the new baby. He must not have received her announcement before penning his own note. But what if he had, and hadn't known what to say? Or worse, what if he didn't want the baby?

As if reading her mind, Violeta adjusted her pitch up an octave, saying, "And how's my little sister this afternoon?" She walked over and rubbed Margarita's belly in a circular pattern.

"She's fine, querida. Hungry as always."

"Did you eat your snacks today? All three of them?" Violeta looked earnestly up into her face.

Margarita smiled. "I sure did. Thank you for taking care of me. We're going to be just fine, the three of us."

Violeta paused her rubbing. "You mean the four of us."

"Of course. I just mean that only three of us are together right now." Margarita felt her face grow warm. She took a step back from her daughter. "Look what I did today." She walked to her chair and lifted up the three dresses of her own that she had let out. Soon, she'd have to switch into her maternity wardrobe of looser-fitting gowns, with aprons over the top to hold them in place.

"Ooh, pretty, Mami." Violeta lifted the hem of a blue dress and held it up to her own waist. "No, wait." She grabbed an acorn squash from the middle of the table and held it against her stomach, smoothing the dress over it. With too much in her hands, the squash came tumbling out, thumping against the wooden floor and rolling under the table.

"Violeta!" Margarita raised her voice. "Now the squash is probably bruised!" As she started to bend to reach for the rolling vegetable, Margarita tripped on the hem of her dress and tumbled to the floor. Whimpering, she rolled to her side, cradling her belly.

Violeta threw herself on the floor. "I'm so sorry, Mami. Is the baby okay? I'm so sorry. Let me get it."

"No! I'm already down here," said Margarita, pivoting onto her knees and grabbing the squash. "I thought you were my helper but guess I have to take care of myself after all."

When she was again standing, she saw Violeta looking helpless at the end of the table, tears in her eyes. "Look, Violeta," she said. "I'm sorry. Things are just a little hard right now. I'm scared about the baby, and I'm not hearing from Papi ..." She broke off and settled her weight into a dining chair.

"You never used to yell at me," said Violeta in a small voice.

Margarita let her eyes travel to the worn wooden bowl that held yarn balls in various colors: deep berry, cornflower, goldenrod. She blinked and looked back at her daughter. "I know. I'm sorry."

Violeta came over and crawled into her lap, her long legs spilling off one side and her arms off the other. They exchanged a smile as Margarita tried to hold her, her growing abdomen in the way. "I'll try harder," said Violeta. "I'll try to help more."

You shouldn't have to, thought Margarita, stroking her daughter's hair. *Jorge should be here.*

38

Silvia awoke the next morning to sunlight shining on the walls of the tent. She had been dreaming about Socorro and her bisabuela's hopes and fears, many of which Silvia shared. Hopes of growth and reunion. Fears of separation and deportation.

After the storm passed during the night, the siblings had returned to the campsite, taken down the dripping tarp, and spent what remained of the night in the tent. In truth, it had only been shortly after midnight when the storm abated, but Silvia's eyes burned as if she had only slept for a few hours. Lucy lay beside her, breathing deeply on her stomach, arms under her makeshift pillow. Sebastián's spot was empty.

Silvia pulled on her tennis shoes and unzipped the tent, emerging into a dewy, brilliant day. The storm had ushered in a major weather change, and the fresh morning air finally felt like autumn. For the first time, Silvia spotted a greenish cast on the dirty ground; there was actually a noticeable fuzz of grass in the desert beneath her feet.

The rain had managed another transfiguration as well. Rather than splashing more mud onto the mobile homes, it had power-washed them. Even the most yellowed of the trailers sparkled in the new light of day.

Sebastián was seated at the picnic table, head bowed over his maps. Unexpectedly, he also had the diary to his left, with his water bottle weighting it open to a chosen page. He looked over at his sister, who was smiling at him with eyebrows raised.

"I just need one more minute, Silvi. Just one more." Sebastián was obviously in the middle of something that required his concentration.

"Okay. I'll go to the bathroom and come back."

Silvia walked the few yards to the restroom building where they had taken shelter the night before. Its cinderblock exterior, too, had been washed clean by the storm, and its formerly grimy windows were gleaming in the dawn sunlight.

When she returned to the campsite, Sebastián was beaming proudly, one hand on the atlas and one on the diario, like Moses with his tablets.

"I know what we did wrong, Silvia, and I know how to fix it," he announced.

"What? How?" Silvia asked.

"Look here," said Sebastián, sliding the two books over as his sister sat down beside him. "You said that nothing looked right at the park yesterday, didn't you?"

"Yeah," said Silvia. "But it was just that I didn't find the right spot on the river yet. I saw some coyote willows, but not near the mesquite trees. Margarita must have lived farther inland. Or farther upstream."

"You can say that again. And yesterday at the mission you were confused because you couldn't see the Rio Grande or the acequia from there, right?"

"Well, yes, but maybe when they shifted the river's course … I don't know. It's been eighty years. We'll just have to look again."

"True. Only this time we should look in the right state!" Sebastián announced triumphantly, bouncing in his seat on the picnic bench.

"What do you mean?"

Lucy had come out of the tent and was standing behind Silvia, looking over her shoulder. "Yeah, what do you mean?"

They all paused as they heard the gravelly sound of a car approaching. All three turned toward the vehicle. Silvia could feel herself tremble at the sight of the state badge on the side of the dark green pickup truck. But when she felt Sebastián start to jump up from the picnic table, she laid a hand on his thigh and gently held him down.

"It's all right, Seba. It's just a park ranger."

Sebastián settled back onto the bench and took a deep breath. He looked over his shoulder and said "Hello, Lucy," like a professor coolly greeting a tardy student. Then he turned back to Silvia to continue. "Well, you read the diary and expected there to be water in view from the mission. But I was following along on my map on the bus. I knew

that we would come to the mission first, and then the river much later."
He paused to let that sink in. "Also, all day you were looking for hills,
but there weren't any. And on my atlas of this part of Texas, there are
hardly any hills at all, so I couldn't understand why you thought you'd
find them near the river."

"It's because Bisabuela said they'd be here," said Silvia weakly.

"I know." He patted her hand in imitation of one of their mother's
characteristic gestures of comfort. "It was all so confusing that I decided to take a look at the maps myself this morning. I found the one in
the diary that Bisabuela had drawn, you know, the bird's-eye view of
Socorro?"

"Sure," said Silvia. It's in the middle."

"Right. So I looked at the map, and noticed that everything was in
the wrong place. Even the Rio Grande was on the wrong side of town."

"That's true, Seba, but I've been thinking. It's because Bisabuela
was drawing it facing south instead of north like your maps."

"Nope, because look." He took the water bottle off of the diary and
pointed to a spot on the open map. "See the arrows? This is the current,
flowing down the map. So she had to be facing north." He looked back
and forth between Silvia and Lucy as earnestly as only a first grader
can, and explained, "We learned about currents in school, and everyone
knows the Rio Grande flows down into the Gulf of Mexico."

Silvia studied the maps in panic. "Oh no. Oh no no no. Bisabuela's
maps aren't going to help us at all! What have I done?" She held her
head in her hands.

"Yes, they are!" said Sebastián, grinning. "Listen!" he insisted,
shaking Silvia's shoulders until she raised her head. "I remembered from
the index that there are many places named Socorro. And so I looked
again this morning, and there are two states with Socorros! And they're
both on the Rio Grande!" He looked expectantly at his sisters, waiting
for them to solve his riddle.

"I got nothing," said Lucy.

Silvia shook her head.

"New Mexico!" shouted Sebastián. "Look!" He proceeded to point
the town out to them on his atlas, then compared its site on the west of

the Rio Grande to Margarita's sketch. "According to my atlas, there's even a mission there! And acequias!" He signaled each with his finger.

"Well, I'm convinced," said Lucy.

"Hermano!" said Silvia, kissing her little brother on the top of his head. "You're amazing!" She looked around the campsite at the pathetic fire ring and splintery picnic table. "Now what do you say we get out of this dustbowl and into the mountains?"

While Sebastián and Lucy jumped up to pack their blankets and clothes into their backpacks and shake out and fold the tarp, Silvia pulled out her laptop and searched for transportation to Socorro, New Mexico. Getting there wasn't going to be easy, since their destination was another town that had been bypassed by not only the railroad but largely by buses. But Silvia found a workable timetable that would get them there by late afternoon.

"Okay, y'all. If we hurry, we can catch the 9:16 Greyhound to Albuquerque."

"Why Albuquerque?" asked Lucy.

"It's the largest city near Socorro," said Sebastián.

"Guess we're following Seba's instincts from now on. Right, hermana?" Lucy elbowed Silvia, who returned the jab with a hug.

"Apology accepted," said Silvia. "I'm sorry, too. But we're on the right track now, thanks to our brilliant brother. Let's salvage this trip."

"And this treasure hunt!" said Sebastián.

39

Forty-five minutes later, they were again at the El Paso bus station, this time with tickets to Albuquerque. Just like the railroad, they would bypass Socorro, New Mexico, on their way, arriving in the big city in the early afternoon. There, they'd walk to the train station to catch the New Mexico Rail Runner Express, which linked smaller towns south of Albuquerque. They would get off in the little city of Belen, still north of Socorro. From there, they would try to connect with Socorro's minibus shuttle, a twice-per-day service that Silvia found on the town's homepage. The entire trip would take them eight or nine hours, giving Silvia plenty of time to make them a camping reservation and research Socorro using the bus's Wi-Fi.

Since it was Saturday morning, there was little traffic leaving El Paso. Silvia looked out the window watching the flat terrain of Texas go by and thinking about how she had struck out completely in the town that she had thought would be the solution to their problems. She had thought she had done her research well and that finding Bisabuela's land wouldn't be too hard. Now, leaving Texas, she realized that she needed to rely on more than just her own reading and research. Like Sebastián, she had to question what she saw rather than blindly pursue an obviously incorrect lead. She also learned that she needed her siblings' help.

Realizing that they were heading north, though, Silvia felt her heart sink. The border was behind them, growing ever more distant. That meant that Mami was also behind them somewhere; they were driving away from her. Silvia began to sweat a little, and rubbed her palms to dry them off. This was going to be okay. This was all going to be okay.

Somehow crossing the border into New Mexico calmed her a little, with the knowledge that they were at least taking a step toward getting Mami back. Exhaling slowly, Silvia watched the familiar flat terrain gradually fade as Route 25 followed the course of the Rio Grande upstream. By the time they reached their first stop, there were mountains on at least two horizons and Silvia relaxed in her seat.

"Las Cruces!" called the driver.

Silvia startled out of her relaxation at the sound of the town's name. Las Cruces. That was where the immigration raid had occurred that she and Dr. Cisneros had been talking about last week. She pressed her face to the glass as they pulled into the station. Everyone looked normal; children were excited, their parents, laden with duffles and suitcases, less so. Silvia wasn't sure what she had expected to see—maybe some visible sign of the terror that Mexican Americans were under due to ICE? Maybe ICE itself? She sighed in relief. Life was just going on as usual, for some people at least.

She must have dozed during some of the next seventy-five miles after Las Cruces. When she awoke, they were pulling out of Truth or Consequences, the last stop before Albuquerque. The landscape had dramatically changed while Silvia had been napping. Outside her window, the countryside was now consistently hilly and extremely arid, with scrubby trees dotting the slopes and an absolute absence of undergrowth. Silvia knew from her botany course that they were now in the Basin and Range region of New Mexico, where they would see an increasing variety of plant life due to the proximities of both the river valley and the mountains. She strained to see the Rio Grande to the east out of her window, but it was not in sight.

Still one hundred fifty miles from Albuquerque, Silvia began searching online for campgrounds. She settled on one just to the north of Socorro, Escondida Lake. There, they would be on the river, in sight of the mountains, and within easy reach of the locations they needed to access in Socorro. Silvia didn't mind the few miles they would have to travel to get to town; they had just enough cash left, and after Sebastián's discovery and good humor on this difficult trip, he at least deserved a real camping experience.

Just after noon, her phone rang. Silvia hesitated at the unfamiliar number but picked up the call anyway.

"Hello?"

"Querida?"

"Mami!" Silvia yelled, waking up her brother and sister in the next seat. "Dónde estás?"

Their mother spoke several long sentences, but the reception was so bad that Silvia could only discern a few words.

"Mami, you're breaking up. I can't hear you." Silvia enunciated clearly, hoping her mother would understand her.

She heard a few more syllables, then a complete sentence: "Can you hear me?"

"Yes, Mami, I hear you. We're in the mountains. Escucha, don't go anywhere yet, please! Stay there, Mami."

Silvia pressed the phone to her ear, but heard nothing, so she continued. "Call us before you do anything. I might have big news." Silvia was sure that the entire bus could hear her yelling into her phone, but she didn't care.

"… you … brother … forget what I … call you soon …" was all Silvia could make out of her mother's final sentence before the call was dropped. She slammed down the phone onto her lap and glared out the window at the canyon walls that had come between her and her mother. Then she turned across the aisle, where Lucy and Sebastián were looking at her expectantly.

Silvia shook her head, then massaged her temples with one hand. "I couldn't understand her. I heard that she's still in Mexico, and that she'll call us soon." Silvia paused and noticed her brother's and sister's serious faces. Fortified by her mother's voice and remembering her duty as caretaker, Silvia took a deep breath. "She's definitely safe. As long as she heard me, I don't think she'll try to cross yet. I think we'll get to talk to her at least one more time before then."

"We kind of have to hurry, don't we, Silvi?" asked Sebastián, with his brow wrinkled.

"Yeah, we do. But now, let's have lunch and talk about camping." She exhaled in relief and smiled a genuine grin at her brother.

The three enjoyed the last hour and a half of the ride as best they could, and Silvia's planning paid off with a smooth arrival into Albuquerque. They spotted a nearby convenience store and restocked their cooler with the cheapest foods they could find. Silvia checked her cash before they left the store: three hundred seventy-six dollars and no way to use the credit card. Tightening her lips, she led her siblings out the door with their supplies.

Then they began to walk the few blocks to the light rail station. After they left the immediate vicinity of the bus station, the streets were fairly quiet. They crossed Silver Avenue, causing Sebastián to chatter about treasure as they traversed the remaining two blocks. Nearly every building they passed along the way was made of adobe in the mission style, with arches and garden walls. Alvarado Transportation Center was the most impressive of all, sitting right at the end of Gold Avenue ("More treasure!" shouted Sebastián) and boasting multileveled towers, red Spanish tiled roofs, and covered walkways under sequences of arches as even as a perfect smile. Silvia knew that she had mistakenly felt a similar excitement back in El Paso when she thought she was near her bisabuela's land, but this time was different. It really felt like they were somewhere exotic and new, like they had finally escaped the nightmare of stress and fear at home in San Marcos and had entered the dream of possibility and hope in Spanish Albuquerque.

To Silvia's satisfaction, the train trip from Albuquerque went as well as she had hoped, and they pulled into the Belen station exactly as the shuttle bus they were hoping to catch arrived. The siblings had no more than a moment to take in the tiny train platform paved in brick beside a large commuters' parking lot. Across the lot, tall trees shaded what looked to be a neighborhood of small houses. In the other direction, across the tracks, they could see another parking lot and more houses. But then they were off, stepping into the small white minibus that served as the shuttle to Socorro.

"Goin' to Socorro, right?" the driver asked Silvia.

"Yes, please," she answered. "Would you be able to tell me how to get from there to Escondida Lake?"

"You goin' to the campground?"

"Yes sir."

The driver scanned the rearview mirror, craning his neck and peering into every seat. "You kids all together?"

"Yes, we are."

"You're the only ones in the van today. Why don't I just drop you at Escondida?" His eyes twinkled at Silvia in the mirror.

She smiled. "Oh, that would be great! Thank you so much." She turned to grin at Sebastián, who returned her smile with an excited one.

After a short while, they rolled into the wooded campsite, and the driver dropped them off at the little cabin that served as the camp office. He unloaded their backpacks, black trash bag, and rolling cooler onto the sandy ground, and said, "Good luck! Have fun out here!" He looked dubiously at Silvia for a moment, no doubt assessing her suitability to be in charge of two kids. Then he smiled and waved.

"Thank you again. Have a great day," she said.

"Yeah, thanks," said Lucy.

"Thank you," Sebastián said with a smile.

Then they turned away and looked around at the campground. It couldn't have been more different from the dusty field in Socorro, Texas. There were abundant tall pine trees and a brook running down the hill toward the lake. Sebastián immediately started running toward the stream, so Silvia checked them in quickly and they walked through the trees toward their campsite.

By dinnertime they had set up camp, Sebastián had chosen the perfect walking stick, and he was leading his sisters along the lakeshore in the diminishing light. Relieved to be on their feet after a long day of travel, they stood munching sandwiches they had bought in the convenience stores and attempting to skip stones on the smooth water. Once the sun went down, they returned to their site and roasted marshmallows over the carefully contained campfire that Silvia built with wood from the camp store and only a little struggle. That night, Silvia put Sebastián to bed equal parts exhausted and contented, tucked in with his blue elephant, wearing his Nature Trekker hat. She smiled to see him so happy. Things were finally going well. She finally had real hope.

40

It's early spring and we expect Jorge any day now. I normally find out when the men are coming back either via his letters or through gossip in town, and I haven't heard a word yet. Nevertheless, Violeta and I go about our tasks with one eye toward the road and all our hopes pinned on this summer — the season to begin anew with Jorge.

Both Margarita and Violeta were ready. They had finished all the sewing, mending, and washing. Jorge's repaired work clothes were hanging on the back of the bedroom door, along with a new flannel shirt that Margarita bought for him in town for the early cool days of planting. They turned the last of the bruised apples into sauce, which was waiting in the pantry beside the remaining pickles and stewed tomatoes. Every few days, Margarita baked a fruit or a meat pie, hoping to have Jorge's favorite treat fresh when he arrived. Violeta swept the house daily so that it would be perfect for his return.

Outside, spring had come early, and with no flooding. The kitchen garden's herbs were already sprouting from among last year's brown stalks, and a few green transplants from the attic were nestled into their adopted new land with warming soil and gentle rains. The rose stems were red, and shiny green leaves sprouted from their stalks. Even the new rose on the hilltop had a few dark shoots.

In the field, Violeta had managed to haul the crates of cotton and barley seeds out to their designated spots, and under Margarita's tutelage, she was learning to manage the team of cows to turn the soil in preparation for planting. The little girl talked nonstop about surprising

Jorge with a lightened load and how proud he would be of her skills on the farm. She fell asleep every night chattering about her plans for when her papi came home.

One March night, Margarita had just finished calming Violeta enough to put her to sleep and was leaving the little girl's room smiling, ready to sit down to sew or to write, when there was a knock at the door. Peering through the glass with her eyebrows knitted, she recognized Mr. Carlton from the store in town, his own serious expression looking back at her. As she opened the door for him, she noticed that he was carrying the unmistakable envelope from Western Union.

"I'm sorry to have to disturb your evening, Mrs. Vargas," he said, as Margarita's eyes searched his. "A telegram arrived for you. It's urgent."

She gestured him in and took the paper from his hand. She absently pulled out a seat for him at the table and sank into her own. Her face crumpled as she read its horrifyingly brief contents:

REGRET TO INFORM OF LOSS OF MR. JORGE VARGAS
IN MINING ACCIDENT.
ALL DUE PAY TO FOLLOW.

Margarita laid her head on the table, sobbing silently into her arms. After a few moments, Mr. Carlton stood up.

"Can I do anything for you, Mrs. Vargas?"

Margarita shook her head.

"Do you need me to stay?"

She shook her head again and started to get up from her spot at the table.

"Never mind. I'll see myself out. I'll come back to check on you in the morning. Again, I'm so very sorry." He left, softly closing the door behind him.

Margarita still clutched the telegram paper, and her hand was beginning to sweat around it. With effort, she opened her fingers and looked at it again. *There has to be some mistake*, she thought. *I must have just read it wrong.* But she hadn't. She buried her face in the red kitchen towel that was lying on the table and cried.

Suddenly, she stopped and sat up, clutching her belly with both hands. *The baby! Oh my God. She has no father.* She again muffled her cries in the towel, still pressing against the baby inside her with one hand. Then she stopped again. *How am I going to tell Violeta?* she wondered. *She'll wake up all excited in the morning and then I'll have to crush her with the terrible news.*

She spilled out her grief and memories and hopes until she was dry. Then she straightened her dress, wiped her palms hard down her legs, and stood up to head to the sink for a drink of water. Only then did she look up and see Violeta standing like a ghost in the hallway from the bedrooms.

"What happened, Mami?" she asked in a tiny voice, as if afraid to ask the question.

Margarita's face crumpled again, and she stretched out her arms mutely to her daughter. Violeta ran to her and together they sobbed until the moon was high in the sky and its cold beam stabbed through the kitchen window. At last, Margarita walked her daughter to her bed and stayed with her through the rest of the night, wrapped up together under the quilt that Margarita had made when she got married.

41

The next morning, Silvia awoke to leaf shadows on the nylon sides of the tent and a range of emotions making her stomach flutter. They were in Socorro, the town in which her great-great- grandmother had lived her greatest joys and suffered her most tragic heartbreak. Silvia hoped Socorro would treat her own family well. This could be the day that would change their lives.

She also awoke cold. When they had packed their things in San Marcos for a hurried departure, none of them had anticipated coming to the mountains, and on this late-November morning the temperature was easily down to the forties. Nevertheless, Silvia lay on her back for a moment in her thin fleece throw and listened to the birds chirping and the trickle of water nearby. She yawned and stretched, feeling stiff but relieved to have reached their destination and intrigued by the sounds outside. She unzipped the tent flap as quietly as she could, slipped on her sweater and tennis shoes, and stepped outside.

The first thing she did was try to light a fire so that she would be able to serve her brother and sister a hot breakfast, with coffee for her and cocoa for them. After the cold night, however, the wood was damp with dew that might have been frost only an hour before. Three times, the pine needles and leaves failed to ignite the wood. Silvia growled to herself, clenching her cold hands into fists. Then she straightened out her stiff knees, standing up to look around.

In the silvery dawn light, she saw low trees and shrubs along the trickling brook that led to the lake. She walked downstream a few yards while inhaling the mountain air. A grackle dipped its beak into the stream for an early drink. No other animals seemed to be about at this early hour. Instead, Silvia saw the silvery fronds of coyote willows farther downstream near the lakeshore. Exhaling and closing her eyes for a moment, she knew they were in the right place at last. She could almost feel her great-great-grandmother's footprints beneath hers.

Silvia walked back to the site to try the fire again. This time it lit. *Thanks, Bisabuela*, she offered. Then laughed at herself.

She couldn't wait to get into Socorro and begin their search, but she remembered that it was Sunday morning; most museums and public buildings where they could potentially do research would be closed. They might be able to get into the mission, but that was probably it. Nevertheless, none of them had ever been to New Mexico before, so they would most likely spend the bulk of the day outside exploring. Silvia anticipated her siblings being in good moods and ready for new experiences.

The two younger kids slept late. When they got up, Silvia had a decent breakfast of hot oatmeal and cocoa ready for them. Fortified for their adventure, the three decided to start hiking along the Rio Grande toward town. Traveling on foot would cost nothing and would allow them to ascertain the lay of the land along the way and to hunt for the natural clues that would indicate that they were on the right track. They agreed that, if they got tired on the walk, they would flag down a bus to carry them into town.

To Sebastián's delight, however, their transport took an even more adventurous turn. After nearly a mile of hiking on the riverside trail, they encountered a boat outfitter, who offered to rent them a flat-bottomed canoe from his trailer so that they could navigate the shallow waters down to Socorro. The outfitter would pick up the canoe later that day in Otero Park, right in the center of town.

"Please, hermanota, can we please do it?" Sebastián asked, looking up at her with his wide blue eyes.

Silvia's hand tightened around the money in her pocket. The boat only cost fourteen dollars; surely she could spend a little money to make her brother happy and rest their feet for a bit. She looked at the vendor. "Okay, we'll take one, please."

Sebastián whooped and jumped up and down. Even Lucy grinned

and grabbed him by both hands and swung him around for a little spin.

Sebastián suddenly stopped the spin and grew serious. He pulled out his explorer hat from his backpack and looked back and forth between his sisters. "Can I please be in charge of this expedition? I mean, you can help, but I'll be in charge."

"Certainly," Silvia said, assuming a suitably serious expression. "I mean, aye aye, Captain."

Sebastián looked pleased with his new title. "Okay, listen, hermanas. Let's pretend we're the first people to ever see this land. You two can paddle and I'll sit in the front and make observations." He pulled out his notebook and pencil as Silvia and Lucy exchanged smiles.

Once they were equipped with life jackets and paddles and had taken a crash course on steering, the three stepped carefully into the boat and shoved off. Silvia was not entirely unfamiliar with boating, having paddled a canoe with her father on some of their fishing expeditions when she was little. The water was shallow and the current gentle, so they were able to look around comfortably while they drifted southward.

Sebastián spoke his observations as he wrote the key words in his notebook: "Wide, shallow river … lots of plants—Silvia, what are those bushes on the riverbank?"

"They're coyote willow, hermanito," said Silvia, casting a meaningful smile in his direction.

Sebastián clearly recognized the diary's first clue.
"Great! *C-o-y-o-t-e*."

Silvia smiled at how her brother's back bent in concentration.

Sebastián continued his observations aloud. "Hilly country, rocky, very dry … brownish-red soil with maybe a stripe of white … Hey! That's quartz! *Q-u-a-r-t-s*."

"*T-z,*" said Lucy from the front bench, in rhythm with her paddling.

"Okay, *z*. Ahead, a cliff overlooking the water," said Sebastián.

"I wouldn't really call that a cliff," said Lucy. "More like a rise." Lucy stopped paddling for a moment to take her sweater off. The temperature had warmed into the sixties already.

"It's a cliff. *C-l-i-f-f*. And look, Silvi! It has trees on top, like you were hoping!"

Silvia stopped paddling to gaze up to the right. The small hill above the river did have some actual trees at its peak, not just shrubs. She couldn't tell from that distance whether or not they were mesquites, but their dark bark signaled the possibility. She also spotted some spiky green plants in the undergrowth beneath the trees, and made a mental note to return to the site on foot to determine whether they were the soapweed yuccas that her great-great-grandmother had written about so frequently. *All three!* she thought. *And it's only the first hour!*

Sebastián now had his atlas open in his lap. "Look, Silvi. The map shows an acequia next to us." He looked up and to the right. "It must be just on the other side of the cliff."

"Rise," corrected Lucy.

"Lucy, it's fine," said Silvia in a low voice. "Let him call it what he wants." Louder, she called to Sebastián, "Good job, hermanito. Keep counting up those clues."

"I am!" he announced, holding up his pad to show his sisters that he had filled three pages of his notebook with nature observations in his careful printing.

The riverbank on their right was now consistently high, with occasional treetops visible over the rise. If Sebastián was right about the acequia, they now had possibly four of the geographic keys from the diario in place.

Eventually they floated into Socorro and easily surmised the location of Otero Park by the families out running their dogs or fishing from the banks of the river in the fall air. Willowy shrubs grew along most of the bank, but one spot appeared sandy, so they hauled the canoe out of the water and threw themselves onto the grass to relax. There, the riverbank was shaded by relatively tall trees and there was a picnic table, so after a few moments they moved to the table to eat the peanut butter sandwiches they had prepared before leaving the campsite.

After lunch, Sebastián found a sign only a few steps from their picnic spot, indicating where they could leave the canoe for pickup, so they were nearly ready to head into town on foot.

"Give me a minute first," said Silvia. "I want to download a map of town and a few other websites while I have cell service."

Lucy, too, took advantage of the signal to check in with her friends, while Sebastián threw stones into the river and pet the dogs that came up to him as he waited. After a few minutes, Silvia had their route plotted; they had only to walk a short distance from the park to Otero Avenue and then follow that directly into downtown Socorro. Their first destination would be the San Miguel Mission.

Leaving the river behind, they almost immediately crossed a small bridge over the acequia that Sebastián had seen on the map, and then crossed another irrigation ditch. Silvia and Sebastián exchanged smiles and the three continued onto the dirt road that bisected flat, dry fields with houses at their farthest edges. Silvia breathed deeply as she saw that many of the trees lining the road were mesquites. Ahead, the land rose sharply into a single mountain, which must have been the one that Margarita had referenced so frequently in her writing. The siblings walked quickly and lightly, encouraged to see, in three dimensions, so many of the elements Margarita had described.

As they entered town, Otero Avenue suddenly became San Miguel Street and the mission stood directly in front of them. Silvia froze in her steps when she spotted it, awed to realize that this actually was the soil that her bisabuela had trodden, the land where she lived and worked and wrote. *This is nuestra tierra.* Sebastián grabbed her hand and they proceeded at a jog to the historic site.

42

San Miguel Mission stood symmetrical and simple, of sand-colored adobe instead of whitewashed like its Texan counterpart. Its enclosed bell towers rose in two tiers on either end, crowned in copper domes and topped with simple crosses. Another cross adorned the center of the roofline, sitting atop a graceful arch. Directly below the cross, various ornaments highlighted the symmetry of the building's construction: a rose-shaped plaster piece, an arched stained-glass window, and a white-painted arched doorway with double doors beneath, also painted white. The contrast between the sand and the white drew the eye to the door, creating a welcoming feeling. Like the mission they had visited in Texas, the property was surrounded by a low adobe wall, however this one contained not a large parking lot, but instead a sparse meditation garden. To Silvia, the entire site was perfect and filled her with a sense of peace.

Mass had apparently ended not long before they arrived, and the siblings found the church door unlocked. As they had in Texas, they entered quietly and observed the simple adobe walls, statuary recesses, wooden ceiling, and altarpiece before sitting down in a pew to read a historical brochure about the site that they picked up at the entrance.

Silvia read aloud, *"The Socorro Mission (later renamed San Miguel) was founded in 1615 and was the namesake of the Socorro Mission in Texas; the Indigenous Americans and Spanish that fled to El Paso did so from this site in 1680. During that exodus—"*

"What's an exodus?" asked Sebastián.

"It's when everybody leaves a place all at once." Silvia continued reading. *"During that exodus, the mission's priest famously hid the church's solid New Mexico silver communion rail and other objects—"*

"Wait! Silver? Like treasure?" Sebastián's eyes were glowing with excitement.

"Yes, but listen. *The priest drew a map of the hiding place for future recovery.*"

Sebastián jumped up. "A treasure map?"

"Shhhh," said Lucy. "We're in a church." She slumped backward against the pew.

"Nevertheless," continued Silvia, *"the treasure was never found, even though searches continued into the 1980s."*

"Are you done?" asked her brother.

"Now I am," she said.

"Good. Here's what we're gonna do. Since we're already explorers, let's add on this new treasure hunt!" Sebastián looked back and forth between his sisters' faces, waiting for them to approve his plan.

"Fine," said Lucy.

"I'm just glad you're having a great adventure," said Silvia, putting her arm around her brother and giving him a squeeze.

Before exiting the mission, they paused to view the few historical items on display. One was a set of property maps detailing the layout of structures and open spaces on the site in three different decades. On each map, a central feature was the acequia Madre, the irrigation ditch that made life in the mission community possible. Silvia studied the documents, noting that the ditch was present on all three of the maps on view, yet they hadn't noticed a channel outside. She snapped a photo of the most recent map with her phone and turned to show Sebastián, since he was too short to see the maps hanging on the wall.

"Let's go outside and check for this acequia that shows up on the maps, okay, Seba?"

The three siblings passed through the wooden doors out into the brilliant New Mexico sun. Together, they walked the route that the ditch must have traversed.

"Looks like it's now covered by El Camino Real Street," said Sebastián, checking the image on Silvia's phone against the sign at the corner where they stood.

"Yeah," said Silvia. "Hmm. I remember from my school trip to San Antonio that lots of times acequias were rerouted through pipes during modern construction."

"Why?" asked Lucy.

"I guess as cities grew, street property became more scarce. They were able to gain more buildable land by channeling the acequias underground."

"Makes sense," said Lucy. "I'm just going to peek around the other corner of the building."

"No!" said Silvia and Sebastián in unison, remembering Lucy's disappearance after the last mission they had visited.

Lucy looked back and forth between them. Her eyebrows drew together and her mouth curled down. Then she burst out laughing. "Okay, okay, I won't go anywhere. Geez, you two are so serious."

Silvia stuck out her tongue at her sister. Then she stood tall and gave one last look around. "Well, I'm satisfied. It looks like the reality on the ground here matches what I know from Margarita's diary. What do you say we go back to the campsite and spend the afternoon exploring?"

"Yes!" shouted Sebastián.

"And I could use a nap," said Lucy.

"Yeah, you've been up for almost six hours," said Silvia, rolling her eyes.

43

They took a bus back out to Escondida Lake and were soon busy with their respective afternoon occupations. Lucy crawled straight into the tent and pulled her hair over her eyes to block out the afternoon light. Silvia walked Sebastián to the lakeshore to start his explorations, and then took the short walk back down the path to the campsite. She planned to read through some of the documents and websites she had downloaded to her phone when she'd had cell service in town, and then return to Sebastián for a nature walk.

She started with the diario, retracing the clues they had found so far. The mission that Margarita so frequently mentioned perfectly matched the reality of San Miguel, including the presence of an important acequia on site. It was an easy walk from the mission to the Rio Grande, where there were also acequias. Along the river itself were plentiful colonies of coyote willow. The west side of the river was overlooked by a hilly bank, and nearly every hill was topped with dark, thick-trunked trees that appeared to be old mesquites. Beneath the trees were spiky plants that Silvia was fairly certain were soapweed yuccas. She flipped through the diary to several of the pages she had marked with keywords. Her readings confirmed her conviction that they were, in fact, in Margarita's Socorro. Silvia felt like everything was in place and she could move on to her great-great-grandmother's final keywords and ultimately the only ones that might matter: *título* and *escritura*.

She opened to one of the diario's maps, and alongside it pulled up the pages from the Socorro County website that she had screenshotted onto her phone. While she was able to see some historical plans reflecting the early land grants in New Mexico, she learned that the more relevant records from the first half of the twentieth century could only be viewed in the County Clerk's office. Silvia accepted this limitation with a grimace. It was still only Sunday afternoon!

Even more frustratingly, without internet access at the campground, she couldn't search the databases of census, marriage, and tax records on the government site. Sighing, she made a quick to-do list for the next day, culminating in *Find the título,* which she underlined three times. Then she closed her book and phone and went to check on her brother.

She found him sitting on the shore of the lake, arms wrapped around his knees.

"Hey, buddy. What are you thinking about?"

"Just Mami," Sebastián said in a little voice. The corners of his mouth trembled, but he remained composed.

Silvia gazed over the still water. "She would like it here, huh?"

"Yeah. She'd love it."

"Well, Seba, this is our homeland. This is where our great-great-grand-parents lived and where our Mami's abuela was born. I love it here, too."

"Me too. I wish we could live here. I don't want to go home. It doesn't feel as safe there now."

Silvia knew he was thinking about their hasty departure. "I know, but it'll be okay. We just have to keep taking care of each other. But for now, let's enjoy the time we have here, all right?"

He nodded.

Silvia suddenly thought of how to cheer him up. "Hey, what do you say we get some pizza at the camp store for dinner?" She had seen on the menu that pizzas were only five dollars and thought that they could afford to celebrate, since everything was going so well.

"Yeah!" shouted Sebastián, jumping up. "Let's go!"

They stopped at the tent to pick up Lucy on their way, who was awake from her nap, leafing through a fashion magazine she had picked up at the bus station in El Paso. The three siblings walked the short distance to the camp office, which sold basic necessities, charcoal for grilling, and surprisingly aromatic pepperoni pizza. While they waited the ten minutes for their pie to be ready, they poked around the little store. Sebastián picked out some fifty-cent gummy worms for his dessert, but Lucy was frozen at the newsstand.

Silvia approached her. "What's up, hermana?"

Wordlessly, Lucy pointed to the picture on the front page of *El Defensor Chieftain*. It showed a girl of Mexican descent on a stretcher, surrounded by immigration officials, with nurses looking on horrified in the background. One nurse was photographed mid-scream, trying to reach the girl while two officers held her back.

Silvia picked up the paper and skimmed the article. "They've detained a nine-year-old girl at the hospital in Albuquerque, just as she was arriving for emergency surgery. They're deporting her without medical care. She came here when she was a baby."

Neither girl noticed that Sebastián had slipped in between them and was looking on, silently wiping his eyes.

Lucy began trembling. "So we're not safe here, either."

Sebastián began to cry in earnest.

"Okay, hang on." Silvia left her brother and sister standing forlornly at the newsstand while she walked to the counter and paid for the personal-sized pizzas, the gummy worms, and some ice for the cooler. Counting up her money after the purchase, she saw that they had just over three hundred fifty dollars left. The campsite cost ten dollars per night and they'd have to save sixty-three dollars each for bus tickets back home. That meant that they had about one hundred thirty dollars left to work with for the trip. When they got back to San Marcos, Mami would be able to come home and they would be all right. *Unless things don't work out here*, she thought. *Then I would have to quit school and get a job. Who knows if I would ever finish?* She shook the thoughts away.

Returning to her siblings at the newsstand, she said, "Come on. Let's get back to the campsite," and ushered them out the door and down the path.

Sitting them down on the picnic bench, she placed a triangle of cheese pizza before Lucy and a pepperoni slice in front of Sebastián. "Look, kiddos." She saw Lucy stiffen at the word, and revised. "Look. These things are happening all over the country right now. All we can do is keep a low profile."

Lucy said, "Mami's plans just don't work anymore."

"Yes, they do!" Sebastián said, eyes flashing. "Mami's plans always work."

Silvia kept her opinion to herself and tried a different tack. "We've got each other. No one knows we're here. No one is looking for us. We're fine."

"Except Mami," said Sebastián. "She's looking for us."

"Not yet," said Silvia. "She heard me say that she should stay where she is." Silvia glanced at Lucy's face, then repeated in a quieter voice. "I'm sure she heard me."

They ate their pizzas in silence, the doubt in Silvia's words presiding over their table. Silvia took a bite of greasy crust. How could she assure them that they were safe when she didn't believe it herself? She looked at the two of them. "We need a distraction. Who wants to watch *Frozen*?"

Sebastián loved that movie so much that Silvia had downloaded it onto her laptop for him to watch months ago. He had probably seen it forty times by now and Olaf's antics still cracked him up every time. Lucy, too, obviously loved the music, even though she always made sure to make it clear through her attitude and complaints that she was too old for animation. They gathered around the firepit on blankets, Silvia successfully lit a fire, and they ate marshmallows and gummy worms while they watched.

When Sebastián's eyes at last grew heavy, Silvia helped him into the tent and held him until he was asleep. When she came out, Lucy went in to bed.

Silvia sat up for a while longer, staring at the campfire and trying to figure out how to make this feel like a vacation. Silvia hated that she couldn't protect her siblings from the fear, no matter where they went. What the three of them needed were parents, but parents with rights. They had no father, and their mother was stripped of her rights, just like the parents of the little girl at the hospital. Parents without rights were parents without power.

Teetering between despair and determination, Silvia chose the latter one more time. Channeling her mother, and from what she could tell, her bisabuela, too, she set her jaw: *Well, we're just going to have to take our power back. Starting now.*

44

The days since we got the news have been a blur: telegrams, a money transfer, arrangements. I learned that the mining accident was an explosion; there were not even any remains to send home. Violeta and I met with Fr. Rodríguez at the mission, who, in addition to offering comfort, emphasized the importance of a memorial ritual for closure, even when there is no body. We've planned a simple service for next week.

In the meantime, there were still chores to be done. Violeta was excused from school for two weeks so that she could help her mother and mourn. She lay for hours on the floor of the attic among the seedlings, but always refused when Margarita offered to pass her the sprinkling can to water them. She sat at the piano, but Margarita never heard a note. Instead, Violeta passed her time grooming and caring for the dog, the chickens, and the cows. She seemed comforted by not having to communicate verbally.

Margarita handled the finances and the housework. She wrote and cleaned and kept busy. She finished the batches of soap that she had started, but didn't begin any more. Neither she nor Violeta had much appetite, so they barely cooked. In fact, the morning after they received the news, they began eating for mere sustenance, not pleasure, finding it too painful to make the switch from baking for three to baking for two. In unspoken accord, they began to eat only one meal per day: rice and beans that simmered independently on the stove regardless of the attention they were or were not paid.

Thankfully, the baby did not protest the change of menu or activity.

Margarita knew that she was fine, for she still kicked from time to time and rolled inside her, but her belly ceased shifting and bulging in conjunction with the pleasure of sweets or the thrill of motion. Somehow the baby seemed to be allowing space for Margarita to mourn.

Eventually the house was in order and the service was over. A package of Jorge's belongings arrived from the mine, supplemented by a collection that the men had taken up for the family. Only two other men had died during the accident, and the enclosed note indicated that the crew was able to send money to each family.

Finally, fifteen days after receiving the news that shattered their lives, Violeta had to return to school and Margarita was obliged to go into town to the store. Despite the many meals that neighbors and friends had delivered to them, they were in need of basics: rice, cheese, dried beans. Mother and daughter bundled up against the spring chill and the vulnerability of being in public, and walked to town.

"Okay, querida," said Margarita, smoothing her daughter's hair, "I'll meet you at home this afternoon."

"Sí, Mami." Violeta kissed her mother, holding the hug a bit longer than usual. Then she separated herself and walked into Mt. Carmel without looking back.

Margarita continued on to Socorro's main street and entered Carlton's shop. The bell hanging from the door clanged loudly as she opened, and she took her time trying to close the door noiselessly. Standing in the main aisle, she looked toward the counter, where a few of her lifelong friends were standing and talking. They fell silent as they saw her, but one of the women walked over to welcome her with a warm hug.

Margarita's frozen composure threatened to thaw with the woman's embrace, but she pulled back, patted the other woman on the arm, and managed a smile. "I'm okay, everyone," she said, her gaze taking in the circle of friends. She smiled. "Now, what are we talking about?"

Her group of friends seemed to breathe a collective sigh of relief. "Well, mi amiga," said one of the women, "the usual, I'm afraid. The protests and riots in California. The sad state of the Mexican schools." She looked around the circle. "And the Border Patrol."

Margarita raised her eyebrows. "What about the Border Patrol?"

"Well," said her old friend Willy, "seems they've been straying a bit farther from the border recently. Did you hear about the trains?"

Margarita looked back and forth among her friends. "What trains?"

"The repatriation trains," said Willy. "From Chicago."

"Chicago?" asked Margarita. "No, I haven't exactly been keeping up with the news lately."

Willy's wife put an arm around her. "Of course you haven't, sweetie."

Willy continued, "From what I've read, trains from Chicago, Detroit, and even New York are carrying Mexicans who are being sent back from up there, picking up more in the Southwest on their way. Seems the Border Patrol is now the national anti-Mexican patrol."

Another man continued, "They say that entire barrios of Los Angeles, San Francisco, and even El Paso are empty after the trains go through. All the families are either repatriated or they left before the Patrol could get them."

Margarita frowned at the mention of the city names. She thought of the man who had harassed them at the movie theater. She remembered her daughter's face when she realized they couldn't go see the show. *How smug he must be*, she thought, *now that he's getting what he wants.*

"And many of them were born here!" said one woman.

"How can the Border Patrol operate in places like Chicago and Detroit, so far from the border?" wondered Margarita aloud.

"They're aided by local sheriffs and anti-Mexican groups, from what I hear," said Willy.

"But it's even more complicated than that," said his wife, laying her hand on his arm. "President Hoover says that aid to Mexicans in the States, including any help for the unemployed, is soon to be cut off. People are scared, so they're just leaving. Look at our own town. Six more families gone this month alone."

"Where are they going?" asked Margarita.

The shopkeeper interjected, leaning across the counter: "A few have left forwarding information with me. I guess there's a lot of opportunity deep in Chihuahua state for farmers, miners, teachers, everything. Lots of families are moving there. They take the train—the regular train—south from here."

"That's just what happened after the United States annexed all of north Mexico," said Margarita, "in my great-grandfather's time. Tens of thousands of Mexicans walked south across the border because they didn't want to be US citizens."

"Only now it's the US that doesn't want *us*," said Willy.

"This too shall pass," quoted his wife.

But walking home that day, hand on her belly, Margarita knew that Willy's wife was wrong, that this would *not* pass. From her family's stories, her research and reading, and her and Jorge's own experiences, Margarita knew that anti-Mexican sentiment had become part of the fabric of American culture. She wasn't sure she had the strength to fight it anymore.

At the end of the road from town, the farm rose before her, empty and cold. No smoke breathed from the chimney of the little house; *I'll have to build a fire to warm the house before Violeta gets home*, she thought. For the last two weeks, their life had been moving forward bolstered by practical thoughts like that one: what needed doing, what needed cleaning. But at that moment, standing on the edge of her parents' and grandparents' and great-grandparents' dormant land, Margarita knew that the house would never be warm again, regardless of how many mesquite logs she burned in the iron stove. Without the hope of Jorge ever returning and making them a family of four, the house would remain cold for her no matter how she heated it, the land would remain barren to her despite all her planting, Socorro would remain unsafe for her, just like the country was now. In that moment, she decided.

45

On Monday morning, Silvia woke up jittery about the day's potential discoveries. She checked the date on her phone: November 20th. If Mami hadn't heard her pleas during their bus conversation, she'd be making arrangements to cross the border right now, maybe even looking to hire a coyote. Silvia could have laughed ironically at the word *coyote*, but she was too scared.

Swallowing her panic, Silvia tried to focus on action instead of worry. She went over the day's plan in her mind: they would go to the County Clerk's office the moment it opened, check the records, and then head to their great-great-grandmother's land. If Silvia had her way, by the end of the day they'd have the título in hand and could finally work on getting their mother back legally. She just hoped it wasn't too late.

Stretching, she rested the back of her hand on Lucy's fleece blanket and found it empty. *Maybe she's making breakfast*, Silvia thought. Sebastián still lay sleeping peacefully. She pulled on her sweater and moccasins and slid out of the tent.

Lucy was not in sight, so Silvia decided to get their morning meal and lunch ready while she waited for her siblings to arrive at the breakfast table. When she opened the cooler, she found a note sitting on top of the package of cheese:

Couldn't sleep. Went for a walk. Back by noon.

Noon? Silvia's jaw fell open and her hand holding the note dropped to her side. *I can't believe her. She knows that today is the day I've been waiting for to do research and try to save Mami.* Heart pounding, she snatched the cheese, turkey, and bread out of the cooler and slammed the lid shut. She made the sandwiches that they would take into town that day, wrapped them in plastic, and put them back in the top of the cooler. She pulled out cereal and milk for Sebastián and left the campsite to go for a walk by the lake and clear her head.

When she returned, she scanned anxiously for Lucy, hoping she had come to her senses and returned, but she hadn't. Instead, Sebastián was sitting at the picnic table wearing his pajamas with a sweater over the top, finishing his last spoonful of granola.

"Where's Lucy?" he asked.

"She's out. She left me a note saying that she went for a walk." Silvia sank down onto the picnic bench beside her brother, frowning.

Sebastián scanned her face. "And that's bad?"

Silvia sighed. "Yes, don't you remember?"

The little boy shook his head.

"We were supposed to get into town early to start our research! Today's the day we might find Bisabuela's land."

"Oh yeah! Well, we can do it when she gets back, right?"

Silvia admired the six-year-old's calm acceptance of circumstances as they were. She did not feel the same way. "Right. Well, I guess that means you get the morning to play around here."

"Great! With you?"

The last thing Silvia felt like doing was taking up a walking stick and pretending she was a wilderness explorer. Still, she recognized that the morning would only creep along if she sat around waiting and growing angrier with Lucy. She sighed. "Sure. Let's get our gear."

Sebastián went into the tent and emerged with his flashlight, trowel, binoculars, notebook, and pencil. He shoved them all into a plastic bag that he tied to his belt, and they were off. They spent the next two hours exploring in the woods, digging up "fossils," throwing stones into the lake, and identifying plants. Periodically, Silvia would break character to survey the visible section of road just beyond their campsite or glance at her phone, ignoring the fact that she had no service at Escondida Lake.

Eventually, Silvia and Sebastián returned to the site, she frustrated and he hungry. It was past eleven o'clock and there was no sign of their sister.

Silvia set her brother up at the picnic table with his lunch while she walked to the camp store to see if the ranger had talked to Lucy that morning. She was starting to have a gnawing feeling in the pit of her stomach that could not be remedied by turkey sandwiches.

The door jingled as she entered and the ranger looked up.

"Good morning, Miss. Another beautiful day!"

"Yes, it is," said Silvia, approaching the lacquered wooden counter decorated with stickers from national parks. "I was wondering; did you see my sister this morning? Young girl who was in here with me last night, dark hair probably in a ponytail?"

"Sure, I know her. I called her a taxi this morning."

Silvia tried not to raise her eyebrows or in any way allow her face to register the shock that she felt at her sister going off on her own, and also evidently having taken money from the family's dwindling stash. "Oh. Do you recall where she was going?"

"Yes. Just into town. The center of town, I remember her saying. Why? Is something wrong?"

"No, not at all. I just couldn't remember where I was supposed to meet her," Silvia said. "Would you mind calling me a taxi as well, please?"

"Certainly. What time?"

"Right now, please. I'll just get my brother from the site and we'll come right back." Silvia was already at the door, face turned back to make sure that the manager had gotten her instructions.

"You got it, Miss. See you in a moment."

Silvia jingled out the door, being careful to not let it slam behind her. She ran the tenth of a mile down the road to the campsite and was already talking when she arrived.

"Seba, grab your stuff! We're going into town. Lucy's there."

Sebastián wiped the crumbs from his sandwich off his chin and jumped up. He joined Silvia in the tent and switched his plastic explorer bag for his backpack, which already contained his maps and blue elephant. Silvia made sure her laptop was in her backpack for the afternoon's research and crawled out of the tent with her brother. She grabbed the two remaining sandwiches from the cooler, tossed Sebastián a juice box, and they left the campsite at a jog.

The navy-blue Crown Victoria taxi was pulling into the gravel parking lot in front of the camp store when they arrived. They slid into the back seat and Silvia reached into her pocket. She pressed her lips together as she squeezed the shrinking wad of cash.

"Good morning. Or good afternoon, I guess. To Socorro town center, please," she instructed the driver.

"Yes, Miss."

They pulled out of the camp driveway and onto the highway. "Where are we going?" whispered Sebastián.

"I don't know exactly. The ranger at the camp store said that Lucy took a taxi to the center of town this morning. Let's try the mission first."

"Oooh, now we're on another treasure hunt!" said Sebastián. "For our sister!"

Silvia growled. "Let's hope it's easier than the other one."

They got out of the taxi at the mission and checked inside, then split up and circled the exterior—at a run because Silvia felt uneasy having Sebastián out of her sight while they were in town. They met at the back and then proceeded to walk San Miguel Street in the direction of Otero Avenue. They reasoned that they should check the sites they had visited yesterday since they were familiar to Lucy. On the way, Silvia texted Lucy several times, and tried calling as well. There was no response.

As they walked, Silvia's concern grew. She peered up and down each street that they crossed: California Street, 6th Street, 5th Street. By the time they were crossing under the CanAm Highway, she felt positively sick to her stomach. Sebastián, too, had grown quiet and was plodding along at her side, clearly tired.

They crossed Chaparral Drive and entered the fields that sat in the flood plain of the Rio Grande. This last part of their walk was barren, hot, and seemed futile, but Silvia didn't know what else to do. Somehow a portion of her brain remembered to wonder about the lands they were passing through. Could any of these fields have been their great-great-grandmother's farm?

"I wonder if any of these was Bisabuela's farm." Sebastián echoed her thoughts.

Silvia scowled. "We should have been finding that out today, instead of wandering around town wasting our time."

"It's not a waste, Silvi," said her brother kindly. "I like it here. It's good to get to know the town. Although my feet are kind of hurting."

Silvia glanced at his little feet, dusty in his sports sandals. "Come on, Seba. Get on my back." She switched her backpack to the front and crouched down for him.

"Yay!" He hopped on overenthusiastically, tumbling Silvia forward onto her knees and sliding off her shoulder to the ground. Silvia caught herself with her hands, one of them landing on a spiky rock.

"Geez, Seba. You can't do that to me! If that's what you're going to do, I'm never carrying you again!"

Behind her, the little boy began to cry. Exhausted, Silvia remained on her knees, and folded forward into child's pose on the rocky roadside. In a moment, Sebastián realized she was crying, too, and he flopped onto her back a little more gently to hug her.

"Lo siento, Silvi. It was an accident."

Choked with tears, Silvia managed, "I know it was, Seba. I'm not mad at you." She gently slid her brother off her back and sat back on her heels, pulling him around to her front. For a long minute they embraced awkwardly around Silvia's backpack, crying on each other's shoulders. For the second time that week, Silvia felt like she could just cry forever and never stop. In some ways it would be a relief to just give up and surrender to the exhaustion, the fear, the sorrow. She could finally stop being in charge of everyone. She could just stay there on the road forever, drowning in tears.

Sebastián was the one to pull back first. He pushed on Silvia's forehead to raise her eyes to his. "Hermanota, I'm not mad at you, either. Let's get up. Come on." He tugged at her arm. "Come on! Hey! How about I carry you!"

This last line made her laugh, and it was as if the sun burst out through a rainstorm. Silvia wiped her eyes on her sleeve and pushed her hair back. Then she switched her backpack to the back and picked up her brother in her arms, like when he was a baby. He rested his cheek on her shoulder and they traversed the two long blocks to Otero Park.

Silvia set Sebastián down as they crossed the acequia at the entrance to the dusty parking lot, and he ran the short distance to the shade under the mesquite and cottonwood trees. For a long while, they simply lay in the shade, Sebastián sipping from his juice box and Silvia staring at the undersides of the leaves, dappled with sunlight. Eventually, she sat up, had a drink of water, and told her brother she had a plan.

"Ooh, good. Another plan like Mami," he said, leaning toward her.

Silvia ignored the pangs of loss she felt at the reminder of her mother and her plans, and by extension, of Melinda's criticisms …

"I have cell service here in town," she said. "So we're going to call a taxi and take a ride through the city to look for Lucy one more time. If we don't find her, we're going back to the campground to see if she's returned."

"Perfect," he said. "But do we have enough money?"

"We'll make it work," said Silvia, deeply upset with Lucy for wasting their time and money.

In twenty minutes, a taxi arrived, piloted by the same driver who had brought them into town earlier. Settled in the air-conditioned back seat, Silvia peered out the passenger's side and Sebastián, the driver's side. For nearly thirty minutes, they crisscrossed Socorro's grid of streets, passing hotels, grocery stores, restaurants, bodegas, salons, churches, and banks. They circled the town's historic plaza, then made the large Fisher Avenue to Grant Street loop, coming back into the town center via Church Street. Silvia stole frequent glances at the taxi's meter, ticking up at a steady pace. She noticed with clenched teeth that they passed the Socorro County Clerk's office, where they should have been doing their research all day. Instead, it was midafternoon and there was no sign of Lucy.

Eventually even the driver was concerned. "Miss, do you want me to call the police?"

"No!" said Silvia and Sebastián together.

"I mean, no thank you. I'm sure it was just a miscommunication," Silvia said.

She directed the driver back to Escondida Lake. She didn't tell Sebastián, but her plan was in fact to involve the police if Lucy was not back at the campground. Trembling, she pulled the silver door handle after the car slowed to a stop in front of their campsite. She gave the driver the $34.17 taxi fare that they absolutely couldn't afford and burst out of the car, pulling Sebastián along behind her.

Lucy's backpack was on the picnic table. Silvia looked around frantically and saw Lucy's shoes sitting outside the tent, the zipper slightly open from the bottom. Mustering all the self-control she had, she asked Sebastián to please go play at the lakeshore for a few minutes while she worked things out with Lucy. Cheered, he ran down the path toward the shore and Silvia stalked to the tent. She roughly tugged the zipper open. Lucy was inside, lying on her back, one knee crossed over the other, reading. Instantly, Silvia metamorphosed from worried mother to enraged sister.

"Where have you been?" she screamed. Tears sprang into her eyes as her face crumpled into angry tears.

Lucy was calm, even coolly annoyed. She laid her magazine down slowly across her stomach. "Here. I got here at, like, one and you guys were gone." She sat up onto her elbows and furrowed her brow. "I should be asking you the same question. Where have you been? I've wasted the whole day waiting for you in this tent in the middle of nowhere."

Silvia's shock instantly dried her tears. "*You've* wasted the day? *We've* wasted the day searching for you! Do you know what we did?" Silvia looked around, suddenly feeling claustrophobic in the nylon tent. "Follow me. Now!" she growled.

Lucy took her time getting her shoes on and crawling out of the tent. Silvia towered imperiously over the tent exit, determined to reclaim her power in the argument.

"We walked the entire route we traveled yesterday, looking for you in town. We took a taxi around the city, searching up and down each and every street for my thirteen-year-old sister who was probably out getting naked with 'new friends' or buying drugs from strangers!"

"What?" yelled Lucy. "That's what you think I—"

Silvia cut her off. "No, you don't talk now. You listen. We spent the last of our money searching for you. And you must have taken some to get into town! We don't even have enough to buy food! We'll be lucky to get home at all!"

Lucy stared at the ground, jaw clenched.

"Look at me!" Silvia screamed.

Lucy raised her eyes, narrowed and cold.

"I called you and sent you messages. Your little brother walked all the way to Otero Park." Silvia's voice cracked, thinking of their shared meltdown on Otero Avenue.

"Silvia, you—"

"No!" Silvia yelled, unable to stop her rant. "You ruined this day. You spent our money. You wasted the time we were supposed to spend finding the legal rights to our land. Our land, Lucy! It's yours, too, so you should care!"

"Wait!" Lucy shouted, taking a step toward Silvia.

Silvia stepped back. "No! I'm done waiting! Do you know that with each day we let pass by, there's a greater chance that Mami will cross the border with some coyote and possibly get captured or killed! This is our only chance to save her! You wasted the one chance we had to prove that Mami belongs here and bring her back! I knew you were a selfish teenager, but I can't believe you are selfish enough to put our mother in danger!"

"Silvia!" yelled Lucy, eyes blazing, stomping her foot and simultaneously pointing at something behind Silvia.

"What?" Silvia screamed, turning around. There, on the path from the lake, stood Sebastián, face crumpled in a grimace of grief, soaked with tears, Blue Elephant dangling from his hand.

46

Tuesday morning dawned with the relentless optimism of New Mexico sunshine, but the memories of the day before crashed down on Silvia's stomach like a lead weight. They had spent the rest of the afternoon and night in near silence. Silvia had taken her brother aside to comfort him at one point, but she insisted that Lucy do all the explaining of the complicated situations that Sebastián had overheard, since it was Lucy's fault that he heard it in the first place.

After a pathetic dinner of more turkey sandwiches, Silvia said, "I'm going to bed."

"But why, Silvi?" Sebastián asked. "It's not even dark yet!"

Silvia glanced at Lucy, sitting with her back to the two of them at the picnic table.

"Can I at least walk you to the bathhouse?" he asked, his face drooping.

"Sure, kiddo."

Silvia stopped in the tent to grab her toothbrush and towel. Then she took Sebastián by the hand and together they walked through the trees toward the small brown log cabin. The lights were already on in the restrooms at either end of the building, pinkish fluorescents bouncing off the institutional white tile, defying the soft greens and browns of the woods just outside.

Silvia sighed and squeezed her brother's hand. "You know, you were very brave today."

"When?" he looked up at her.

"While we were searching for Lucy."

"And after, too, right?"

Silvia knew he was thinking about their fight. "Yes, after, too."

Sebastián smiled and returned his gaze to the path.

"I'm going to need you to be brave a little bit longer, you know," Silvia said.

"That's no problem. I'm practically a superhero."

Silvia grinned in the dusky light. "Well, good, because I could use a superhero about now."

Her brother pulled away from her, spread his arms, and ran the rest of the distance to the bathhouse. "See?" he shouted back from the doorway, swatting at a moth that was fluttering around the screen door to the family restroom. "I got this!"

I'm glad somebody does, thought Silvia, following him into the log cabin.

When they got back to the site, Silvia hugged Sebastián and grunted a good-night to Lucy at the picnic table, before crawling into the tent. When her head hit the pillow, angry tears followed, splashing down onto the cold pillowcase until sleep overtook her.

Now she stretched and consciously did some deep breathing to try to wake up and to relieve the weight of anxiety on her solar plexus. She breathed in to the count of three, then out to the count of five. When she was satisfied, she stretched her arms to the sides, bumping Sebastián on one side and an empty fleece blanket on the other.

Instantly her breath caught in her throat and she sat upright, visually confirming her sister's absence. Quietly, she pulled on her sweater, unzipped the tent with trembling fingers, and crawled over Sebastián's form in the sleeping bag, landing in her sneakers outside. She zipped the tent closed as silently as she could, then straightened and surveyed the campsite. Lucy's backpack was sitting on the picnic table, so Silvia allowed her breathing to relax a bit.

She's probably in the bathhouse, she thought. Good. I'll go in and apologize for yelling at her and maybe we can salvage this trip. It's only Tuesday, after all, and the County Clerk's Office opens at nine.

But Lucy wasn't in the bathhouse, nor was she at the campsite when Silvia returned. Silvia laid a hand on her chest, trying to calm her heartbeat. She peeked in one of the tent's screened windows to confirm that Sebastián was still asleep in the tent, then decided to take a walk by the lake to keep her head clear and the panic at bay.

As she approached the water, a stiff breeze blew up suddenly. Silvia pulled her sweater around herself and crossed her arms. She scanned the path in either direction. To her left, halfway down the shore, Lucy was standing with her back to Silvia, facing a tall tree stump. She was busy with something in front of her, and Silvia thought, with a roll of her eyes, *Leave it to the middle-schooler to find the pocket of Wi-Fi in the wilderness.* As she approached, however, she saw that Lucy had an array of little baggies spread out before her, along with a folded paper and a small plastic cup.

"What exactly do you think you're doing?" she demanded, stalking up behind her sister.

Lucy jumped and hurriedly began gathering up her items. "Geez! Why are you sneaking up on me like that? Can't I ever have any privacy?"

"Not after yesterday! No you cannot!" Silvia's voice cut through the breeze and rang through the trees, too loud for the early dawn. "I can't believe you brought this here, after all the conversations we've had, after all the times I checked your backpack!"

Lucy was stuffing the bags into a little box.

"What is that? What do you have? You may as well show me, since Mrs. Black already told me, anyway!"

Lucy looked over her shoulder, mouth open like a mountain lion. "Told you what?"

"About your ... habit!" Silvia screamed out the last word and then began sobbing, against her will. "Now here we are in the middle of nowhere and you're endangering us with illegal substances!" She began running back up the path, into the wind and away from Lucy.

"Silvia! It's not what you think ..."

Silvia whirled around to face her sister again, hands clenched. Her hair broke loose from its bun in the wind and she shook her head violently to move it away from her eyes. "Oh, it's exactly what I think!"

"Nope, wrong again, Miss College Student! You think you have it all figured out, but you're always wrong! You were wrong about Mami and you're wrong about me!"

Silvia lowered her voice to a deep octave. "What about Mami?" she spat.

"You said she had a plan to keep us all safe until she got back. Well, she didn't. Either that or you were just too stupid to follow it. Because we're not safe!"

Silvia blinked at the insult, then screamed, "You're right: we're not safe here! Because of you! This is about you, remember! Not me, not Mami."

Lucy turned back to her packing, but her hands stilled over her supplies. Her shoulders slumped, she heaved a deep sigh. Then she began dumping everything out again on the stump. "Okay, look! See for yourself! See how wrong you are—again!"

Silvia shook her hair back and walked back to the stump, feet growing heavier with every step. This was it; she couldn't be in denial about Lucy's problems any longer. Her hands were shaking, so she stuffed them in her pockets as she came in sight of the stump. Piled on it were seven or eight little zipped baggies, some with green or brown flakes inside, some with white dust, one with yellow powder. Lucy's cup and disposable spoon were both coated with a greenish liquid. Silvia laid a hand on her chest, trying to quell her rising nausea. Then she set her jaw and looked Lucy in the eye.

"Well?"

Lucy stared down at the stump. She spoke quietly. "It started a few months ago. I was having irregular bleeding and really bad cramps and I didn't know what to do about it. I was scared to go to the doctor because I knew we were short on money. Plus, what if something was seriously wrong? How could we have afforded to get me treatment?"

Silvia blinked at Lucy, trying to comprehend. "So you started … this," Silvia's sweeping gesture took in the array of supplies, "to escape from your problems."

Lucy met her eyes. "No! I started this to solve my problems."

Silvia curled her lip and stared at her sister. Nothing in their upbringing had ever suggested that turning to drugs was a way to solve problems. She was going to have to figure out rehabilitation for Lucy once they got home. She wouldn't even know where to start! Suddenly exhausted, she sank down onto a rock along the sandy path.

"Silvi, just look." Lucy brought a handful of the baggies over to her sister and thrust one toward her. "This one's turmeric. It's supposed to help shrink cysts if there are any."

Silvia raised her eyebrows and looked at the fine golden powder. "Okay …"

"And this one?" Lucy crouched down and showed her a bag of a crushed brownish substance. "It's cramp bark. I'm supposed to drink it mixed with water three times a day. It's for, well, cramps."

"Who gave you these?"

"Well, *these* I got in town yesterday. That's where I went, to the herb shop. It opened later than I thought, so that's why I was late." Lucy's eyes searched Silvia's face. "But I was originally prescribed them by my friend Susana's tía. She's a curandera. She's half Cherokee and half Mexican. She's sort of a shaman. I've been seeing her at her house over in Blanco Gardens since September."

Silvia paused to put it together, remembering that Agent Randolph saw Lucy on that side of town. "Oh my God, Lucy. Why couldn't you have just told me? Do you know what I thought?"

Lucy's stood up over Silvia. "Of course I know what you thought! That's why I was too mad to talk to you about it. I couldn't believe that's what you thought of me." Lucy paused, her eyes filling with tears. "But I was scared, too. I am scared. I still don't know what's wrong with me."

"Okay, do you promise me that this is really it? That there's nothing more to your secrecy than this?"

"I swear."

"And no more running off? And no more lies?"

"Promise."

Silvia flopped backward, then yelped as she landed on a spiky pine cone. Both girls laughed, probably more than they ordinarily would have. Lucy reached out her hands and pulled Silvia up off the ground.

Silvia hugged her. "Okay, then. We're going to take you to the doctor when we get home and find out what's wrong. It'll be okay. I've been a bunch of times and it's really not that bad. I'll go with you."

"I just need Mami."

"Yeah, you do. We all do. But for now, you'll have to deal with me." Silvia tried a smile. "I'm sorry I've had to check up on you. And I'm sorry for all the yelling, yesterday and today. But seriously, no more secrets, okay? I can't take any more of this. Plus, I can only help if I know what's going on."

"I know. I'm sorry. But don't tell Seba, okay? About my cramps and stuff?" Lucy wiped her eyes.

"Of course I won't."

Lucy tucked her paraphernalia into her backpack and they strolled back to the campsite arm in arm. Sebastián was awake and waiting for them, sitting on the picnic bench, staring toward the trees.

"Where were you? I thought you had both left me!"

"We just went for a walk, Seba. It's all good." Silvia rumpled his hair, then went to the cooler to get their breakfast out. There was hardly anything left, but she found some milk and half a bag of cold cereal. As she brought the food to the table, she remembered their plans. "Let's eat quick! We've got a big day ahead!"

They ate, then packed apples for lunch. At close to nine o'clock, the three walked to the camp office to call a taxi to take them into town. Ten minutes later, their ride arrived and they headed directly to the Socorro County Clerk's office, armed with the laptop, the diary, the atlas, and the screenshots Silvia had taken on her phone.

Once they reached the correct office, a smallish carpeted corner room with two round work tables and Wi-Fi, Lucy and Sebastián settled down at a table to log in and begin searching the online census and marriage records. Silvia headed to the Public Records desk and asked the clerk on duty, a friendly woman in her thirties, for the files on all land parcels in Socorro with frontage on the Rio Grande. When the woman returned with a considerable stack of legal files, Silvia sat down at one of the wooden tables to read.

She opened the first folder and leafed through the documents it contained: certificates of occupancy, building permits, a deed, and a survey record. A few of the documents were from the first half of the twentieth century, but most were newer. She began to flip through the other files, checking the dates. Two she was able to eliminate immediately for being new construction.

After nearly ninety minutes, Lucy and Sebastián called her over to their work table. They had found Margarita's marriage record but weren't able to find her name in the 1920 or 1930 census.

"We're looking under Vargas, just like Bisabuelo is listed in the marriage records, but there's nothing there. Do you think they rented their farm and didn't own it?" Lucy asked.

"No way," said Silvia. "First of all, even if you're a tenant, you still get counted in the census. Secondly, Margarita is very clear that this is her land, granted to her ancestors by the Spanish. Also, she wouldn't have a título or escritura if she were just a tenant. There would be no treasure to hide."

This got Sebastián's attention. "No treasure? That's impossible," he said, turning back to the computer. "What if we look under her own name, not her married name?"

"Sebastián, that's it!" Silvia nearly shouted, squeezing onto her brother's chair in front of their laptop. She glanced up at the other clerk at his desk, who was looking at her, unamused, over his reading glasses. Silvia whispered, "If the título was in her name, maybe they did the census in her name, too, just to be sure the records matched. I know from the diary that she was worried about losing her land, like so many other Mexican Americans in town." Silvia's hands hovered over the keys. "Wait. I don't know Margarita's last name." She looked at her brother and sister in turn.

"The marriage record!" Lucy and Sebastián said together.

Silvia and Lucy quickly changed places at the computer and Lucy reopened the database of marriage and death records that they had used a few minutes before. She keyed in *Vargas* again. "It's Rosas!" she announced.

All three siblings froze for a moment. Rosas, like their mom's first name.

"Wow," said Silvia quietly, her voice thick. "Mami got her name."

"Now let's get her land!" said Sebastián, slapping his hand down on the table, bringing them back to their task.

Silvia looked again at the clerk, mouthing "sorry" at him to apologize for Sebastián's noise. "Okay, let's try," she said to her siblings.

Lucy clicked open the census file for 1920 and keyed in *Rosas*. Several records came up. She read each address aloud and Sebastián marked each one with an X on his map. In the end, they narrowed the results down to the only two possibilities near the river.

Together, they ran over to Silvia's table to look at the property files for each one. Both were on the river, both had acequias running through them. According to the surveys, however, only one of the properties showed a change in elevation, leading Silvia to posit that Margarita's hillside with its mesquite tree could only be there. Furthermore, that property, located on Riverside Road, seemed to be large enough to have been a farm at the time of the census, while the other was much more modest.

Just then, the female clerk who had retrieved the files for Silvia came over to their table and whispered something in her ear. Silvia drew back and looked at the woman, brow knitted and mouth open. The woman nodded and hurriedly gathered up the files from the table.

Silvia stood up. "We've got to go. Now!" she said to her siblings.

47

Catching Silvia's urgency like a virus, her brother and sister gathered their backpacks, closed the computer, and stood up from their chairs. Silvia shoved the laptop into her bag and the three headed toward the back stairwell where the kind clerk was holding the door open for them.

"Be careful," she whispered to Silvia as the three passed through the doorway. She pressed something into Silvia's hand.

"Thanks," said Silvia, pressing her lips together. As she passed through the door, she looked down at the ten-dollar bill that the woman had given her.

"What's going on?" demanded Lucy, once the fire door had closed behind them.

As they rattled down the two flights of stairs to the back parking lot, Silvia explained that the clerk had told her that she had overheard her colleague on the phone with Immigration. He was suspicious of the three "Mexican kids" looking at all the town records and was sure they were up to no good, maybe even domestic terrorism. From experience, the clerk thought that ICE could arrive within a very few minutes, so she called a taxi for the kids and sent them down the back stairs as quickly and as quietly as possible.

"She even gave me taxi money," Silvia finished.

"So what do we do now?" asked Lucy.

"The only thing we can do. Find the deed!" said Silvia, sliding into the waiting car and directing the driver to Riverside Road.

In no more than three minutes they were there, stepping out of the navy-blue town car onto what they all hoped was their family's land. Keenly aware that this might very well be their only shot, Silvia was initially crestfallen to find the land vacant and overgrown with brambles. No house nor structure of any kind was in sight on this land that sloped gently up from the road toward its highest point, a rise in the distance that Silvia knew must overlook the river.

For a moment, the three stood uncertainly at the edge of the field as the taxi drove off. After a beat, Silvia called out, "Let's head toward the rise along the river," and they began to run through the tall grasses.

After only a few steps, Lucy rolled her ankle on a loose stone sitting atop the dry soil.

"You okay?" Silvia called back to her.

"Yes! Keep going!" shouted Lucy, beginning to hop on every third step to give her ankle a rest without sacrificing speed.

About halfway into the lot, Silvia stopped just short of falling into the ruins of a stone foundation. She took a moment to look down over the structure. It was made of layers of river rocks, the gaps between them filled in with sandy cement. A few feet of chimney stood at one end and the entire foundation was no more than twenty by twenty feet.

Silvia took in these details in a flash, then turned sharply to the right to go around the foundation, then back to the left to continue on straight up the rise. Only now she was marching instead of running, and counting as she went.

"Seven … eight … nine … ten …" Sebastián caught up to her and got into step.

"… twenty-one … twenty-two … twenty-three … twenty-four …" they counted together, as Lucy hopped up to join them.

"… forty-three … forty-four … forty-five …" They jumped over the brownish acequia.

"… fifty-seven … fifty-eight … fifty-nine …" Sebastián was beginning to lag behind, so Lucy grabbed one of his hands and Silvia the other. They pulled him along between them as they climbed, all counting in unison now. Lucy seemed to have forgotten her twisted ankle.

" … seventy-two … seventy-three … seventy-four … seventy-five!"

Reaching the top, they peered down the steep bank of the rise at the Rio Grande reflecting blue below. To Silvia's great joy, they were only a few yards away from a gnarled mesquite tree with an impressive canopy and many dangling seed pods. Beneath it was a dense cluster of undergrowth. Panting, Silvia pointed at a plant with spiky greenery.

"Soaptree," she gasped.

"This has to be the spot," Sebastián said.

"Let's start digging," Silvia instructed.

Sebastián pulled out the garden trowel that he had brought in his backpack for rock hunting and began to fight his way into the undergrowth. He scratched at the earth's surface for a few moments while Lucy and Silvia circled the tree looking for the most likely spot for Margarita to have hidden the título.

After a while, Sebastián plunked down in the undergrowth, head sagging. "Ouch!" he shouted, jumping up.

"What?" asked Silvia, rushing toward him, fearing a bee or rattlesnake.

"Thorns," Sebastián said, rubbing his upper left thigh.

"Oh, yeah, mesquites can have thorns," said Silvia, remembering the illustrations in her botany textbook.

"No, it wasn't the tree. It was the ground." Sebastián turned around to look.

At once, Silvia caught a flash of pink beneath all the green yucca fronds. "Move a minute, Seba," she said, sidling her way into the scrub. "Is that ...?"

"A rose!" shouted Lucy, pointing. The three looked at each other in turn, the possibility dawning upon them.

"Rosa!" shouted Sebastián.

"Let's do it," said Silvia, reaching out her hand for the trowel. Her brother and sister crowded in as closely as they could, while Silvia cut away the overgrown yuccas to reveal a thick stem of old rosebush, covered with dense spines. "This has to be the spot," she said, straightening up. "But I'm going to have to destroy the bush to get under it." She looked regretfully at her siblings.

"Do it!" they said in unison.

Silvia gingerly plucked the bright pink rose that had led them to the precise spot and tucked it into her sweater pocket. Then, setting her jaw, she began loosening the dry soil on one side of the thick wood, while stomping on the plant with her boot to attempt to uproot it by tipping. Within a few moments, her whole weight was on the stalk, pinning it toward the ground on one side, while the soil on the opposite side began to heave. With Lucy digging to further loosen the earth, the root ball suddenly popped into sight.

At the same time, they heard a car door slam across the field and turned to see an unmarked black SUV parked along the road and a man and a woman in black track suits running across the field.

Frantically, Silvia hacked through the root ball with the pointed end of the trowel. When she heard a clink, she hacked harder and faster, at last removing a rusted biscuit can from eighty years of underground safety. She tossed it to Sebastián, who stowed it in his backpack and then whirled around to stand with Lucy facing the approaching ICE agents. Silvia came to stand beside them, and together they held hands at the summit of the land and of their dreams.

48

Yesterday I said goodbye to the only home I've ever known—the final closing up of my ancestral home. As a child, I used to so relish closing up the farm, in the days before I knew danger and instability and pain and grief. Back then, closing up had meant that the physical labor and heat of the summer was over, and that my family would soon spend the winter cozied up in the little home that my grandfather had built atop the foundation that his grandfather had built of rocks from the Rio Grande. So for my final closing up, I waited until Violeta was at school, and absolutely every last chore was done.

Margarita paused, her pen suspended. The memories from the last four weeks rushed through her mind as she glanced at Violeta beside her on the train seat.

"Yes, Mami," the little girl had said, standing forlornly by the door.

For a moment, Margarita had stood looking at Violeta, bravely pushing through her grief to face the next phase of her life. On the outside, with her duffle bag and porcelain doll, she looked the same as she had the day they had left for El Paso. But that was terribly long ago, when the scale one measured by was happiness and hope.

Margarita had spent the time since Violeta's return to school doing the most final "closing up" of her life: the unfathomable end of her plan. Before sharing her decision with Violeta, Margarita settled the finances, both obligations and resources. She visited the office of the company she had contracted with to buy her cotton and barley crops, returning their cash and arranging for them to pick up the seeds that she had purchased for direct sowing next month. She went to the bank and withdrew all of their savings from last year and this, including her soap money, their crop earnings, and Jorge's wages.

Then she sat down with Violeta at their dining table. "Amor, it's time for us to have a new adventure."

Violeta looked up with an interest that was rare in recent weeks. "Okay. What is it?"

"Well, I think we need a change of scenery. A new perspective for a while."

"Like a trip?"

"Yes, querida." Margarita laid a trembling hand on her chest to calm her heart. "We're going to take a trip. Soon."

"Do I get to miss school again?" asked Violeta.

"Yes, you do," smiled Margarita.

"Fine." The little girl smiled, but Margarita remembered the last time they were planning a trip, when she jumped around whooping for joy. That little girl was gone, replaced by a much more serious one. "So where are we going?"

Margarita's eyes wandered over to the window above the kitchen sink. She let her gaze fall on the empty window box with just a few dried flowers left in it. "I think we're going to Mexico. I think we're going to go for a long time." She looked back at Violeta for her reaction.

Tears suddenly sprang up in Violeta's eyes. "How long? Who will take care of our animals? What about the planting?"

"Well, very soon I won't be able to work because of the baby. I'm not able to handle the planting this year." She scanned her daughter's face for comprehension. "Which means we won't have money from the cotton or barley. And without Papi's salary—" Margarita broke off.

"But I can do the planting, Mami. You know I'm a good worker!"

"Yes, you are. But even you can't run a farm all by yourself. Soon your sister will be here and I'm going to need your help with her, too. The farm is just too much for us right now."

By then Violeta was openly crying. "May I go to my room, Mami?" she sobbed.

"Yes, you may, hijita."

Margarita waited, wondering if she had handled this right, if she should have told her daughter more about the realities of their finances. Or more truthfully, should she have told her that it was the precarious situation of Mexicans in the United States that had ruined her peace with their land? Could she have made her daughter feel once again that she didn't belong, that because of her skin color and her heritage, she might not be safe in her country? Should she have told her that as a single mother, she worried about their life in Socorro, when so many other families had fled or been deported? Since the conversation in the store, Margarita had decided that she alone was going to be master of their fate, not an angry white man, not a Border Patrol, not a president.

Rather than continuing to lament and analyze their situation and her life as a mother without a husband, Margarita stood up from the table and set to work making Violeta's favorite dinner: arroz con pollo. Trying not to think, she fried the rice in a little oil in the ceramic pot that her mother always used to use. She added a small jar of pureed onion and tomato that she got from the pantry and stirred quickly with her smooth wooden spoon while the mixture sizzled. As she knew it would, eventually the warm aroma drew the little girl out of her room.

Violeta entered the kitchen with red eyes, but smiling bravely. "I'm not mad at you, Mami. And I do love adventures. As long as we're together, I guess we'll be okay."

Margarita walked over to her and crouched down, pulling her daughter in for an embrace. "You are so grown up, Violeta. I hope and pray we can come back, maybe when your sister is a big girl like you. But for now, let's make the most of our adventure." Margarita pulled back to look in Violeta's eyes, pink-rimmed and puffy like her own. They smiled as tears came down both of their faces.

They spent the subsequent days seeing to the care of their belongings. Violeta passed the evenings packing and unpacking her duffle, trying to squeeze in all of her prized possessions alongside her clothes. She brought a favorite dress, scarf, or hat to school nearly every day to give to a friend. So caught up was she in the excitement of giving that she sometimes even smiled or laughed through her grief.

At Violeta's insistence, Margarita handled the redistribution of their animals while the little girl was at school. She entrusted Pastor to the next farmer over, who also gratefully took their two cows. The mission church and school happily accepted the chickens, and on Saturday morning Fr. Rodríguez himself came with a tractor and three men to move the coop into town while Violeta read *Aesop's Fables* in a loud voice in her room with the door shut.

At last, everything was ready and accounted for. Violeta went to school for her last day, and Margarita attended to the task she had most dreaded, the reason she had never allowed herself to even imagine going through with the final stage of her plan: saying goodbye to the only home she had ever known. Since she planned a practical and dry-eyed departure the next morning in order to minimize the pain for her daughter, she allowed herself one day to indulge in the separation ritual that she needed in order to be strong enough to walk out that door.

First, she bade farewell to the house, room by room. She started in the kitchen, her fingers tracing the wooden cabinets that her grandfather had made. She looked out her window between the curtains she had sewn of the fabric that Jorge had brought home last summer, his last summer. Angry tears burned her eyes as she realized how cheated she felt, cheated out of the new start they could have had, the father her girls would have had, the additional babies she would never have. Her hand dropped to the counter at that last sudden realization. She could have had more babies, more girls. Violeta could have had more sisters. Four weeks since Jorge's death, and she still couldn't accept the injustice.

Wiping her eyes, she dropped her gaze to the vacant window box just outside, and then to her herb garden below, dormant in the late spring chill. Before she left the kitchen, she grabbed her rosebud knife and tucked it into the pocket of her apron, fingers tracing the smooth carved handle as she continued her farewell tour.

A few steps later, she rubbed her hands over the long wooden dining table that Jorge had made for her and where she had sewn her baby's clothes and written out her hopes and fears in her diary. Closing her eyes, she leaned both hands on the table and allowed herself to remember. She heard the laughter of little Violeta as she played with her father, and the determined notes of her "Long, Long Ago" on the piano. The scents of the meals they'd shared there wafted through her consciousness: turkey or roast beef during the times of abundance, beans and chili during the leaner years. Slowly she opened her eyes, recording the golden hue of the shiny pine, each curvilinear grain mark. Her tears dripped onto the shiny surface, and she left them there to dry.

After a moment, Margarita straightened up, rubbing her belly, and walked past Jorge's chair near the door. She went down the tiny hallway with three doorways. The one on the right was the pantry door, tucked under the stairs to the attic. She opened it, peeking in at the remainder of their winter stash. With one finger, she traced the metal lids of the last few jars of stewed tomatoes, pickles, onions. Her hand stopped and her breath caught on an empty Uneeda Biscuit tin, the yellow-jacketed boy peering out from the label. The touch of the can brought back a series of memories all at once: her father joyfully returning home with a can for her from the big city, Jorge's smiling face as he pulled a tin from his pocket to hand to her, and that one special can stuffed with precious documents that she had buried nearly a year ago under the rose root. She picked up the tin and tucked it into her apron pocket beside the knife.

The door on the left was Violeta's room, which Margarita had many times imagined that her two girls would share. Violeta's bed was neatly made with the purple blossom–strewn calico spread that Margarita had sewn for her. A potted bean seedling sat on her windowsill; Violeta had insisted that one of the "babies" live with her. A bedside table held the *Aesop's Fables* book and a lamp. Violeta's porcelain doll reclined on the bed, not yet willing to be stuffed inside the duffle that sat on the floor by the door. Margarita smiled. This room was the perfect reflection of a girl with dreams.

She sighed and approached the center doorway, the one that opened to her and Jorge's room, where their babies had been conceived, where countless late conversations of dreams and plans had occurred. And where stony silence had stood between them last summer on too many nights. With the mix of feelings washing over her, Margarita didn't think she knew how to say goodbye to that room. She'd be sleeping there

Sara A. Leman

that night, anyway. She exhaled and pulled the door closed.

She then ascended to the attic, creeping up the pine steps that her husband had built two years ago—before their problems—so that she could sow their dreams and tend their future through the long winters while he was away. She stood under the peak of the roof, feeling an agonizing guilt that she was condemning innocent baby plants to die by negligence. She pictured them reaching up toward the skylight then shriveling when its heat seared their dehydrated leaves. Eventually they would be nothing more than crusty brown remnants of life, aborted before even feeling the breeze or tasting the rain.

Margarita rubbed her belly as her baby kicked inside her. Impulsively, she bent over her bulging stomach and lifted one of the trays of seedlings, the green beans. Since she hadn't watered them since making her decision to leave Socorro, the tray was alarmingly light. Carefully, she backed down the stairs, holding the tray in front of her and setting it on a stair when she needed to rest. When she reached the solid floor of the house, she turned and brought the tray outside, laying it on the sun-warmed soil of her kitchen garden.

At least here they'll have a chance at life, she thought, returning to the house for the next tray. *Life without us.*

Margarita spent all morning in a flurry of transporting and then transplanting beans, tomatoes, lettuces, spinach, broccoli, cabbage, cauliflower, her spirits rising like the seedlings toward the April sun. Once they were all in the ground, she brought a pail of water from the acequia, watered them, and tucked them in with dry leaves from the mulch pile in hopes that they would be shielded from the remaining spring cold. She knew that they could easily push through the leaves in their quest to reach the sun. She imagined, if not neighbor children finding and eating their fruits, certainly deer, raccoons, mice, and birds benefitting from the little legacy that she was leaving behind.

Flushed but smiling, she turned to face the high point of the land, the rise with her mesquite tree on top. Wiping her hands on her apron, she began to walk, and then to run, hands under her baby to shield her from the bouncing. She automatically counted the steps:

"One … two … three …"

At precisely seventy-five, she was atop the rise, beside her tree with the new rose beneath it, facing the sparkling river below. The river was high with runoff and rain, but the Rio Grande's normally brown waters reflected the blue sky and gray clouds above. Inhaling deeply, Margarita rubbed her belly.

"Someday you'll come back here, bebé," she whispered, glancing at the *Rosa floribunda* and picturing the documents hidden safely underneath. "A nuestra tierra."

49

The intake officers at the ICE Processing Center in El Paso spoke in low voices. "Weren't they caught in New Mexico?"

"Yeah, but the agents operate out of Texas, so they're here."

"Should we split them up like the others?"

"Just put them wherever there's room."

One officer took Lucy and Silvia by the arms and began to walk them to the right. Another grabbed Sebastián's hand and turned toward the left hallway.

Silvia heard him begin to speak and then almost immediately crescendo to a yell. "No. No! Don't take me away! No! Silvi!"

She twisted around in her officer's grip and spotted her brother pulling with all his small weight against the officer's hand. She saw him throw himself on the floor, screaming and crying for her.

"Oh, whatever, kid," the officer grumbled. "Just go with her. I got better things to do." He kicked with the toe of his shoe at Sebastián's feet, then stepped over him and went back to the intake room, leaving him lying on the white floor.

The little boy pulled himself to his feet and ran to Silvia, throwing his arms around her waist and sobbing.

"It's okay, Seba, it's okay. We're together. I won't let you go," Silvia said, wrenching her arm away from the guard to hold her little brother.

Sebastián had his arms wrapped around his stomach and was still crying softly when they arrived at their holding room. They found themselves in the company of twelve other detainees awaiting "processing." After making sure that her brother and sister were all right, Silvia talked softly with the others and learned that the deportation process could be completed in a matter of days, or could delay for weeks or even several months. Two of the roommates had already been there for four months.

One of them, Mayra, a woman in her mid-fifties, immediately took the three kids under her wing. She spoke comfortably in English as well as in Spanish, so she was able to communicate with Silvia in relative privacy when necessary, as well as with Lucy and Sebastián, who spoke less Spanish. She also had access to paper and pen, so she spent some of the first few hours playing tic-tac-toe with Sebastián and writing simple sentences for him to practice reading in Spanish. When they were done, she gave him some paper from underneath her bunk to draw on, and he lay down on his stomach on the floor looking much calmer than when they had come in.

That night, Mayra reminded Silvia that, if in fact she was a citizen, she was owed a phone call. Although Silvia had no documentation to prove her citizenship, the guards acquiesced to one call, but would not allow her access to her computer or her own phone. The only phone number that Silvia knew from memory was Melinda's, and she prayed that she would answer, and that this time, above all others, she would listen.

"Hello?" came her friend's answer on the line.

For a moment Silvia couldn't find her voice, but she knew this was her one chance to save her siblings. "Melinda, it's Silvia. I'm in trouble."

"Silvi. What's wrong? Where are you?" For once, her friend sounded attentive.

"This is my one phone call so I need you to listen hard. Do you have something to write on?"

"Your one phone call! Oh my God." Silvia heard shuffling on the other end, and then Melinda said, "Okay, go ahead."

"Seba, Lucy, and I are at an immigration processing center. We're in El Paso. That's the ICE Processing Center in El Paso. Got it?"

"Yes, got it." Melinda sounded panicked. "But you're not immigrants! You were born here. Just like me!"

"Not just like you. Apparently not just like you at all. But listen."

"I'm here."

Silvia felt her eyes tear up at her friends' phrase, but she continued.

"They won't let me see my phone or computer, so I need you to get a message to the only person that I think can help us." Silvia's voice was nearly breaking.

"It's gonna be okay, Silvi. Who is it?" asked Melinda.

"It's my advisor at Penn, Dr. Kathleen Cisneros. You'll find her on the School of Social Work's website. *C-i-s-n-e-r-o-s*."

"Okay. Call or email?"

"Both, if you have to, but try calling first. Tell her where I am, that we've been detained, and that we assume they're going to deport us. Tell her we don't have passports or anything, and we need help." Silvia paused, bit her finger hard, and did anything she could to hold back her tears.

"Okay, I will. Right away. How can I contact you?"

"I don't think you can." Silvia's heart raced with panic. Her words came out in a torrent: "Could you ask Dr. Cisneros if she could possibly call someone and get us out of here? I know that she used to work with immigrants at the border. If she knows a lawyer or anyone who can help us, I'll pay the bill as soon as I can. We just need help."

"Okay. Let me call her right now. Just tell me this: Are you safe? Are you in danger right now?"

Silvia looked around the small office at the three men in uniform sitting at desks. A uniformed woman stood by her side during the phone call. "No, we're okay. We've met a woman who is sort of taking care of us, and we have food and beds. The only danger is that they might send us to Mexico. And we don't know where Mami is!" Silvia began sobbing.

"I know. All right. Let me go call now. Hang in there, Silvia. We'll get you out."

Silvia clutched the phone to her ear. "Wait! Tell Dr. Cisneros that more than anything, we need documentation. My records from the university. Oh, and we found our family's land! If there's any way to use that to prove that we're citizens, maybe she can figure it out. I know she wants to help us."

"Got it. Now go take care of Lucy and Seba. I'll handle this," Melinda reassured her.

"Thank you! I love you so much, Mel. I still do." Silvia's nose was completely plugged from all her crying.

"I know. Don't worry. Just keep being brave. I'll fix this."

As the phone clicked to disconnect the call, Silvia hoped that "this," any of this, was fixable.

Silvia told Mayra about her call, and her hope that Dr. Cisneros would send a contact or a colleague to see her at the detention center.

"You know they're not going to allow you any visitors," cautioned Mayra.

"You're sure?" Silvia asked. "I mean, we were born here. We're citizens!"

"Cariño, everybody here is indocumentado until proven otherwise. They are not going to let you see anybody."

Silvia put her head in her hands. She peered under her arm toward her brother and sister, still sitting on the floor napping, leaning against each other like wilting willow saplings.

"But," Mayra paused for emphasis, her eyes twinkling, "they will let me leave a note with the guards in case anyone does come for you."

Silvia looked up. "Really?"

"Sure. I've been here long enough. They know me, and a few of them owe me a favor. Take some paper from my bunk and get to it."

Silvia wondered what Mayra had done to get the guards to owe her anything, but she got two sheets and a pen and went to a quiet corner of the holding cell. For the next twenty minutes, she recorded the history of the last few days. At the end, she included her mother's cell phone number even though it was currently in the hands of her tía, and instructions to take all three kids' personal effects out of the Processing Center's storage. With shaking hands, she directed the reader to open the rusted biscuit canister in her brother's backpack and to please use the information contained inside to help them.

Silvia put the pen down and tightened her ponytail. Who was going to read the letter, if anyone? And who knows what was really in the biscuit can? Maybe all three siblings had been carried away by romantic notions of family treasure and escapist thinking. Or maybe they had been right, but the document that contained their fate had long since deteriorated to powder in its container. All she could do was hope. *And pray that Mami doesn't try to cross back,* she thought.

50

As Mayra had told her four days before, Silvia received no sign of any visit to the facility. If help had come and gone, there was no way to know. And if someone had come, the kids now had no belongings to their name. Should they happen to be among the quick to be "processed," they would arrive in a country they had never seen with no money, no phone, no clothing, no food, and no idea where their mother was. Mayra assured her that this was unlikely, but nevertheless, the night she wrote the note, Silvia stopped sleeping.

Instead, she passed the hours trying to keep her siblings' spirits up. She made up stories with Sebastián about rebuilding their bisabuela's house and adding a geology lab and living and working there as a family forever. They played catch with one of Sebastián's rolled-up socks. He became friends with another little boy in the holding cell and learned some new Spanish words from him. They drew transforming robots and animated them by making them walk up the room's walls or fly through the air and visit other people in detention.

While her brother was amused with his friend, Silvia played Twenty Questions with Lucy, or sometimes they just talked. Surprisingly, Lucy began to open up and share with her big sister her concerns about school, boys, her health, and her feelings about their mother's deportation, topics that she had refused to discuss all that year. It was as if the barriers between them had been removed that morning on the path beside Escondida Lake.

Sometimes Mayra would take Lucy for walks around the perimeter of the cell and they'd talk in low voices and stop to do pushups against the wall, or calf raises. Silvia would see her sister laughing, or even wiping away tears in the older woman's presence, and she smiled with pleasure to know that Lucy had, at least for a moment, what she'd been missing in her life without their mother.

Yet still Silvia didn't sleep. She prayed, she did the yoga stretches that she had learned in high school, she rested her eyes, but she didn't sleep.

Then, five days after she'd written the note, the residents of the holding room were startled by an officer coming down the hall, boots clomping and keys rattling. He opened the metal door and everyone sat up from their spots on their bunks or on the floor.

"Castillo family?"

"Yes?" answered Silvia, pulling Lucy and Sebastián close to her in their corner.

"Get up. You're coming with me."

Her heart racing and eyes wide beneath her knitted brow, Silvia looked at Mayra, who winked and gave her a smile. Crossing the gray floor, their friend gave first Lucy, then Sebastián, and finally Silvia a hug. She whispered in Silvia's ear, "Don't worry. You're outta here."

Silvia pulled back and looked at her. "In a good way?"

Mayra laughed. "Yes, in a good way. Take care of yourselves."

"Come ON," the officer growled. "I'm not standing here all day."

"Bye, Mayra," Silvia said. She glanced as little as possible at the other detainees as the siblings walked over to the officer and out the door.

The sun was brilliantly, joyfully bright when they stepped out of the concrete processing center and into the Texas sun. Blinded, Silvia shielded her eyes and made out the profile of someone standing at the end of the sidewalk. As they approached, she recognized her advisor's face and started to cry. Although this was their first time meeting in person, Silvia ran into her arms and buried her face in the taller woman's shoulder for a moment. Straightening up, she wiped her eyes and introduced her brother and sister. They shook hands all around.

"Thank you so much for coming," said Lucy.

"Yes, thanks," echoed Sebastián.

"I wish I could have done more." Dr. Cisneros's mouth tightened into a slight smile, even as she brushed tears from her eyes. "Get in the car and I'll tell you." She led them to the rented dark blue Subaru.

Climbing into the front passenger seat, Silvia spoke nervously. "We need to pick up our stuff in Socorro, New Mexico. That's going to make the drive even longer. Are you sure you want to take us? We could always catch a bus."

"Well, I'm afraid your stuff in New Mexico is going to have to stay there. I can't take you across state lines right now."

Finding his backpack on the floor of the car, Sebastián pulled out his toy. "Good thing I bring Blue Elephant everywhere I go," he said, hugging the stuffed animal to his chest. "Otherwise he'd still be in New Mexico."

"Open up that cooler bag, too, Sebastián," said Dr. Cisneros, pronouncing his name in beautiful Spanish. "There are sandwiches and drinks in there for everyone."

They passed around the sandwiches while Dr. Cisneros began talking. "First things first. I talked to your mother."

"What? How?" asked Lucy from the back seat.

"Well, when I got the call from your friend Melinda, I knew immediately that I had to come. I have very few contacts left in Texas, but you are my student, and in some sense, my responsibility. I couldn't leave your future up to the hope that some old colleague might help me out. And I couldn't bear the thought of another family I know being deported." She paused. "So I got on the first plane out of University Park."

"I can't believe you came," said Silvia, cleaning her face and hands with the wipe that Dr. Cisneros had included in the lunch cooler. "Thank you so much. And thanks to Melinda."

"Silvia, Melinda said to tell you she's sorry. She said you'd know what she meant."

Silvia swallowed, then answered quietly. "I do. Thanks."

Her professor looked her in the eyes for a brief moment at the stop sign at the exit from the detention facility. Then she continued driving.

"Okay. So, when I got here, I followed all the instructions that you wisely left for me. I got your things out of holding and charged up your phone in my car. I called your aunt in Mexico, but didn't get any useful information. With my social-worker Spanish, I was able to get her to understand who I was and why I was calling. She said she was waiting for a call from your mom and would let her know to call your phone."

Silvia nodded with her mouth full of turkey and Muenster. Sebastián leaned forward from the back seat, waiting to hear more.

Dr. Cisneros continued in a louder voice that would carry to the back seat. "So I kept your phone on, just in case. On the second day, your mother called."

"She did?" cried Sebastián.

"Yes, and she sends her love to all of you. I told her everything that had happened and that I was working on getting you out. I made sure she knew that I was hopeful that I'd get to you quickly. See, she was calling the night before she planned to cross over the border."

Silvia stiffened. "Did she? Is she okay?"

"I got her to agree to stay where she was until further communication. She's safe, you guys." Dr. Cisneros made eye contact with each sibling using the rearview mirror. She'll be calling in a few days."

The younger kids whooped with excitement and Silvia turned around to high-five Sebastián. "See, hermano? I told you it was going to be all right." She glanced back at her professor's profile, but she was unsmiling. Silvia's heart dropped.

"Why don't we pull over for a bit so I can tell you everything before we get there," Dr. Cisneros said.

"Get where?" asked Silvia, frowning.

"I'll tell you in a sec. To understand it, you need to know what I've done up to now."

They pulled into the parking lot of a Circle K and Dr. Cisneros left the car running for the air conditioning. For the next twenty-five minutes, she explained how she had come to the detention facility around three o'clock the day after receiving Melinda's call. She had sat in the rental car to let Silvia's phone charge up while she examined the contents of the biscuit canister that she found in Sebastián's backpack.

She dusted off the tin and found she could still read *Uneeda* and see the iconic little boy in the yellow raincoat through the rust. Prying off the lid, she discovered a layer of red sealing wax underneath and began to chip it off with her house key. Inside, she found the canister as shiny as the day it had been produced, giving her hope that the contents were well-preserved. Tied with scraggly twine was a yellowed roll of paper, which she slipped out of its tie and gingerly opened. One look at the blue New Mexico seal and she wrapped it back up and drove straight downtown to Immigration Court, hoping to arrive before closing time.

She spent all the working hours of the next three days trying to get an audience at the court, speaking to the General Counsel's Office on the phone, and consulting with *pro bono* lawyers present outside the courtroom. She spent the two evenings online and at the library, researching the documents she had found in the biscuit can and the laws that pertained to them. Eventually, she got a call back from an old friend from graduate school, an immigration lawyer who was able to secure an after-hours meeting with a federal judge that evening on the third night. Together, they scrutinized the documents.

Four tightly rolled sheets comprised the family treasure. The first was a copy of the 1816 Spanish land grant showing the divided parcels given to various families. Next was an 1875 confirmation of the grant, dated after the Treaty of Guadalupe Hidalgo and stipulating that current and future residents of such parcels, provided that they were the heirs of the original grantees, would be guaranteed US citizenship. Third was a family tree drawn in pencil, showing the lineage from the date of the land grant through Margarita's generation, clearly included to prove her heritage and rights to the land and citizenship. Last came the anticipated *título*: the contemporary deed to the Rosas family farm in Socorro. It seemed that Margarita had a new deed drawn up during the course of her research, to ensure that all documentation was fail-safe.

"In short, everything in the canister checked out with my research," Dr. Cisneros said, "and allowed me to present a complete file to the judge. The next morning—which was only today, even though in some ways it feels like a lifetime ago—he granted a Stay of Deportation with ICE, which allowed me to get you out immediately."

"This is unbelievable!" said Silvia, glancing into the back seat to share her joy with her brother and sister. Lucy was smiling, but Sebastián had fallen asleep, his head dropped to one side.

Dr. Cisneros's tone turned dry. "Well, unfortunately, that's what the judge said, too."

"What?" Silvia's smile vanished and she turned back around, rotating in the passenger seat to face her professor directly. "What do you mean?"

"He says it's literally unbelievable. He doesn't think a pile of old documents will hold up in court today, and frankly, he doesn't think it should. He filed a stay of deportation as a favor to my lawyer friend, but it's very short-lived. Actually, we have to get you ready to appear in his office tomorrow morning."

Her mouth hanging open, Silvia turned to exchange glances with Lucy. Her sister had tears in her eyes that she was frantically trying to wipe away.

"Okay, but is it just a technicality or what?" Silvia asked. "I mean, we're citizens!"

"When we left the office, my friend stayed behind for a minute. When he came out, he told me that we're lucky we even got the twenty-four-hour stay of deportation. The judge said that if I weren't a friend, he would have deported you kids as soon as your case came across his desk."

Silvia's hand trembled as she brushed unwanted tears off her face as quickly as they spilled out. "But we have the papers. It's all legal."

Professor Cisneros was biting her trembling lip. "I know, Silvia. But it seems that may not matter as much as we had hoped it would. Again, what I've done isn't enough."

Silvia shook her head. "No. I'm sorry." She unbuckled her seat belt and opened the car door. Silhouetted in the doorframe with the hot sun low behind her, she half screamed, half sobbed, "I'm not doing this. I can't do this anymore." She slammed the door and began walking, then running, along Montana Avenue.

As she ran, she continued to be wrenched with sobs. Nearly blinded by the sun and her tears, she repeatedly brushed at her eyes with the backs of her hands. She passed Dunkin' Donuts, Burger King, the Sprint Store. All stupid American chains. Then Taco Bell, Viva Chevrolet, Casa Lane. *They take our food, they take our words, but they won't take us.* Sobbing, she leaned against a bus shelter to try to catch her breath.

"Mami," she moaned as she wept. "Mami, Mami. ¿Dónde estás? You had it all planned but it just didn't work. I just wasn't good enough."

She didn't notice the car pull up beside her and put on its flashers. She didn't resist as Dr. Cisneros put an arm around her and led her back to the Subaru. She didn't care that her professor protected her head from banging on the doorframe as she settled her into the rear of the car. She didn't feel Lucy stroke her hair while she sat crumpled between her brother and sister. Lined up in the back seat like criminals.

51

Socorro, Socorro, my one true home,
Where the future is planted and mem'ries are sown.
Alongside the Rio, rushing fast,
Lie buried the treasures of ancestors past.

Settled into their compartment racing southward that night, Violeta slept and Margarita still held her pen. She looked back at what she'd written: a poem, full of love and anguish and hope for the future. Once she pushed the memories away, the rhymes presented themselves as if precomposed in her mind. The verses grouped themselves in fours, the stanzas held the secrets she had hidden on her land.

She read it again and was amazed. She had never before felt moved to write a poem. She read and reread it as if it were someone else's work, committing it to memory as the desert passed by unseen in the darkness outside her window.

When she was satisfied, Margarita closed her leather-bound journal, feeling its smooth cover under her fingers. For a moment, she stroked it, seeing flashes of all the maps, drawings, and reflections she had written inside it over the years. She knew that she would never again open it. The time for dreaming on paper was in the past. Now was the time for forging a new life.

52

The next morning, they arrived early at the federal judge's meeting room. Silvia couldn't sit still, instead choosing to pass the time looking at the books lined up on the dark oak shelves. One section was all legal volumes that made Silvia's stomach turn, so she quickly redirected her attention to a shelf of literature. She smiled bitterly to herself. *Must be nice to have time to read for pleasure while the rest of us are fighting for our rights.* She read the titles: *The Adventures of Huckleberry Finn, Moby-Dick, The Grapes of Wrath.* All so American. Shelf after shelf of perfectly categorized volumes, alphabetized even, each in the section in which it belonged.

Belonged. She had never before thought of that word as exclusive, excluding. But looking through the titles, she realized that, for all of the warm inclusive connotations of *belong*, it by definition implied an exclusivity, an outside, a whole world of outsiders like her.

She stepped closer to the wall to scan more titles in the dim light from the inadequate windows. Yes, it was just as she thought. No *Cien años de soledad*. No *Como agua para chocolate*. No Darío or Martí or Hernández or Allende. Those did not belong. Just like she did not belong. Not anymore.

Silvia swallowed her guilt as she looked at her brother and sister, whom she had failed to protect. Lucy and Sebastián were so small at the oversized round table, seven unoccupied seats fanning out from where they sat, pulled back slightly from the table as if each were occupied by a ghost. In a different life, the table would have been perfect for a family dinner, maybe a big Thanksgiving meal. She almost laughed, realizing only at that moment that they had spent Thanksgiving motherless and in ICE detention. She hadn't even noticed. Now, she compared the enormous round table before her with their small Formica rectangle at home, around which they had crowded for the best meals of her life.

Tamales, burgers, rice, french fries, guacamole. All the cuisines had coexisted just fine on the kitchen table. It could have stayed that way.

Glancing down, Silvia saw that her jeans still had dirt on the right knee from digging in the red soil in New Mexico, when she'd still had hope. It seemed like ages ago. She pushed up the sleeves of the navy cotton blazer that Dr. Cisneros had picked up for her at Target before getting them from detention, knowing that they'd have to appear in court. Then she pulled it closer around her to try to hide the gray long-sleeved T-shirt underneath, the shirt that she had been wearing on the day that she and her siblings discovered their great-great-grandmother's land and the documents that should have saved them. Instead, they were waiting to find out how soon they'd be sent to Mexico.

"I've been able to do one thing right for you," Dr. Cisneros had said yesterday, once Silvia had finally calmed down.

Silvia had stared at the motel coffee table. "What's that?"

"I arranged for your mother to be waiting at the border."

Sebastián had jumped up. "Really?"

Silvia looked up and saw that even Lucy was paying attention. Although she knew her eyes were swollen and red, Silvia met her professor's gaze directly for the first time since she had fled the car. "You've done so much for us. You really have." She reached across the table and squeezed her hand. "This is wonderful. This will make it possible for us to go on as a family. Thank you."

"No, thank *you*. You're very kind to say that to me, even after all this." Dr. Cisneros had teared up with Silvia then.

Today, though, Silvia's eyes were bone dry and dusty. She looked at her reflection in the glass doors of the bookshelf. Frowning, she tightened her ponytail and tried to contain the unruly waves on the sides, even as she heard footsteps in the hallway.

"Ready?" Sebastián asked in a little voice from his seat at the table. His upturned face held a slight smile of encouragement.

Silvia met his eyes. Seeing his steady gaze, she slowly reached up and pulled out her ponytail holder. She fluffed out her Mexican waves. Then she took her red lip gloss out of her pocket, nodded at her little brother, and turned to face the door.

Gratitude

Socorro exists because of the support of many individuals and institutions. The very first was Kathleen Tynan, my teacher who inscribed "Send me a copy of your first book" in my autograph journal when I was leaving elementary school. Those eight words gave this then-third-grader an ember she would carry inside her with a lifelong, quiet pride: the unwavering confidence that a novel would emerge in due time. This book is dedicated to Miss Tynan, and I have to believe she knows it finally happened.

I started writing *Socorro* in 2017 as a way of speaking out about grave concerns I had and have regarding our nation's policies and tendencies. My passion caused me to share my work early, and my first readers humbled me and showed me how much I had to learn about my craft! Nancee, Eric, Henry, Nicole, Freejay, Jean/Mom, thank you for that and for your stubborn confidence in me and in the process.

Later, I benefitted from the insights of developmental editors Amy Tipton and Vivian Lee, who helped me overhaul the book during its awkward adolescence. But it was Jimin Han and Pat Dunn at The Writing Institute at Sarah Lawrence College that guided it to its maturity. Thanks to their expert leadership, kind approach, and wry brilliance, this book and this author transformed in fundamental ways. I am so grateful to these two teachers for their continuing support, and to the best workshop group I could ever have concocted.

It has been my great joy to develop a friendship and wonderful working relationship with the publisher who rooted for *Socorro* from the moment he saw it. His beautifully conceived house, Nervous Ghost Press, awarded me the first annual Prize for Prose, and it has been my honor to work with Matthew ever since. Writing does indeed save lives.

The news of the Nervous Ghost Prize came while I was attending my thirtieth high school reunion, singing Indigo Girls songs with Bill and Eileen, who celebrated with me in the very moment, forever wrapping them and the rest of my class of '91 friends (thanks, Amy!) up in the wondrous, surreal memory of the night I became a legitimate novelist.

My amazing friend Nancee Adams was both the first and the last reader of the book in manuscript form. Her incredibly thorough and masterful copyedit saved me a lot of shame, but it was her keen eye for detail and logic that polished it for the showroom. I am forever grateful for her gifts.

Finally, my unending gratitude goes to my friends and family who support my writing life: Freejay (whose own creative path gave me hope through all the rejection letters), Giselle (who made me feel like an author from day one), Nicole (who knew how to "be confident" even when I didn't), Henry and Chance (who were my most constant cheerleaders), Chris (who honored me by being the first to get mad at something I wrote), Adrianna (who celebrated every little milestone), and all who never stopped believing and checking in for updates (Mom, Liz, Rich, Peg, Joanne, Christopher, Lisa, Dad, Scott, Jen, Steve). This list shows how blessed I am to be surrounded by such support; I only hope I return it well and forever.

—Sara A. Leman

Sara A. Leman is always writing in her head. She is Professor of Spanish and Associate Dean of the Graduate School of Arts and Sciences at Fordham University in New York City, where she teaches creative writing and literature. She holds a PhD from Boston University and has published five academic books on topics ranging from colonial commerce to contemporary fiction. A recent alumna of Sarah Lawrence College's Writing Institute, Sara writes fiction that offers peeks into topics as "small" as family life and as big as social justice and multiculturalism. *Socorro* is her first novel.

Connect with Sara on Twitter @SaraALemanAuthr and on the web at https://saraaleman.wordpress.com/contact/.

Nervous Ghost Press